JENNY
FINN

WRITERS
MIKE MIGNOLA
TROY NIXEY

ARTIST : CHAPTERS 1-3
TROY NIXEY

ARTIST : CHAPTER 4
FAREL DALRYMPLE

LETTERER : CHAPTERS 1-2
PAT BROSSEAU

LETTERER : CHAPTERS 3-4
ED DUKESHIRE

COVER ART
MIKE MIGNOLA

COVER COLORS

ANDREW COSBY
ROSS RICHIE
founders

ADAM FORTIER
vice president,
new business

MARK WAID
editor-in-chief

TOM FASSBENDER
vice president,
publishing

MICHAEL ALAN NELSON
associate editor

CHIP MOSHER
marketing &
sales director

ED DUKESHIRE
designer

DANIEL VARGAS
publishing coordinator

ISBN-13: 978-1-934506-14-1
ISBN-10: 1-934506-14-1

Collecting Jenny Finn: Doom and Jenny Finn: Messiah
10 9 8 7 6 5 4 3 2 1

First Printing: April 2008
Printed in Korea

CHAPTER ONE

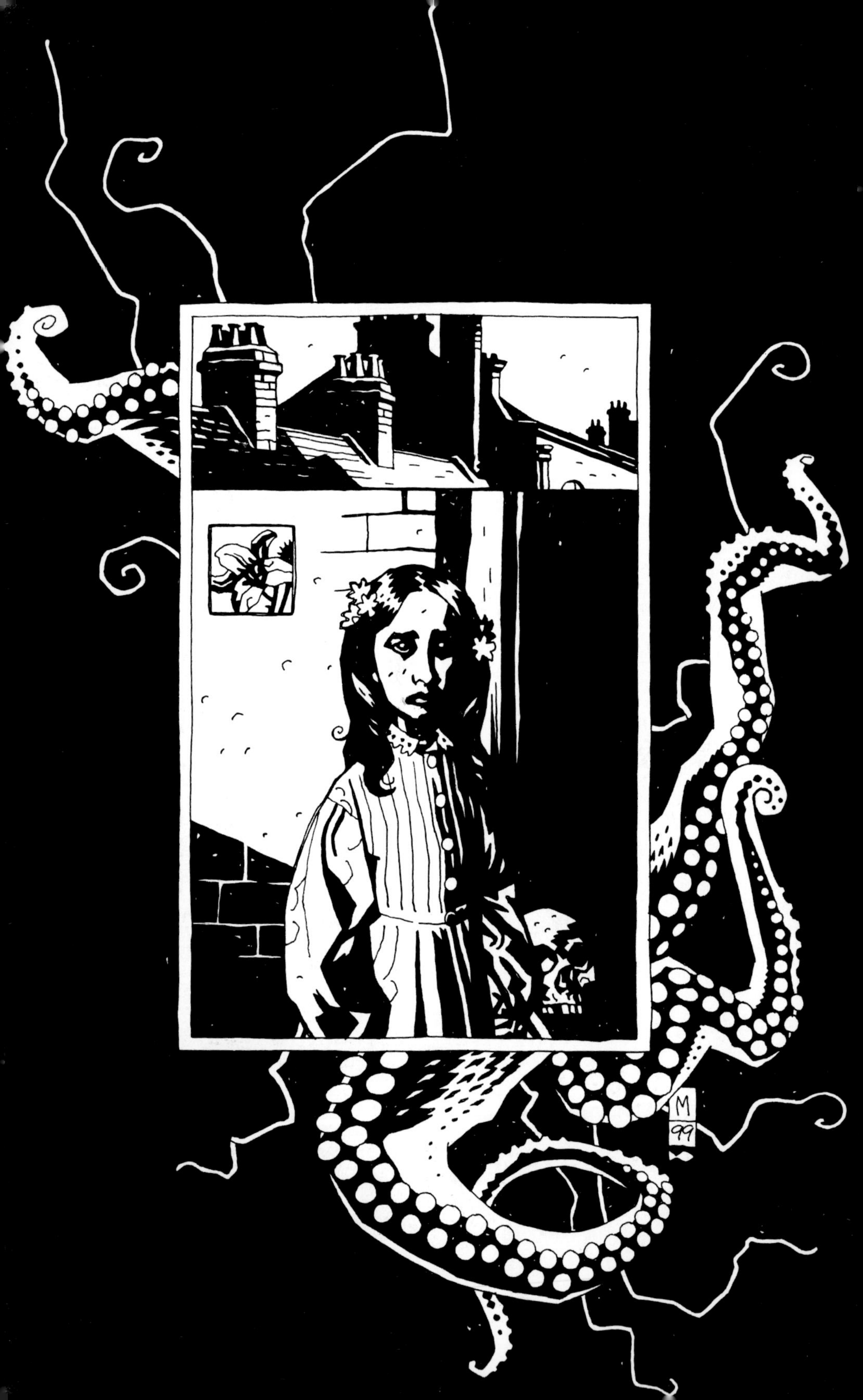
M
99

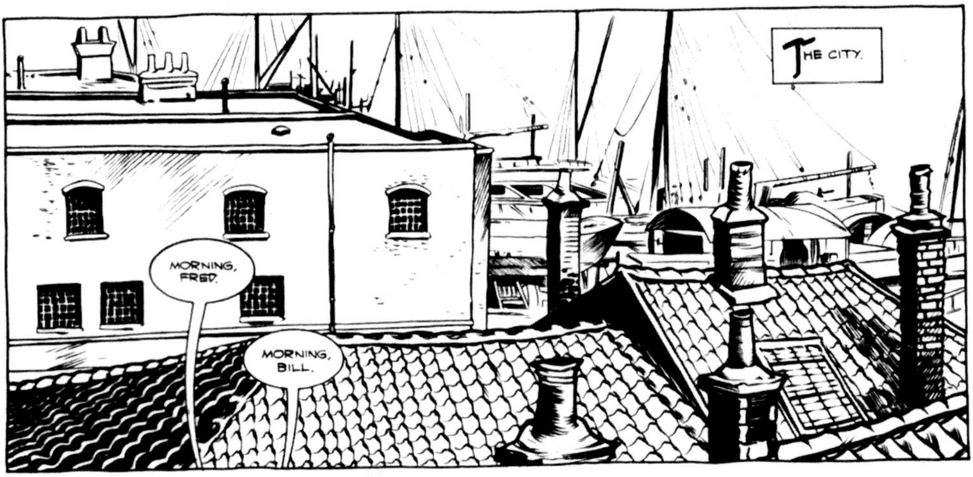
THE CITY.
MORNING, FRED.
MORNING, BILL.

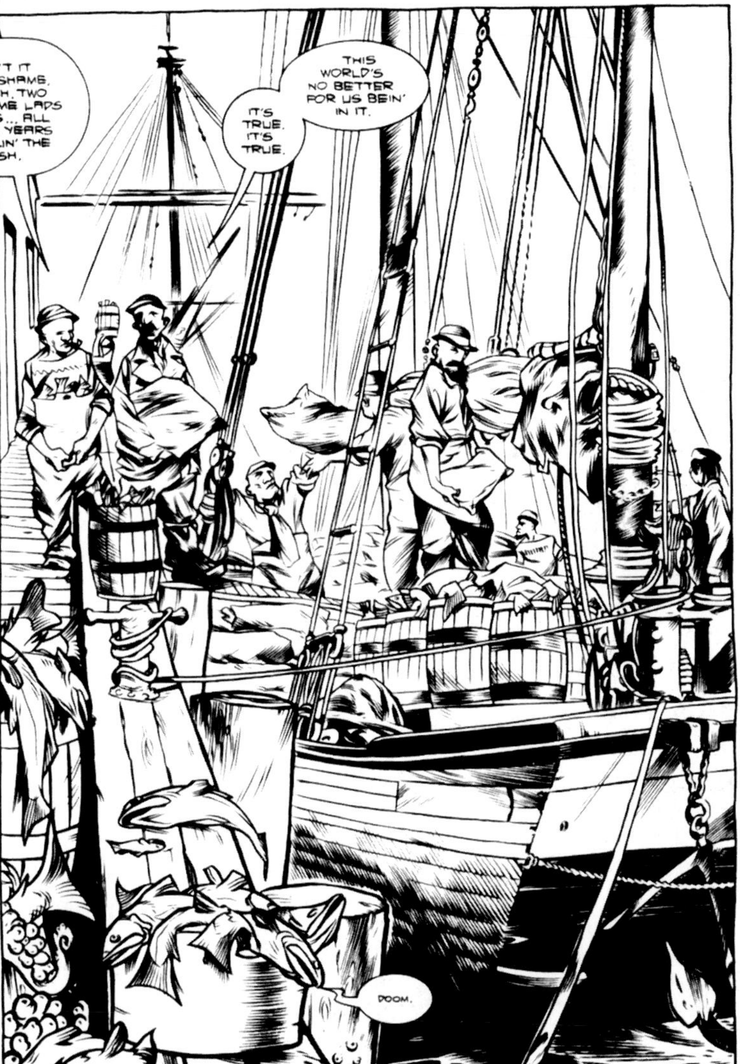
AIN'T IT THE SHAME, THOUGH. TWO HANDSOME LADS LIKE US... ALL THESE YEARS HAULIN' THE FISH.
IT'S TRUE. IT'S TRUE.
THIS WORLD'S NO BETTER FOR US BEIN' IN IT.
DOOM.

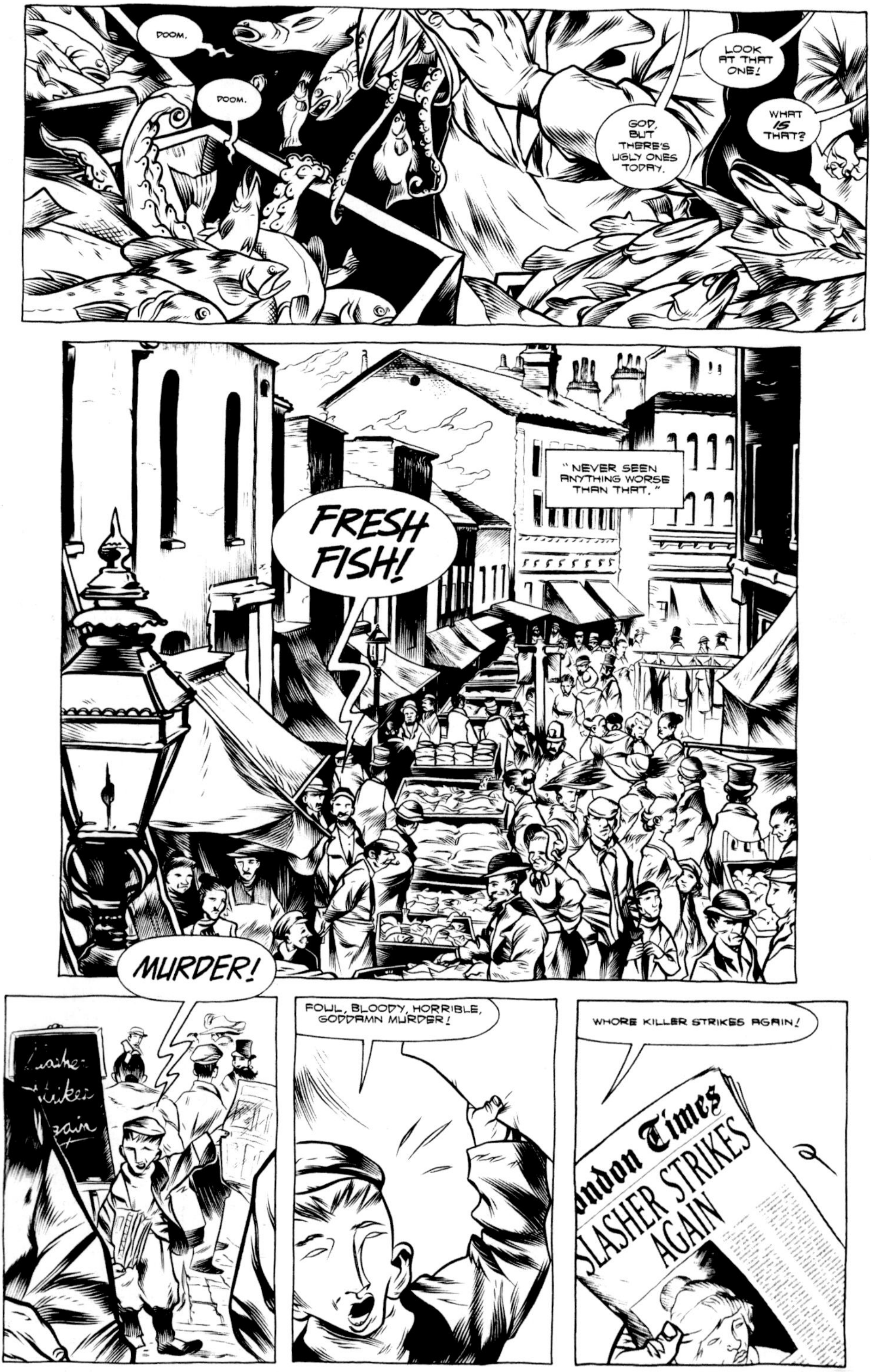
DOOM.
DOOM.
LOOK AT THAT ONE!
GOD, BUT THERE'S UGLY ONES TODAY.
WHAT IS THAT?
"NEVER SEEN ANYTHING WORSE THAN THAT."
FRESH FISH!
MURDER!
FOUL, BLOODY, HORRIBLE, GODDAMN MURDER!
WHORE KILLER STRIKES AGAIN!
London Times
SLASHER STRIKES AGAIN

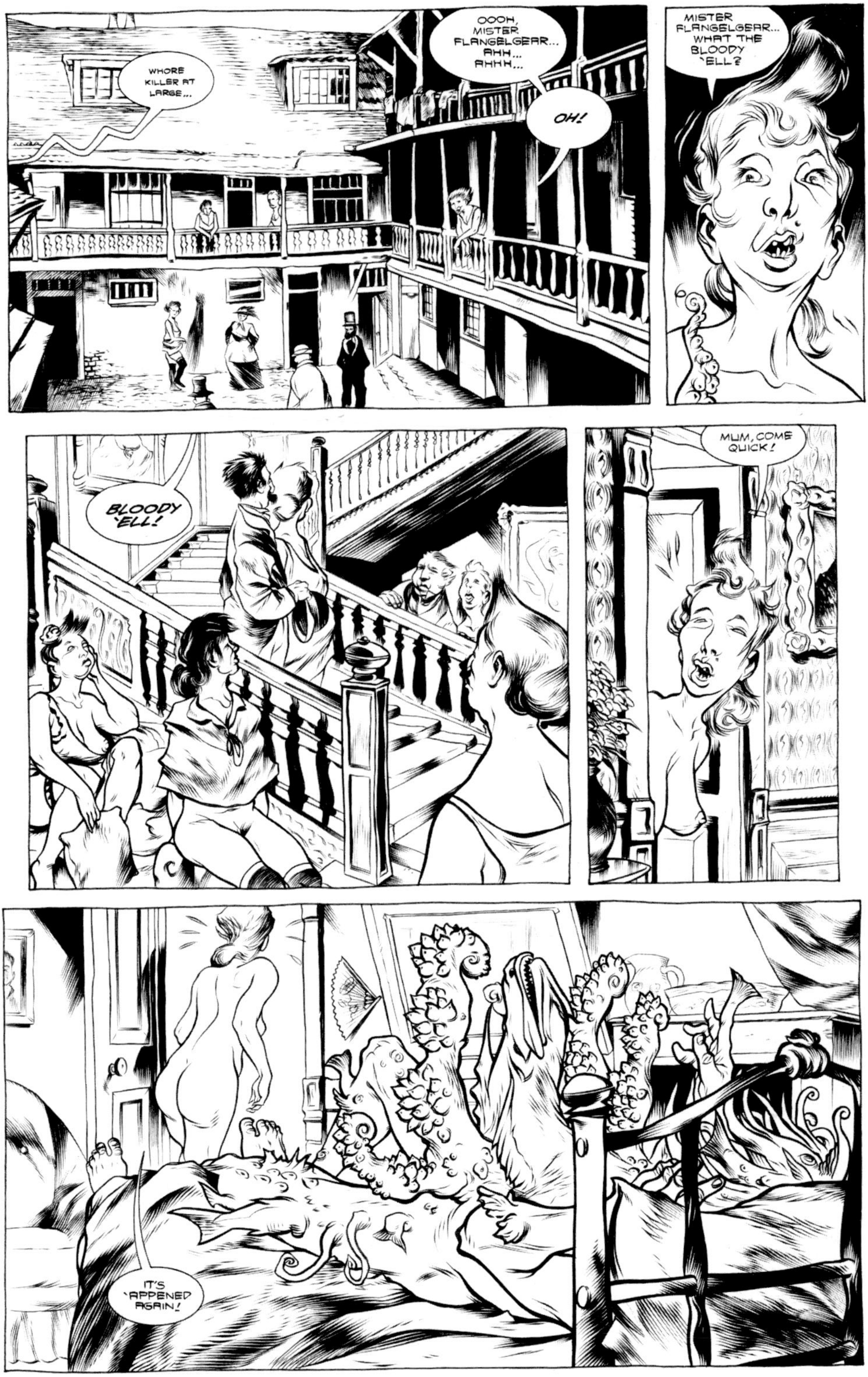
WHORE KILLER AT LARGE...
OOOH, MISTER FLANGELGEAR... AHH... AHHH...
OH!
MISTER FLANGELGEAR... WHAT THE BLOODY 'ELL?
BLOODY 'ELL!
MUM, COME QUICK!
IT'S 'APPENED AGAIN!

THIS IS THE WORST ONE YET.

'E DIDN'T LOOK SO BAD AT THE START...

...OH, A LITTLE SCALY, BUT THIS ...*THIS* COMB ON 'IM ALLA THE SUDDEN.

HMM...

WELL, I HOPE HE PAID UP FRONT.

HE DID...

...BUT THAT ONE ATE THE MONEY.

SNAP

GOD, IT'S A BLOODY AWFUL MESS...

WE'LL DRAG 'IM OUT BACK--

I WILL TAKE CHARGE OF HIM.

PRIME MINISTER...!

TELL ME, WAS HE A "REGULAR"?

I SEEN 'IM IN 'ERE LAST WEEK... WITH THE NEW GIRL.

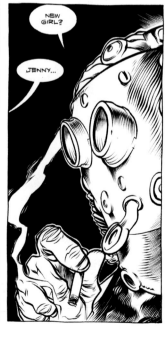

NEW GIRL?

JENNY...

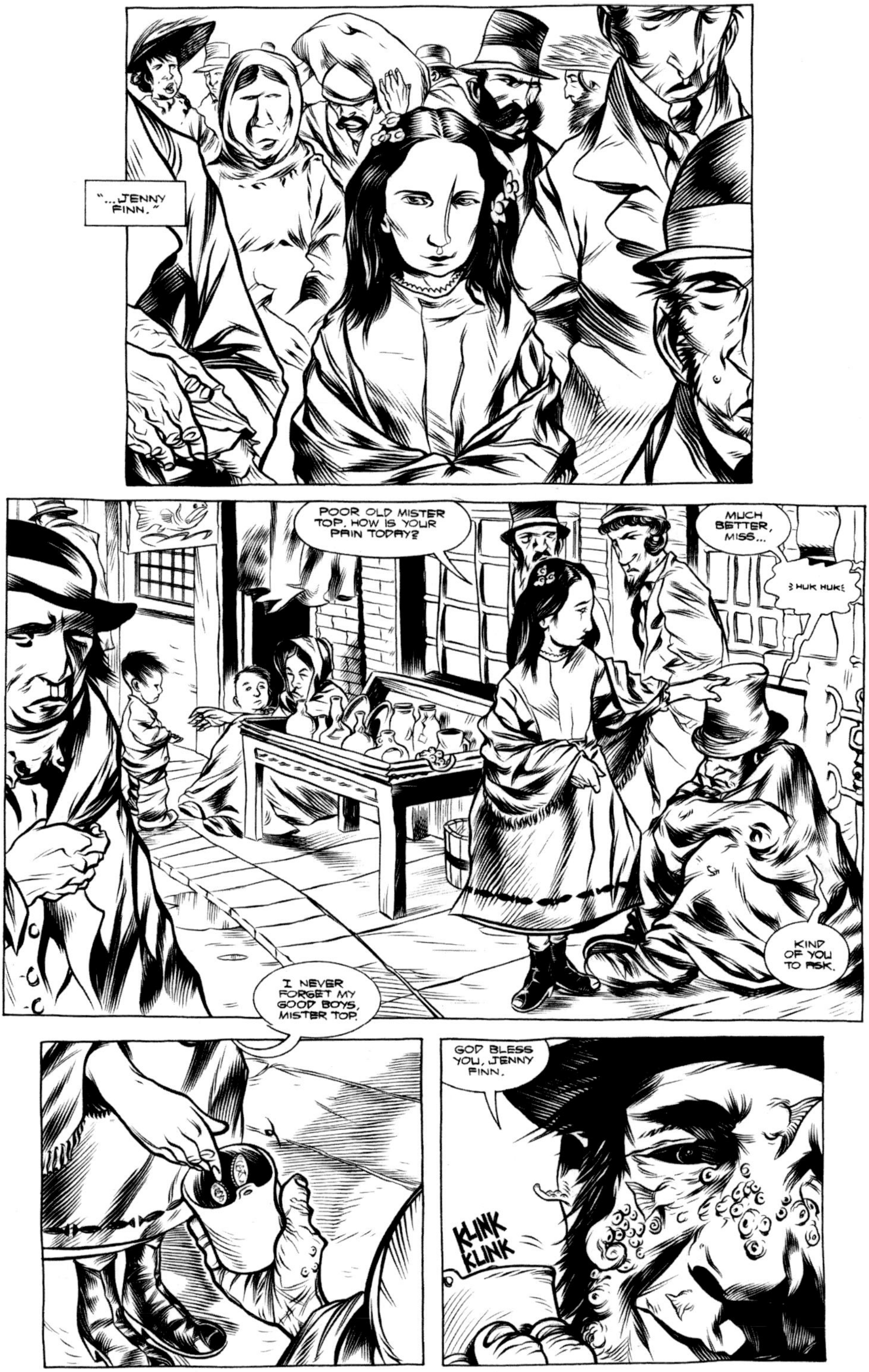
"...JENNY FINN."
POOR OLD MISTER TOP. HOW IS YOUR PAIN TODAY?
MUCH BETTER, MISS...
HUK HUK
KIND OF YOU TO ASK.
I NEVER FORGET MY GOOD BOYS, MISTER TOP.
GOD BLESS YOU, JENNY FINN.
KLINK KLINK

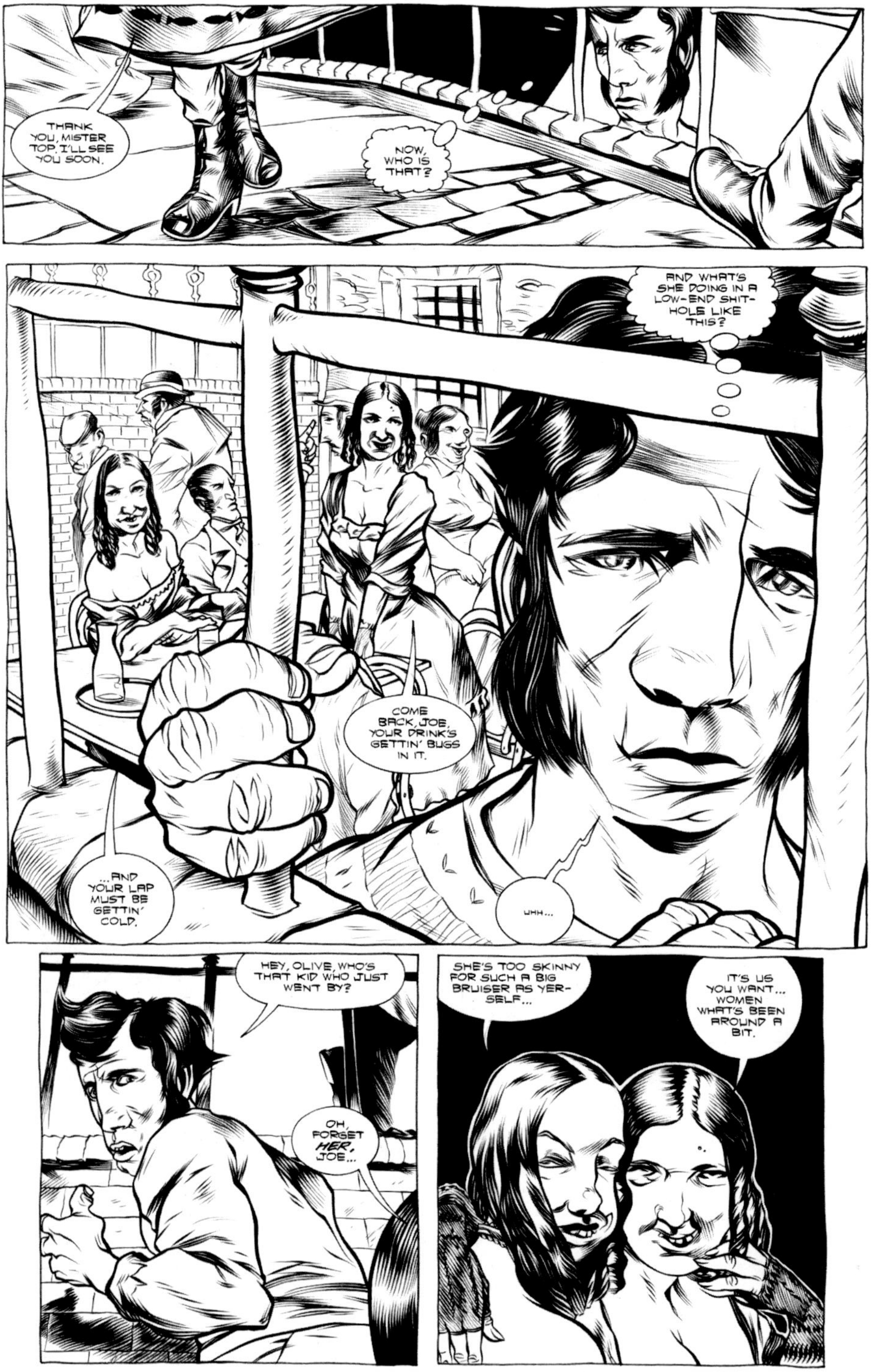
THANK YOU, MISTER TOP, I'LL SEE YOU SOON.
NOW, WHO IS THAT?
AND WHAT'S SHE DOING IN A LOW-END SHIT-HOLE LIKE THIS?
COME BACK, JOE. YOUR DRINK'S GETTIN' BUGS IN IT.
...AND YOUR LAP MUST BE GETTIN' COLD.
UHH...
HEY, OLIVE, WHO'S THAT KID WHO JUST WENT BY?
OH, FORGET *HER*, JOE...
SHE'S TOO SKINNY FOR SUCH A BIG BRUISER AS YER-SELF...
IT'S US YOU WANT... WOMEN WHAT'S BEEN AROUND A BIT.

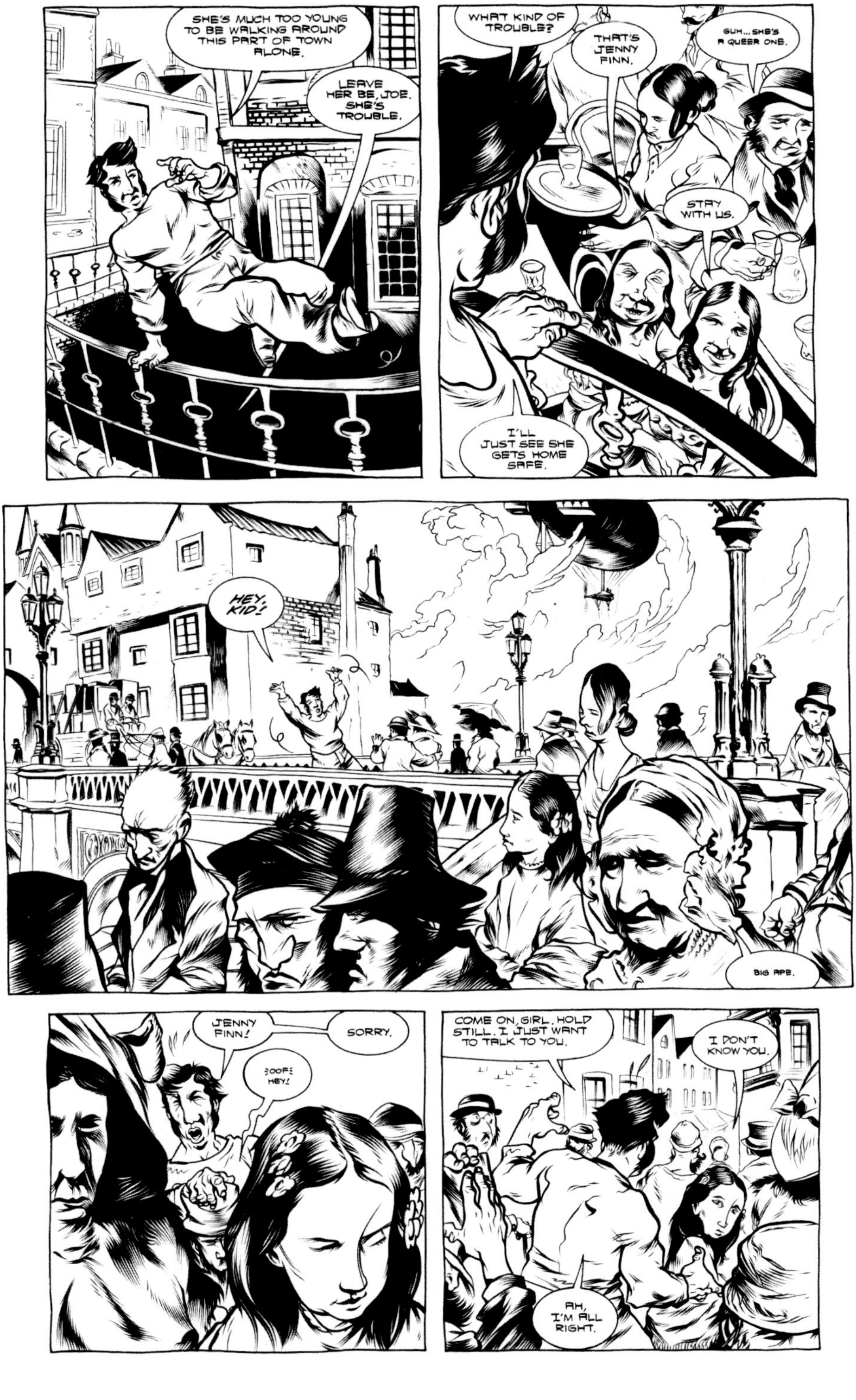

SHE'S MUCH TOO YOUNG TO BE WALKING AROUND THIS PART OF TOWN ALONE.
LEAVE HER BE, JOE. SHE'S TROUBLE.
WHAT KIND OF TROUBLE?
THAT'S JENNY FINN.
GUH... SHE'S A QUEER ONE.
STAY WITH US.
I'LL JUST SEE SHE GETS HOME SAFE.
HEY, KID!
BIG APE.
JENNY FINN!
SORRY.
OOF! HEY!
COME ON, GIRL. HOLD STILL. I JUST WANT TO TALK TO YOU.
I DON'T KNOW YOU.
AH, I'M ALL RIGHT.

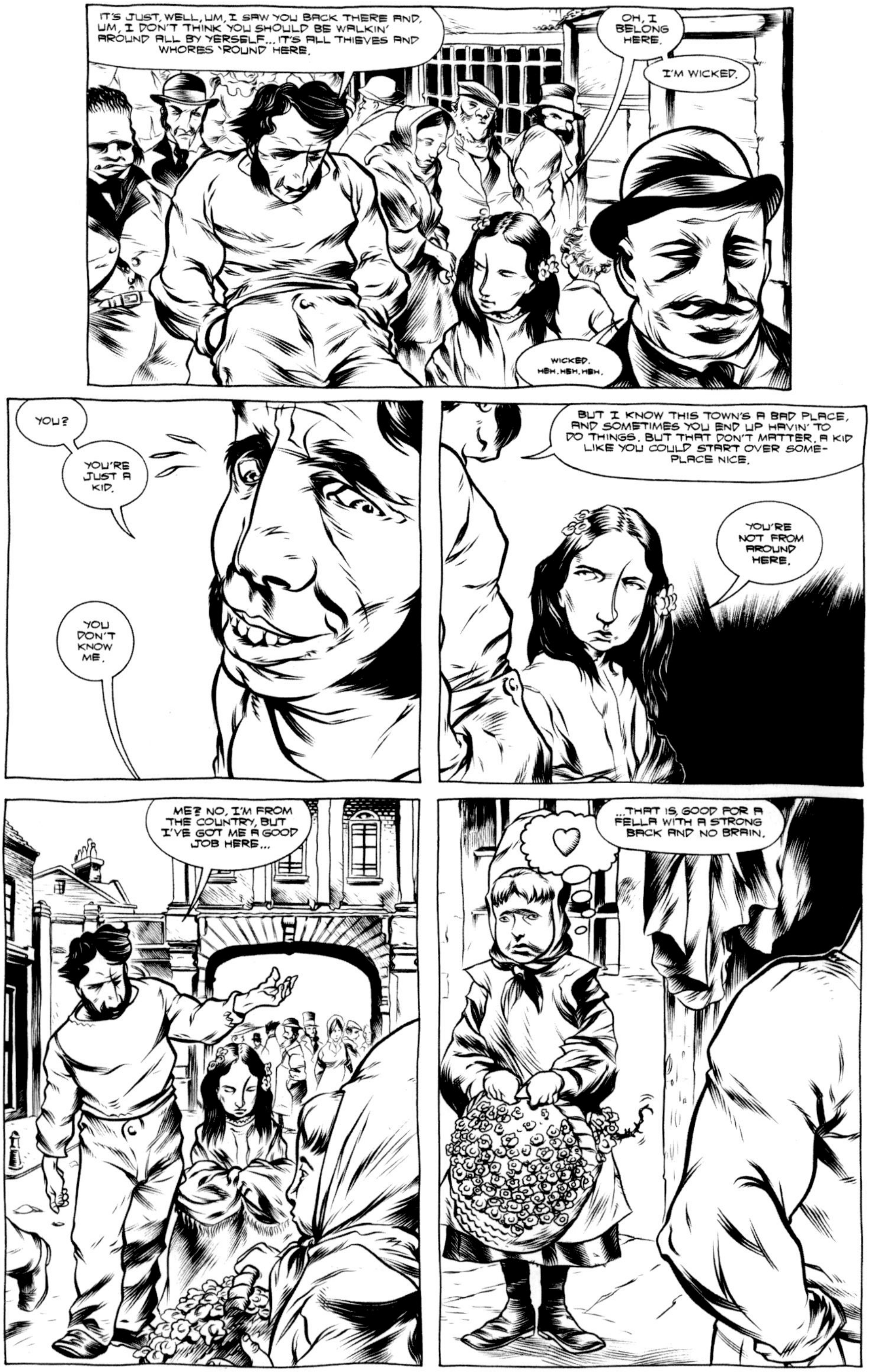
IT'S JUST, WELL, UM, I SAW YOU BACK THERE AND, UM, I DON'T THINK YOU SHOULD BE WALKIN' AROUND ALL BY YERSELF... IT'S ALL THIEVES AND WHORES 'ROUND HERE.
OH, I BELONG HERE.
I'M WICKED.
WICKED. HEH. HEH. HEH.
YOU?
YOU'RE JUST A KID.
YOU DON'T KNOW ME.
BUT I KNOW THIS TOWN'S A BAD PLACE, AND SOMETIMES YOU END UP HAVIN' TO DO THINGS. BUT THAT DON'T MATTER. A KID LIKE YOU COULD START OVER SOME-PLACE NICE.
YOU'RE NOT FROM AROUND HERE.
ME? NO, I'M FROM THE COUNTRY, BUT I'VE GOT ME A GOOD JOB HERE...
...THAT IS, GOOD FOR A FELLA WITH A STRONG BACK AND NO BRAIN.

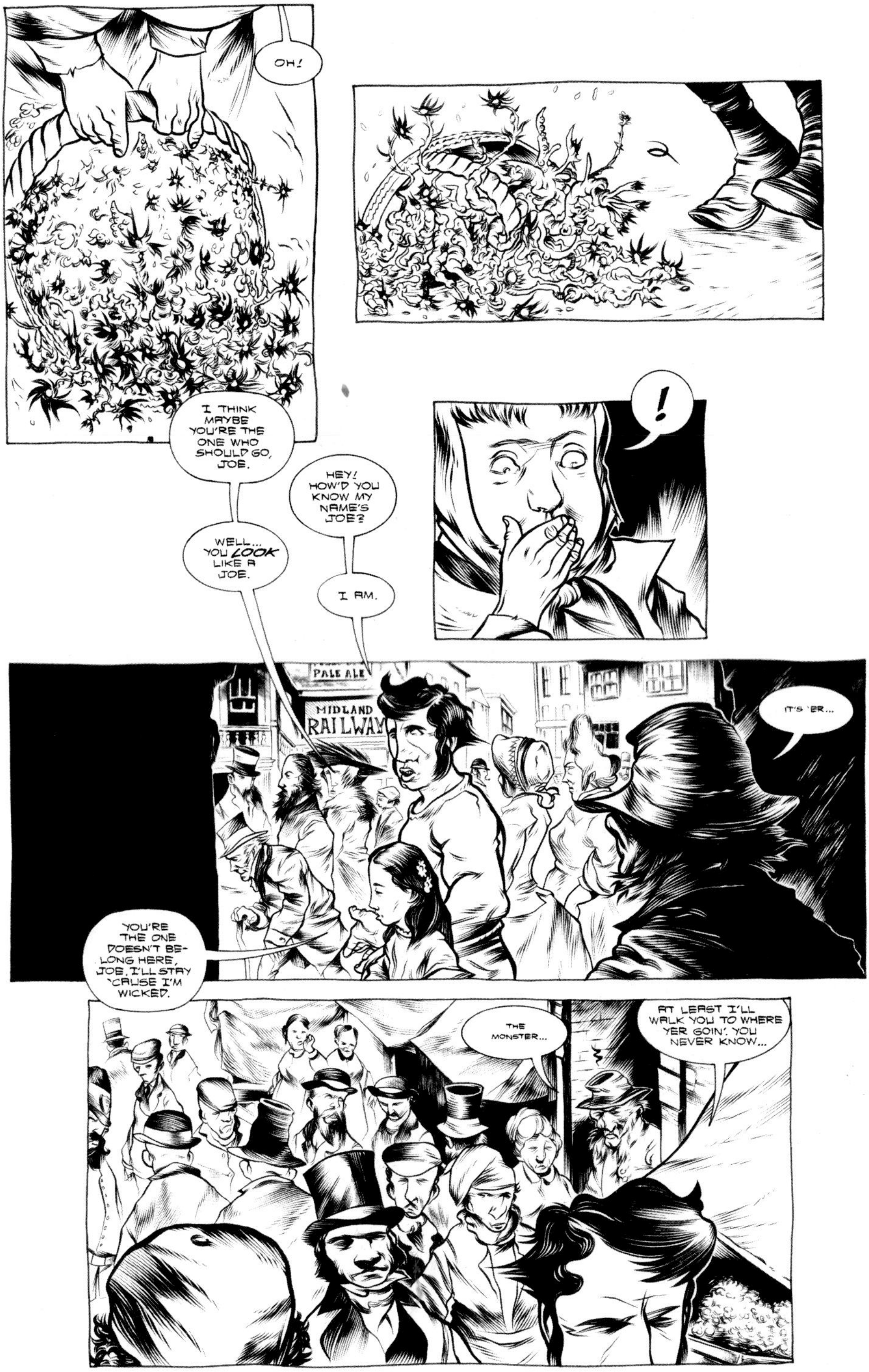
OH!
I THINK MAYBE YOU'RE THE ONE WHO SHOULD GO, JOE.
WELL... YOU LOOK LIKE A JOE.
HEY! HOW'D YOU KNOW MY NAME'S JOE?
I AM.
!
PALE ALE
MIDLAND RAILWAY
IT'S 'ER...
YOU'RE THE ONE DOESN'T BE-LONG HERE, JOE. I'LL STAY 'CAUSE I'M WICKED.
THE MONSTER...
AT LEAST I'LL WALK YOU TO WHERE YER GOIN'. YOU NEVER KNOW...

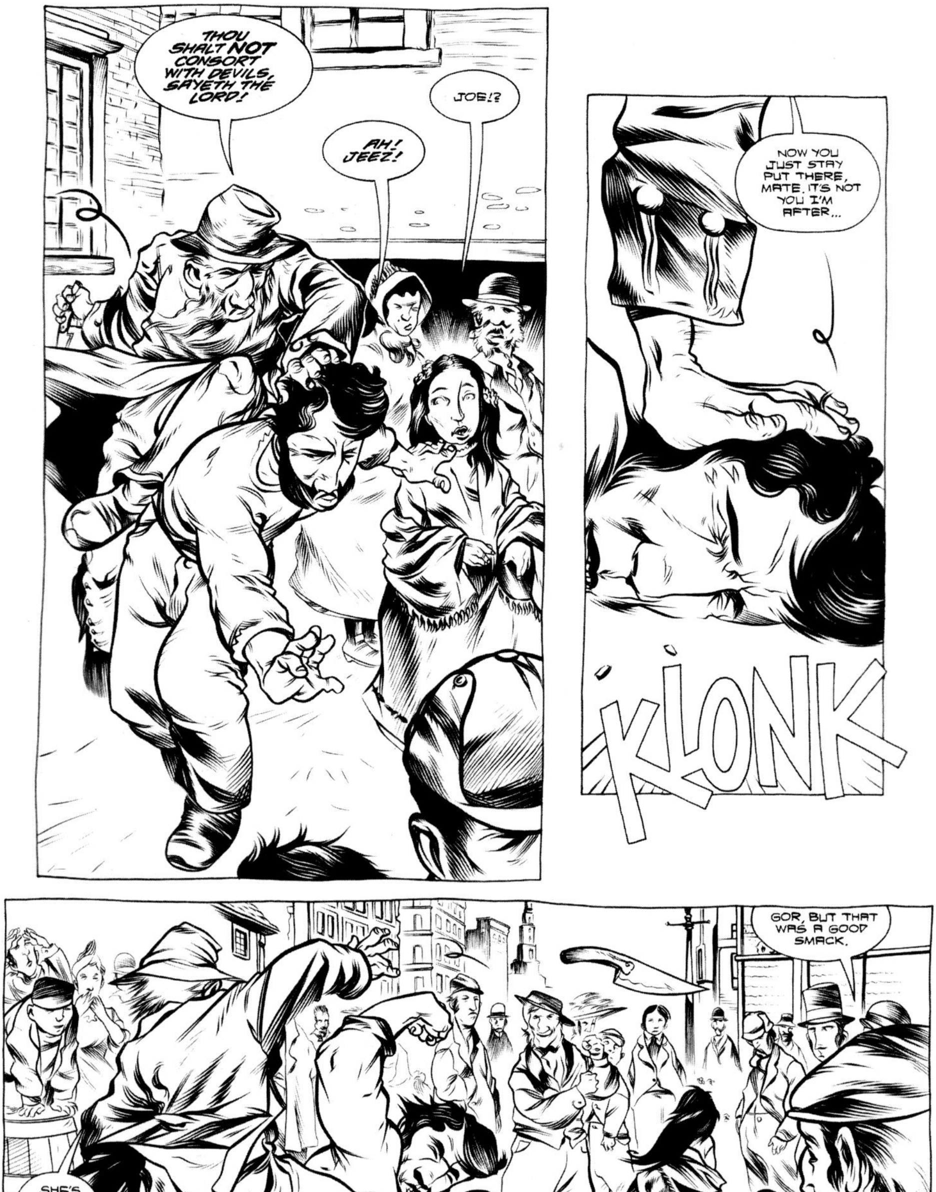
THOU SHALT NOT CONSORT WITH DEVILS, SAYETH THE LORD!
AH! JEEZ!
JOE!?
NOW YOU JUST STAY PUT THERE, MATE. IT'S NOT YOU I'M AFTER...
KLONK
GOR, BUT THAT WAS A GOOD SMACK.
SHE'S THE ONE...
GAH!
DON'T WORRY, KID. I CAN HANDLE THIS GUY.
KEEP'UM COMIN', JOE.

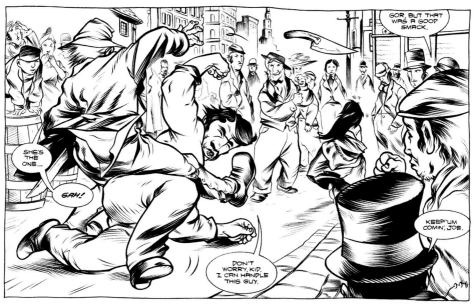

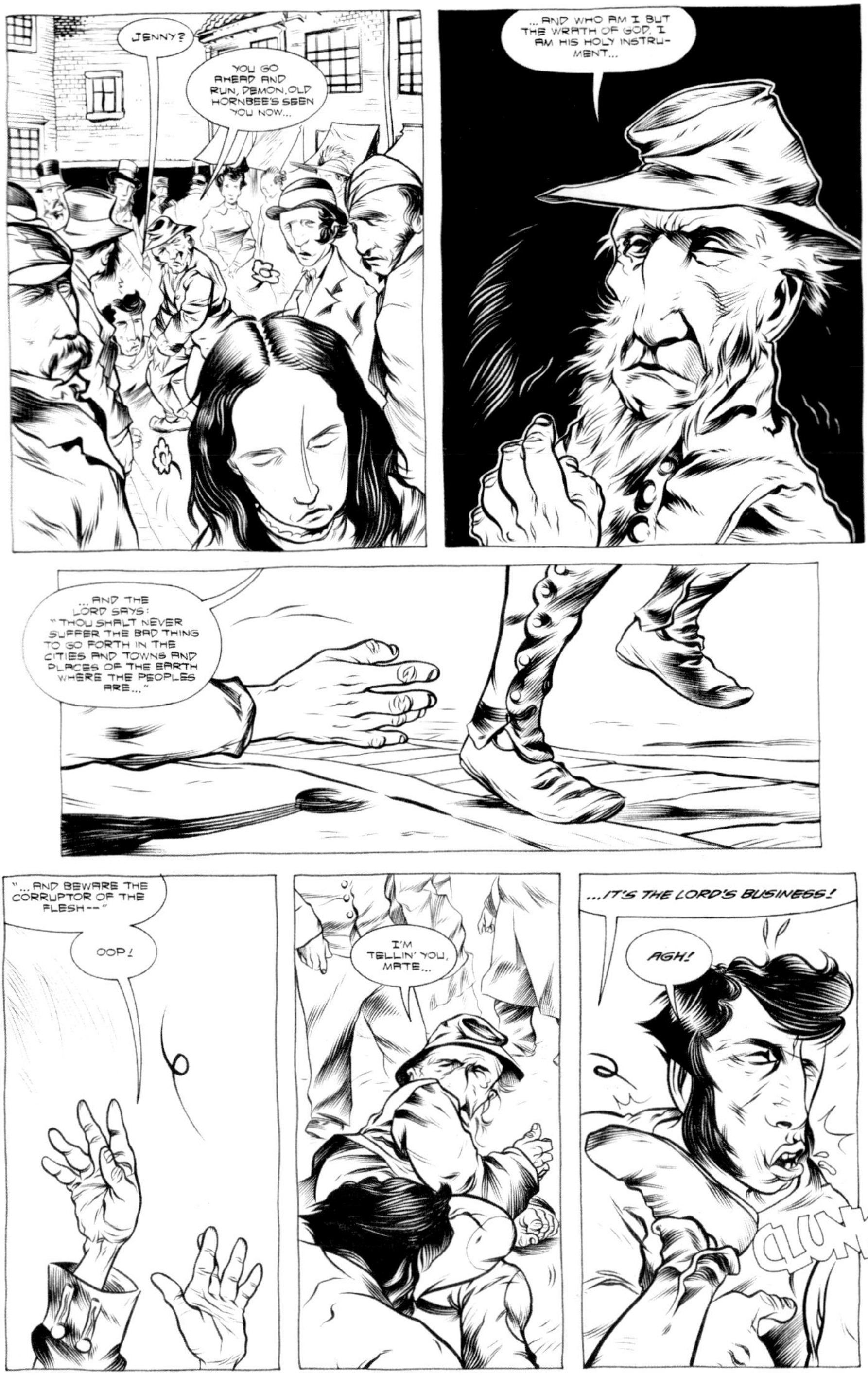
JENNY?
YOU GO AHEAD AND RUN, DEMON. OLD HORNBEE'S SEEN YOU NOW...
...AND WHO AM I BUT THE WRATH OF GOD. I AM HIS HOLY INSTRUMENT...
...AND THE LORD SAYS: "THOU SHALT NEVER SUFFER THE BAD THING TO GO FORTH IN THE CITIES AND TOWNS AND PLACES OF THE EARTH WHERE THE PEOPLES ARE..."
"...AND BEWARE THE CORRUPTOR OF THE FLESH--"
OOP!
I'M TELLIN' YOU, MATE...
...IT'S THE LORD'S BUSINESS!
AGH!
CLUNK

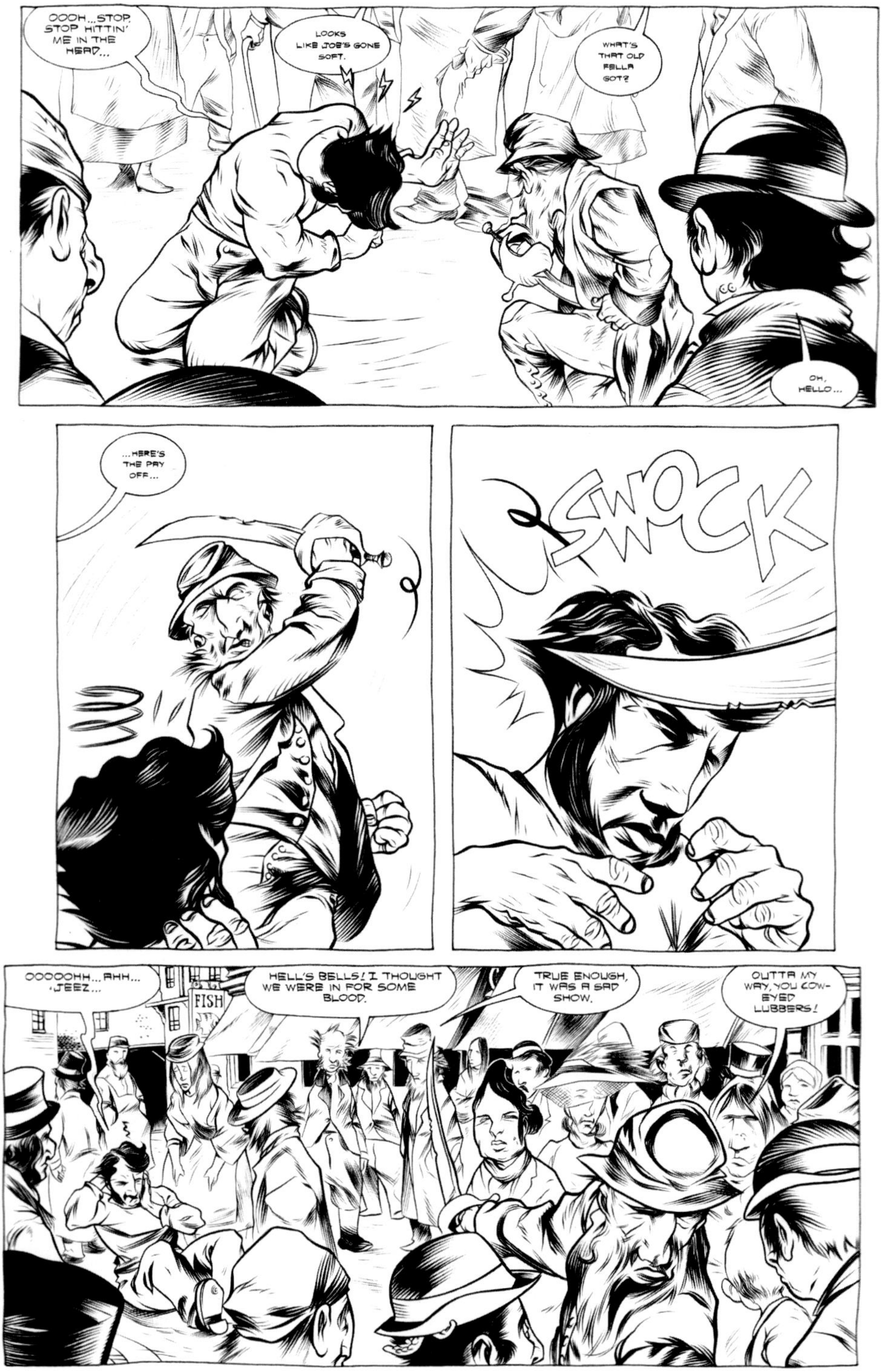
OOOH...STOP. STOP HITTIN' ME IN THE HEAD...
LOOKS LIKE JOE'S GONE SOFT.
WHAT'S THAT OLD FELLA GOT?
OH, HELLO...
...HERE'S THE PAY OFF...
SWOCK
OOOOOHH...AHH... 'JEEZ...
HELL'S BELLS! I THOUGHT WE WERE IN FOR SOME BLOOD.
TRUE ENOUGH, IT WAS A SAD SHOW.
OUTTA MY WAY, YOU COW-EYED LUBBERS!
FISH

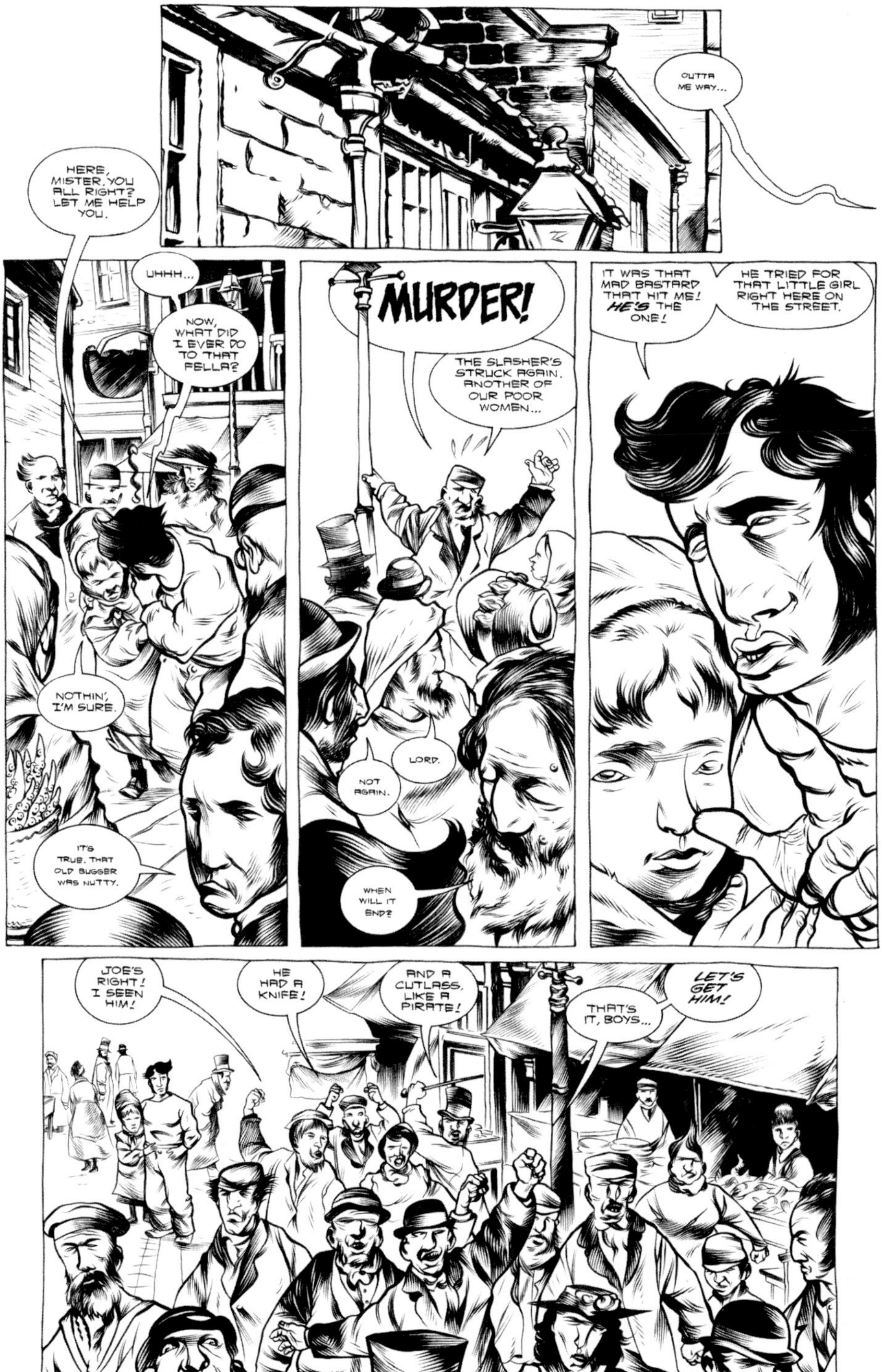
OUTTA ME WAY...
HERE, MISTER. YOU ALL RIGHT? LET ME HELP YOU.
UHHH...
NOW, WHAT DID I EVER DO TO THAT FELLA?
NOTHIN', I'M SURE.
IT'S TRUE. THAT OLD BUGGER WAS NUTTY.
MURDER!
THE SLASHER'S STRUCK AGAIN. ANOTHER OF OUR POOR WOMEN...
LORD.
NOT AGAIN.
WHEN WILL IT END?
IT WAS THAT MAD BASTARD THAT HIT ME! HE'S THE ONE!
HE TRIED FOR THAT LITTLE GIRL RIGHT HERE ON THE STREET.
JOE'S RIGHT! I SEEN HIM!
HE HAD A KNIFE!
AND A CUTLASS, LIKE A PIRATE!
THAT'S IT, BOYS...
LET'S GET HIM!

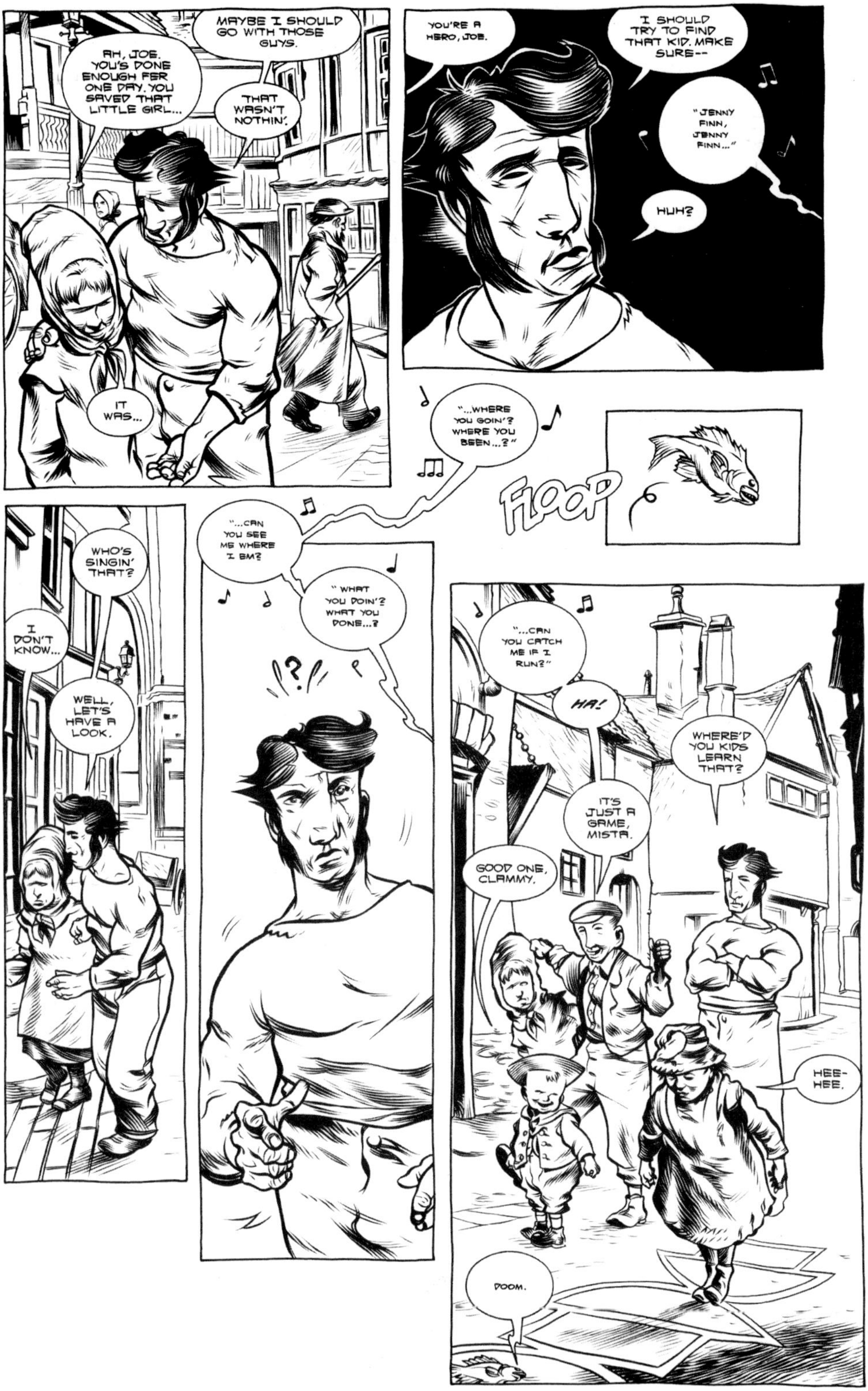
AH, JOE. YOU'S DONE ENOUGH FER ONE DAY. YOU SAVED THAT LITTLE GIRL...
MAYBE I SHOULD GO WITH THOSE GUYS.
THAT WASN'T NOTHIN'.
IT WAS...
YOU'RE A HERO, JOE.
I SHOULD TRY TO FIND THAT KID. MAKE SURE--
"JENNY FINN, JENNY FINN..."
HUH?
"...WHERE YOU GOIN'? WHERE YOU BEEN...?"
FLOOP
WHO'S SINGIN' THAT?
I DON'T KNOW...
WELL, LET'S HAVE A LOOK.
"...CAN YOU SEE ME WHERE I AM?
" WHAT YOU DOIN'? WHAT YOU DONE...?
!?
"...CAN YOU CATCH ME IF I RUN?"
HA!
WHERE'D YOU KIDS LEARN THAT?
IT'S JUST A GAME, MISTA.
GOOD ONE, CLAMMY.
HEE-HEE.
DOOM.

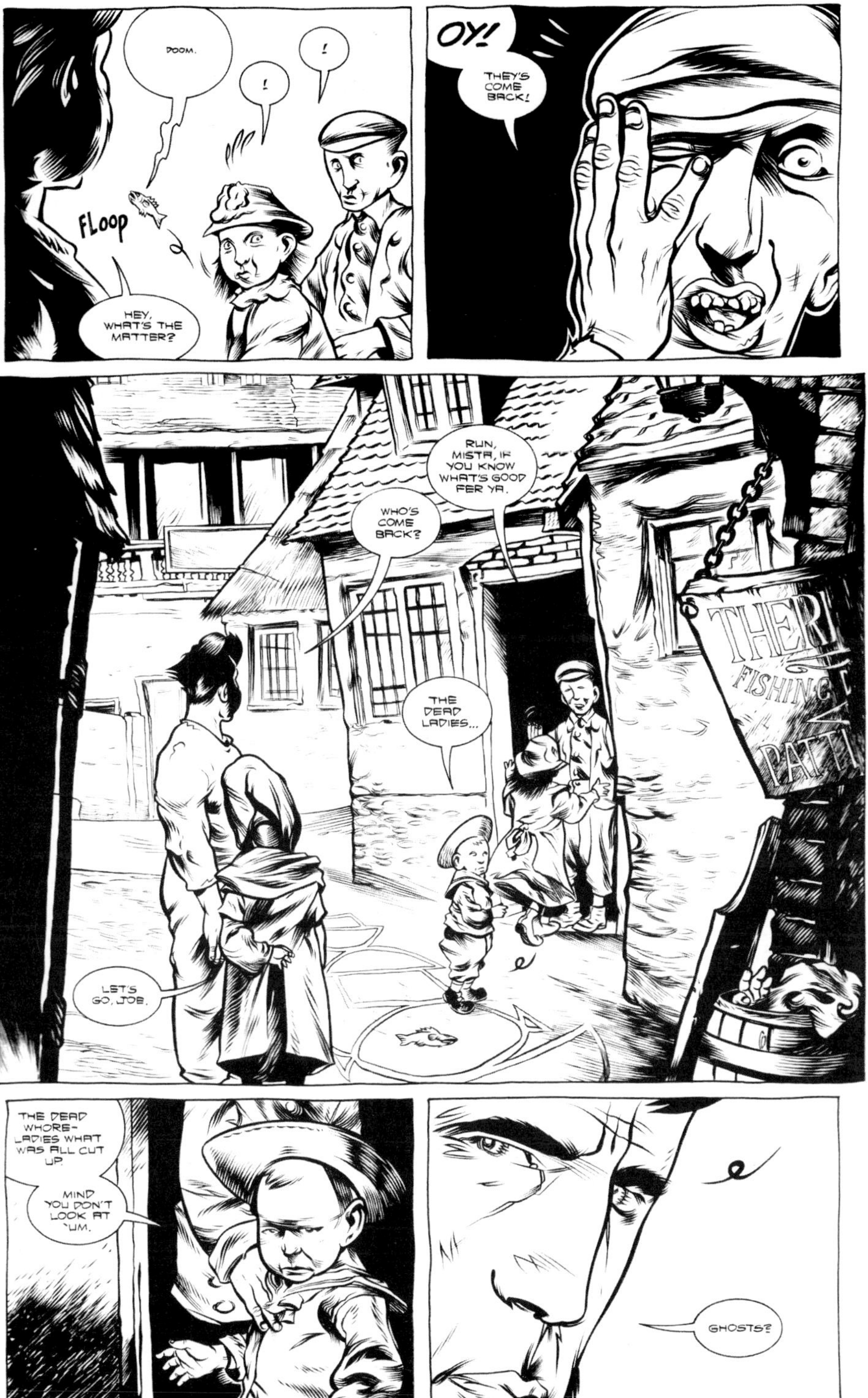
DOOM.
!
!
FLoop
HEY, WHAT'S THE MATTER?
OY!
THEY'S COME BACK!
RUN, MISTR, IF YOU KNOW WHAT'S GOOD FER YA.
WHO'S COME BACK?
THE DEAD LADIES...
THER
FISHING
PATI
LET'S GO, JOE.
THE DEAD WHORE-LADIES WHAT WAS ALL CUT UP.
MIND YOU DON'T LOOK AT 'UM.
GHOSTS?

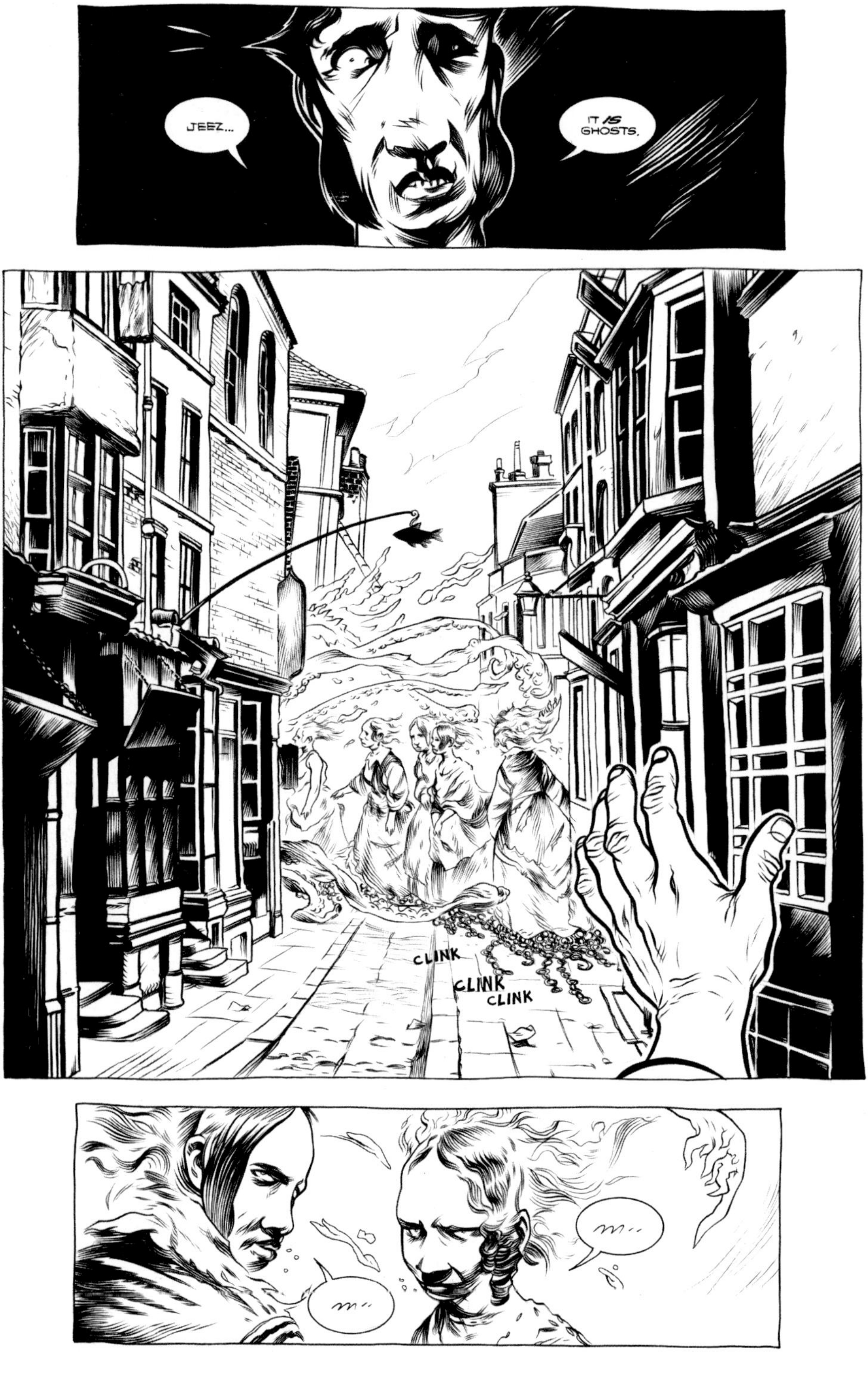
JEEZ...
IT IS GHOSTS.
CLINK
CLINK
CLINK
m..
m..

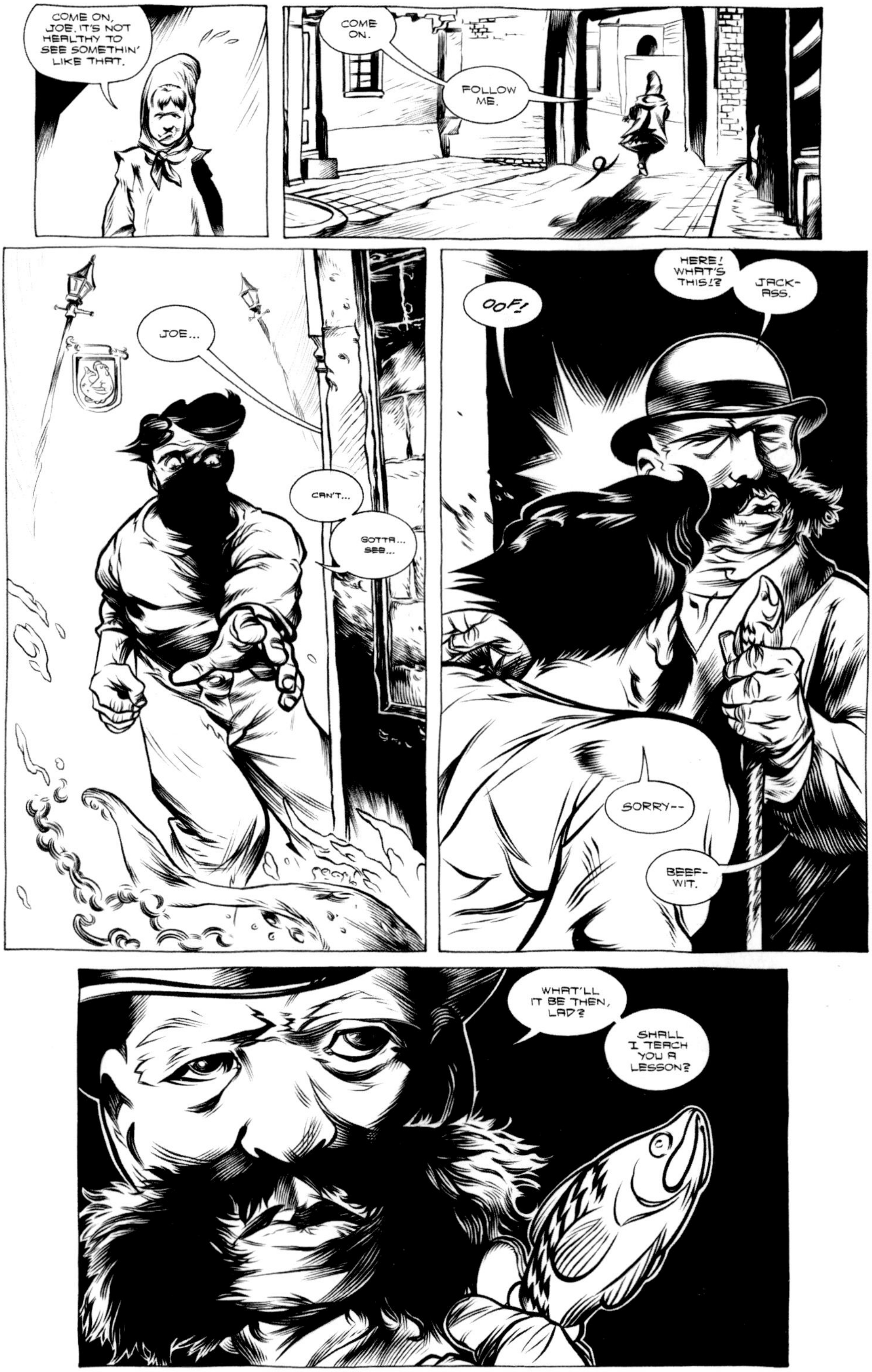
COME ON, JOE. IT'S NOT HEALTHY TO SEE SOMETHIN' LIKE THAT.
COME ON.
FOLLOW ME.
JOE...
CAN'T...
GOTTA... SEE...
OOF!
HERE! WHAT'S THIS!?
JACK-ASS.
SORRY--
BEEF-WIT.
WHAT'LL IT BE THEN, LAD?
SHALL I TEACH YOU A LESSON?

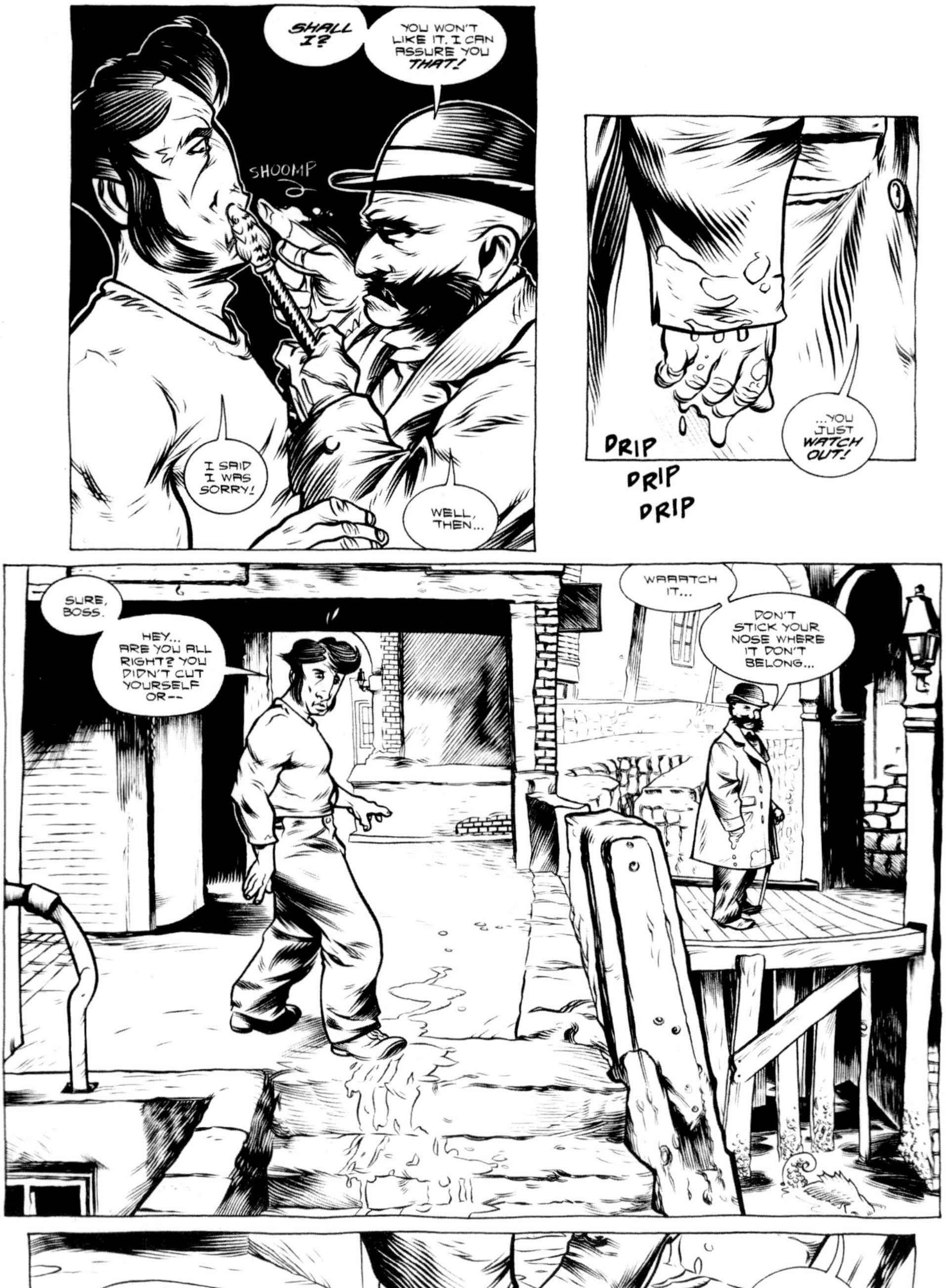
SHALL I?
YOU WON'T LIKE IT. I CAN ASSURE YOU THAT!
SHOOMP
I SAID I WAS SORRY!
WELL, THEN...
...YOU JUST WATCH OUT!
DRIP
DRIP
DRIP
SURE, BOSS.
HEY... ARE YOU ALL RIGHT? YOU DIDN'T CUT YOURSELF OR--
WAAATCH IT...
DON'T STICK YOUR NOSE WHERE IT DON'T BELONG...
...ELSE SOMEONE'S LIABLE TO CUT IT OFF.
SPLITCH

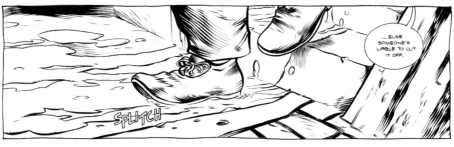

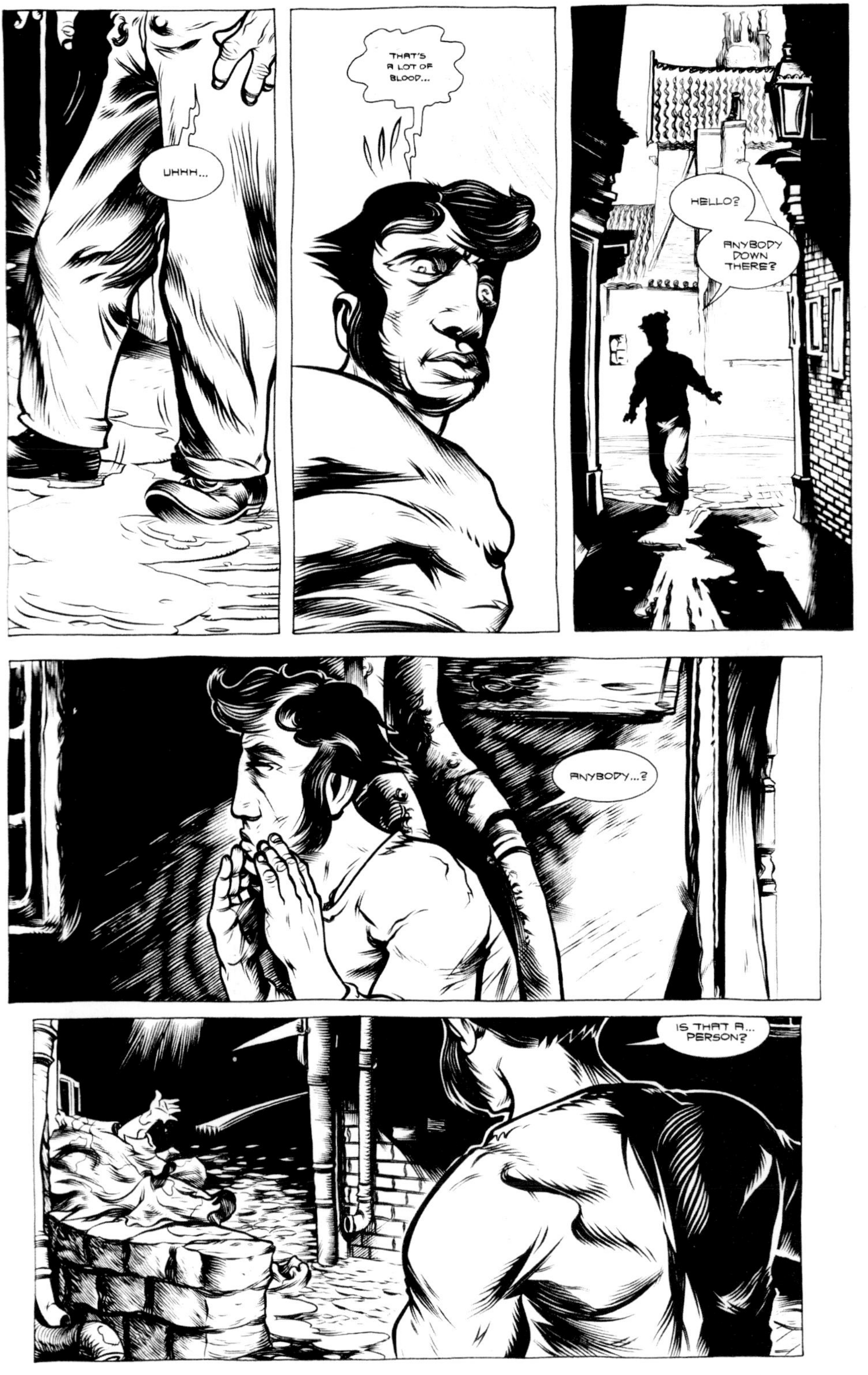
UHHH...
THAT'S A LOT OF BLOOD...
HELLO?
ANYBODY DOWN THERE?
ANYBODY...?
IS THAT A... PERSON?

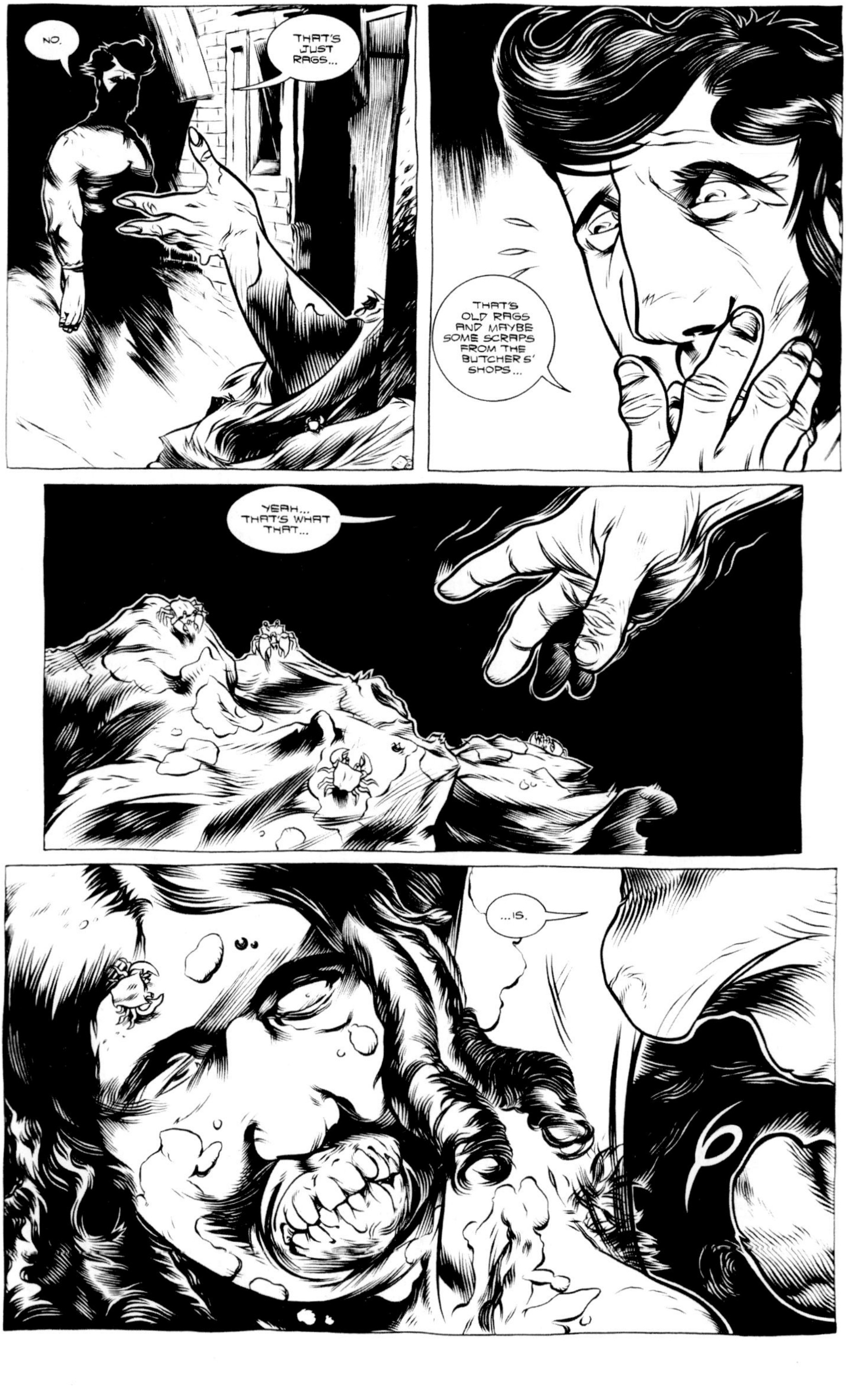
NO.
THAT'S JUST RAGS...
THAT'S OLD RAGS AND MAYBE SOME SCRAPS FROM THE BUTCHER'S' SHOPS...
YEAH... THAT'S WHAT THAT...
...IS.

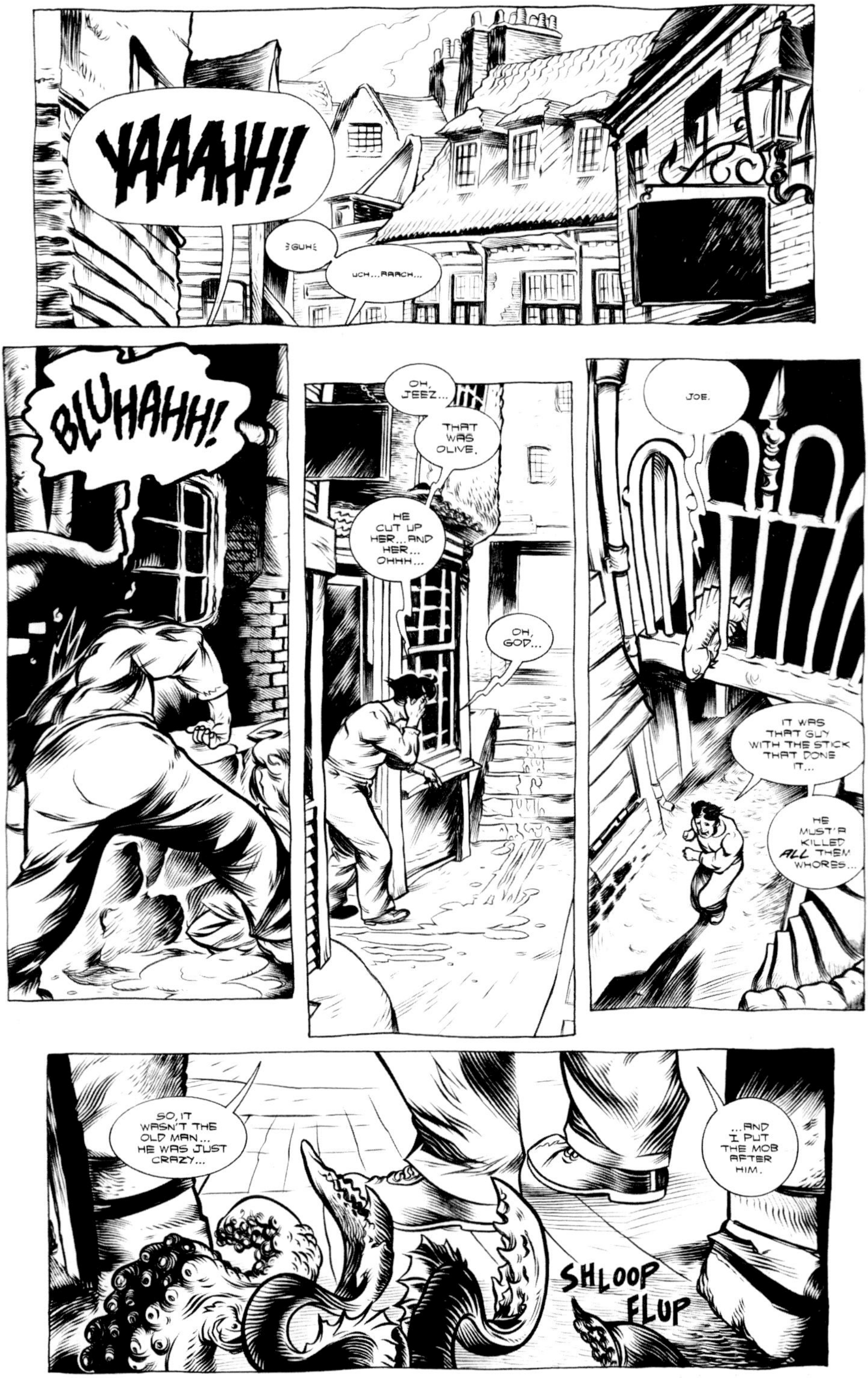
YAAAHH!
GUH
UCH...RARCH...
BLUHAHH!
OH, JEEZ...
THAT WAS OLIVE.
HE CUT UP HER...AND HER... OHHH...
OH, GOD...
JOE.
IT WAS THAT GUY WITH THE STICK THAT DONE IT...
HE MUST'A KILLED ALL THEM WHORES...
SO, IT WASN'T THE OLD MAN... HE WAS JUST CRAZY...
...AND I PUT THE MOB AFTER HIM.
SHLOOP
FLUP

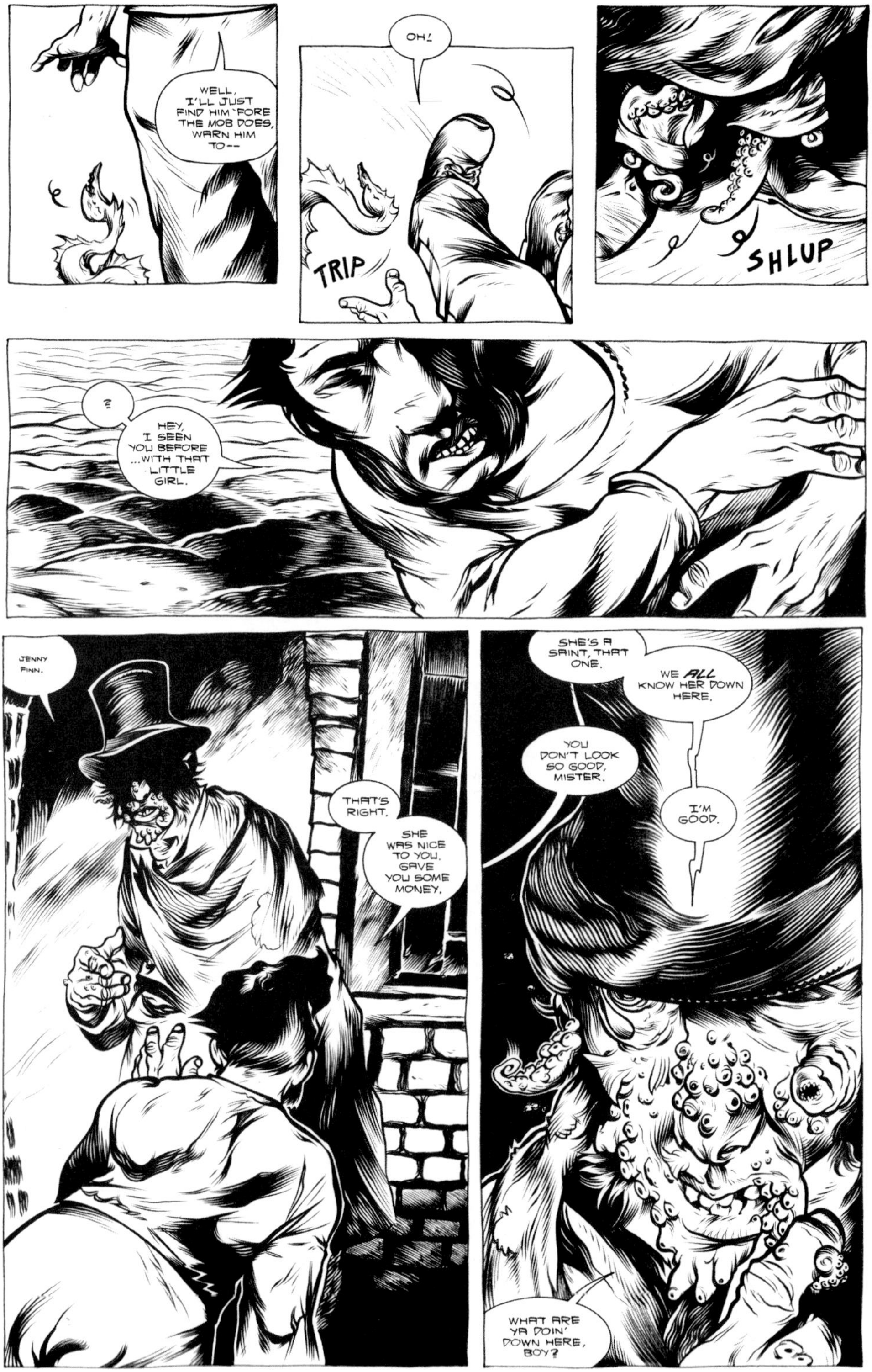
WELL, I'LL JUST FIND HIM 'FORE THE MOB DOES, WARN HIM TO--
OH!
TRIP
SHLUP
?
HEY, I SEEN YOU BEFORE ...WITH THAT LITTLE GIRL.
JENNY FINN.
THAT'S RIGHT.
SHE WAS NICE TO YOU. GAVE YOU SOME MONEY.
SHE'S A SAINT, THAT ONE.
WE ALL KNOW HER DOWN HERE.
YOU DON'T LOOK SO GOOD, MISTER.
I'M GOOD.
WHAT ARE YA DOIN' DOWN HERE, BOY?

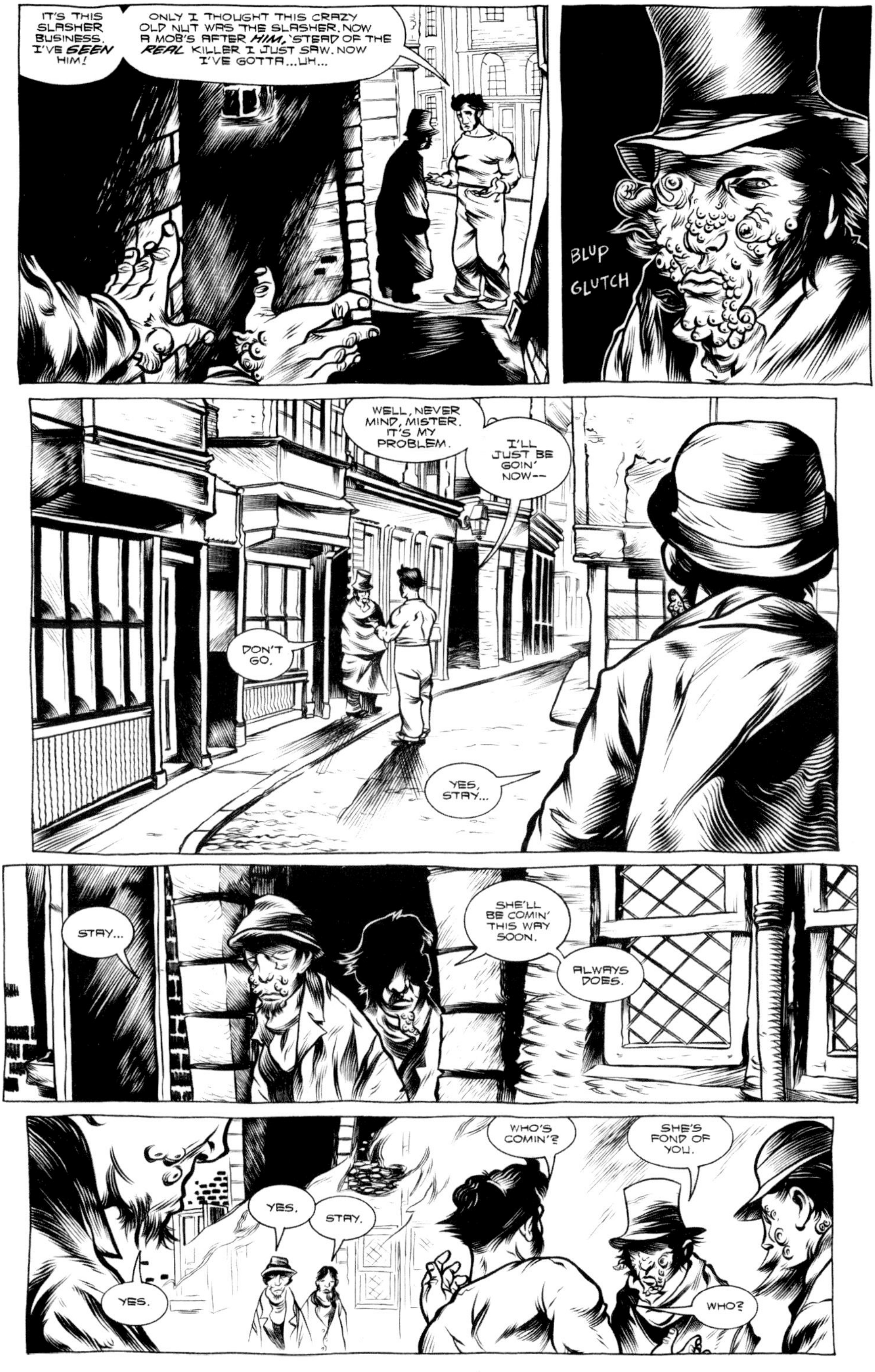
IT'S THIS SLASHER BUSINESS. I'VE SEEN HIM!
ONLY I THOUGHT THIS CRAZY OLD NUT WAS THE SLASHER. NOW A MOB'S AFTER HIM, 'STEAD OF THE REAL KILLER I JUST SAW. NOW I'VE GOTTA...UH...
BLUP
GLUTCH
WELL, NEVER MIND, MISTER. IT'S MY PROBLEM.
I'LL JUST BE GOIN' NOW--
DON'T GO.
YES, STAY...
STAY...
SHE'LL BE COMIN' THIS WAY SOON.
ALWAYS DOES.
WHO'S COMIN'?
SHE'S FOND OF YOU.
YES.
STAY.
YES.
WHO?

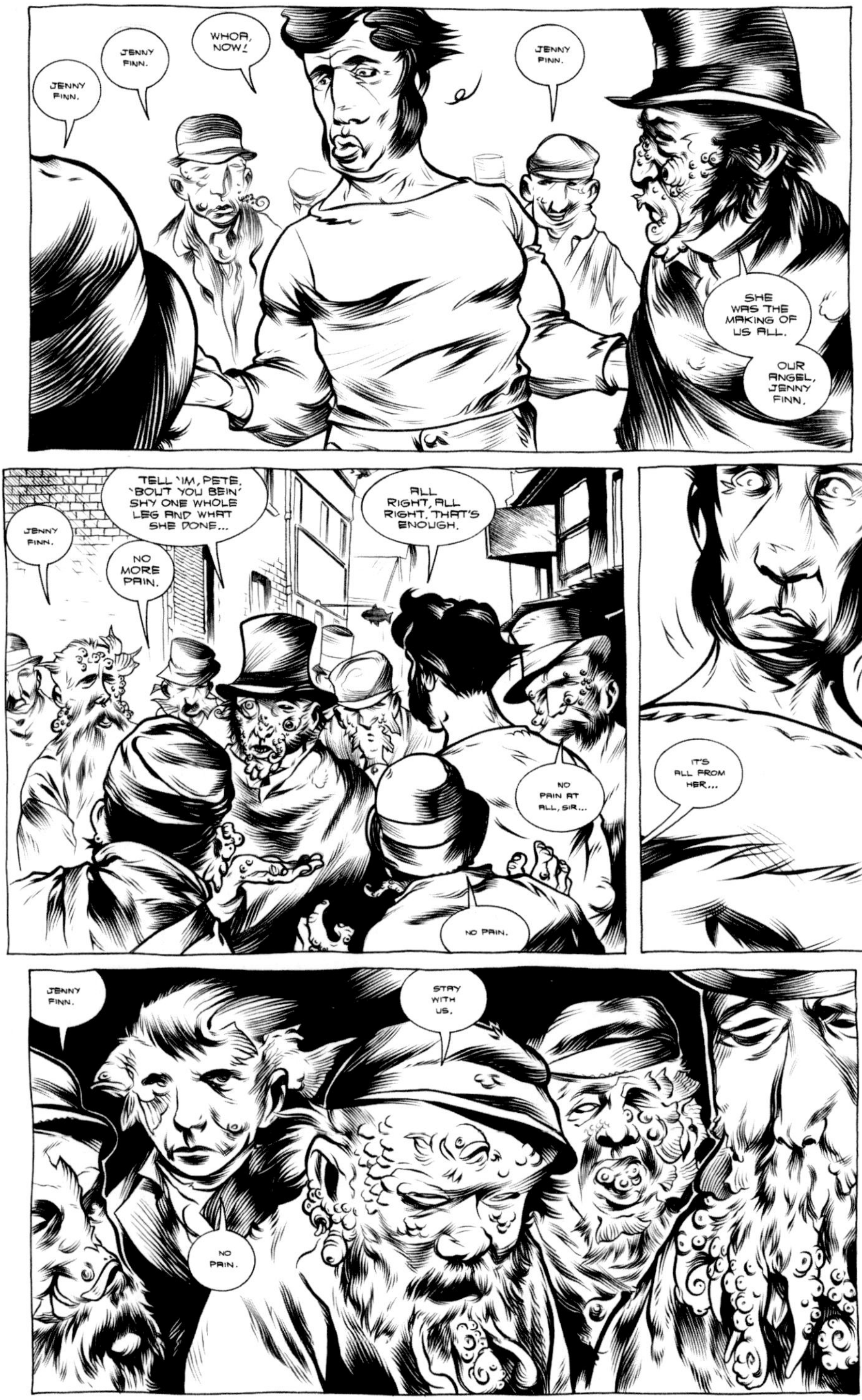
JENNY FINN.
JENNY FINN.
WHOA, NOW!
JENNY FINN.
SHE WAS THE MAKING OF US ALL.
OUR ANGEL, JENNY FINN.
JENNY FINN.
TELL 'IM, PETE. 'BOUT YOU BEIN' SHY ONE WHOLE LEG AND WHAT SHE DONE...
NO MORE PAIN.
ALL RIGHT, ALL RIGHT. THAT'S ENOUGH.
NO PAIN AT ALL, SIR...
NO PAIN.
IT'S ALL FROM HER...
JENNY FINN.
STAY WITH US.
NO PAIN.

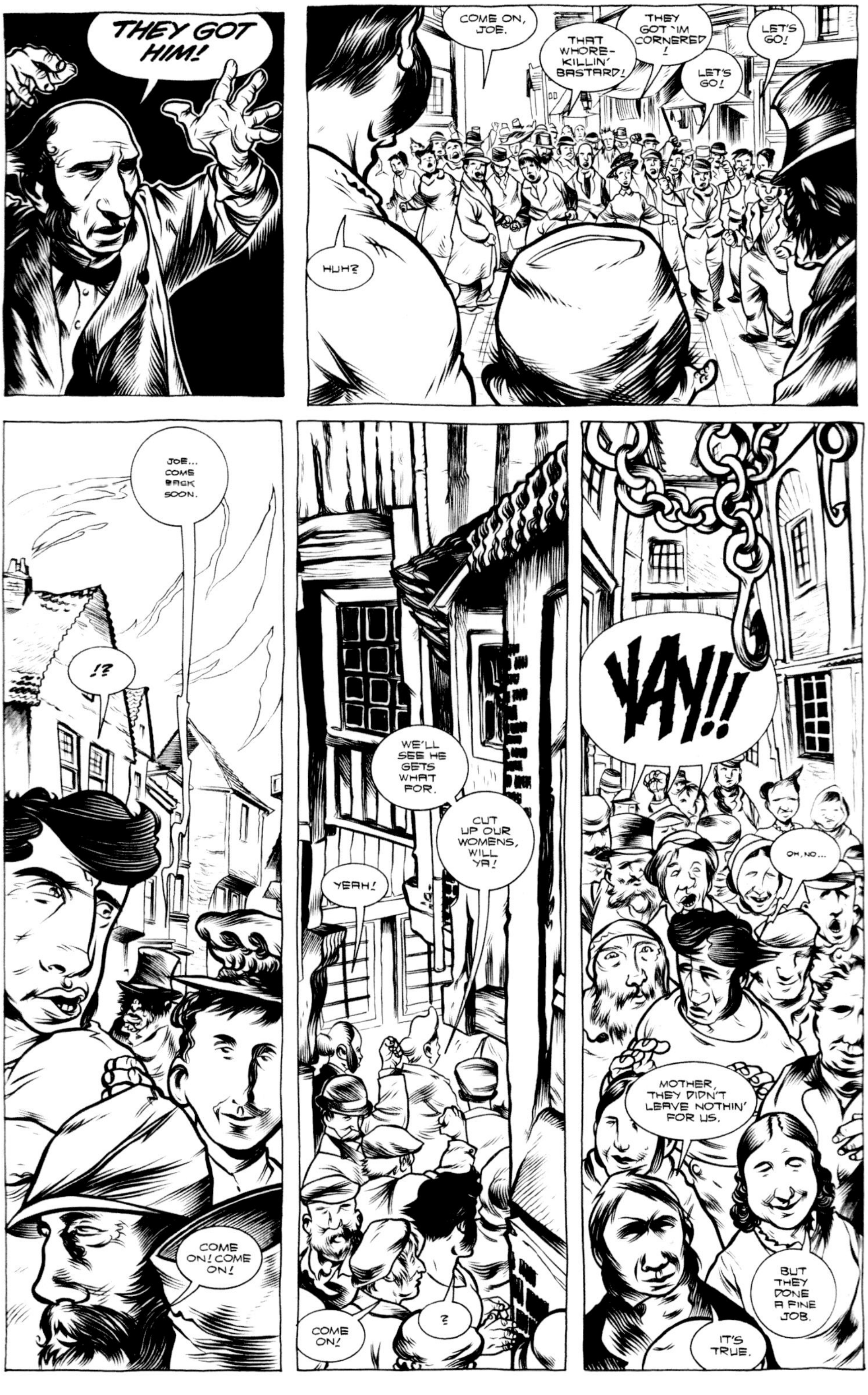
THEY GOT HIM!
COME ON, JOE.
THAT WHORE-KILLIN' BASTARD!
THEY GOT 'IM CORNERED!
LET'S GO!
LET'S GO!
HUH?
JOE... COME BACK SOON.
!?
COME ON! COME ON!
WE'LL SEE HE GETS WHAT FOR.
CUT UP OUR WOMENS, WILL YA!
YEAH!
COME ON!
?
YAY!!
OH, NO...
MOTHER, THEY DIDN'T LEAVE NOTHIN' FOR US.
BUT THEY DONE A FINE JOB.
IT'S TRUE.

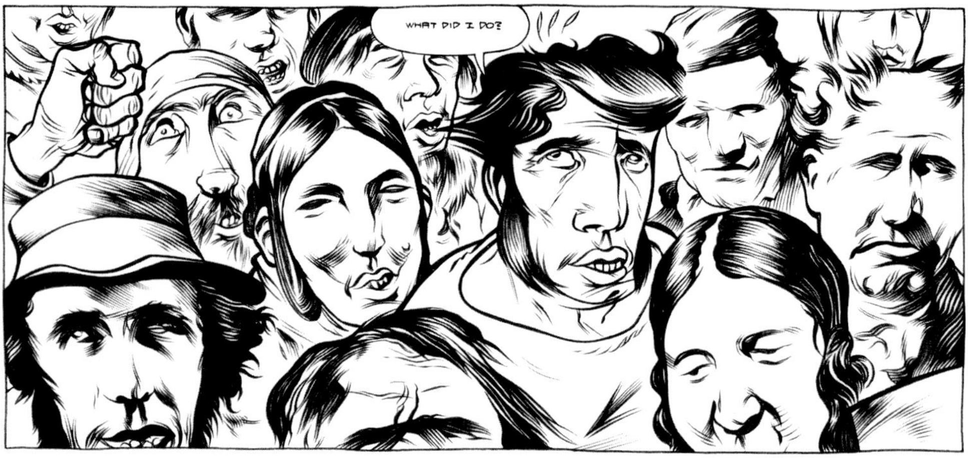
WHAT DID I DO?

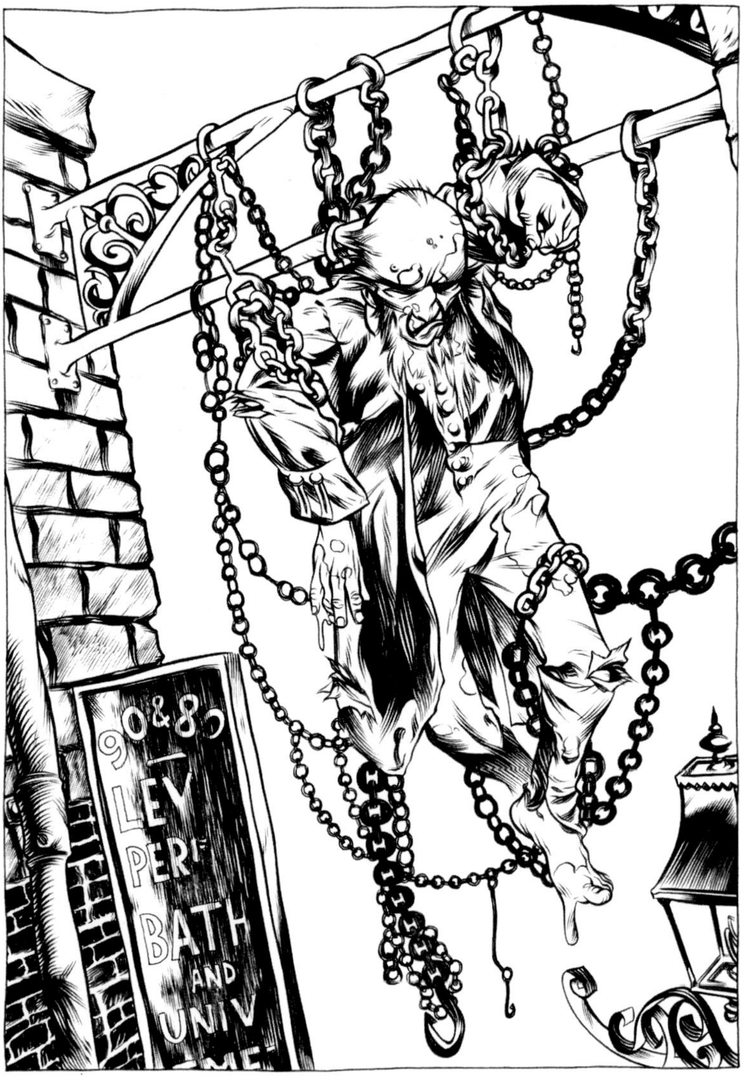
90&85
LEV
PERF
BATH
AND
UNIV

CHAPTER
TWO

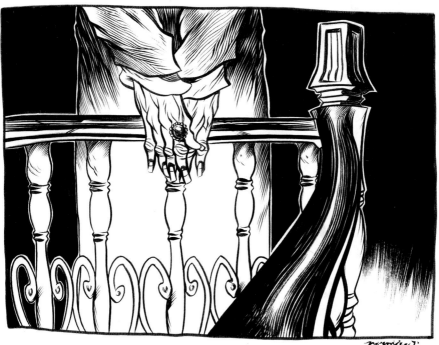

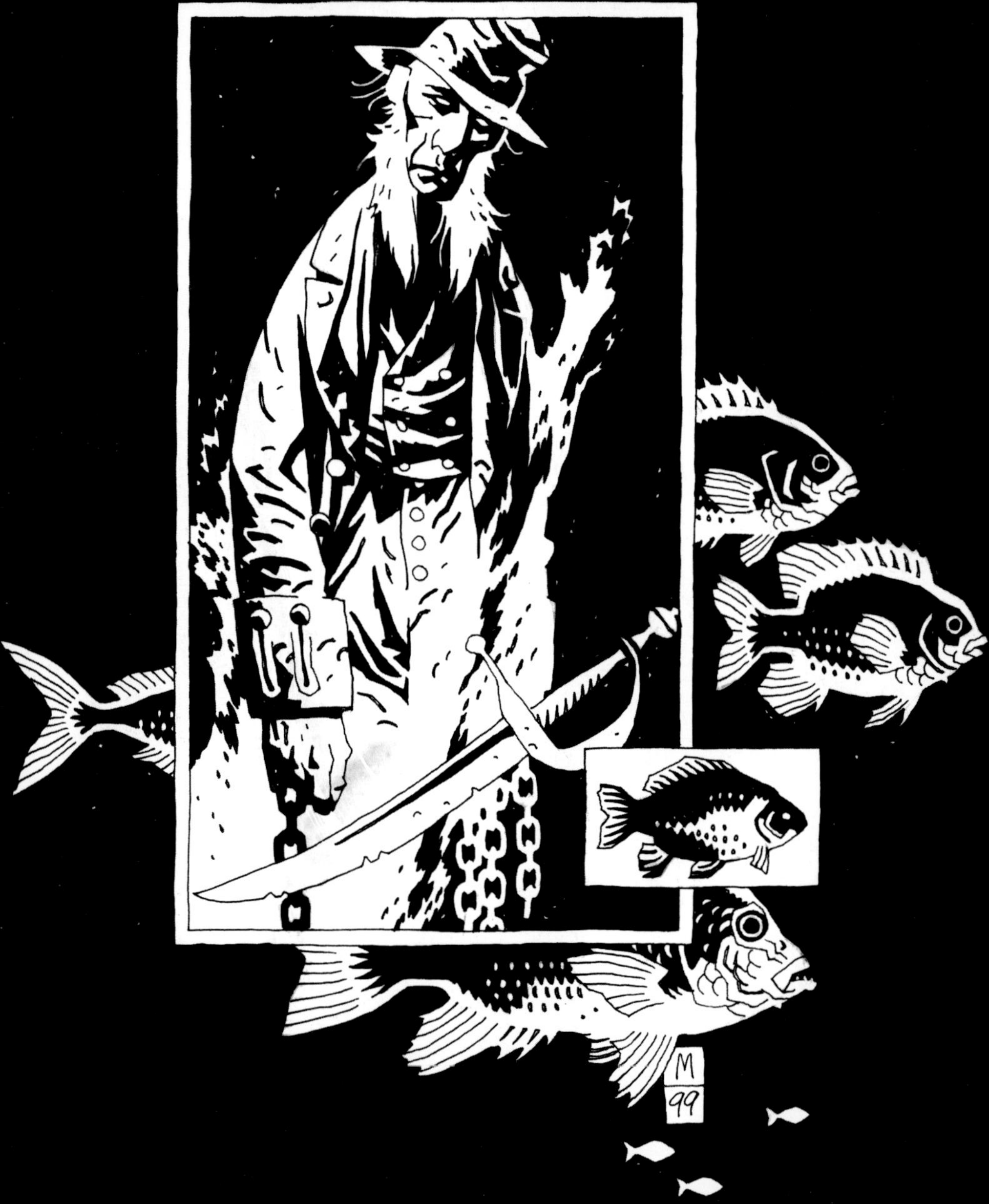
M
99

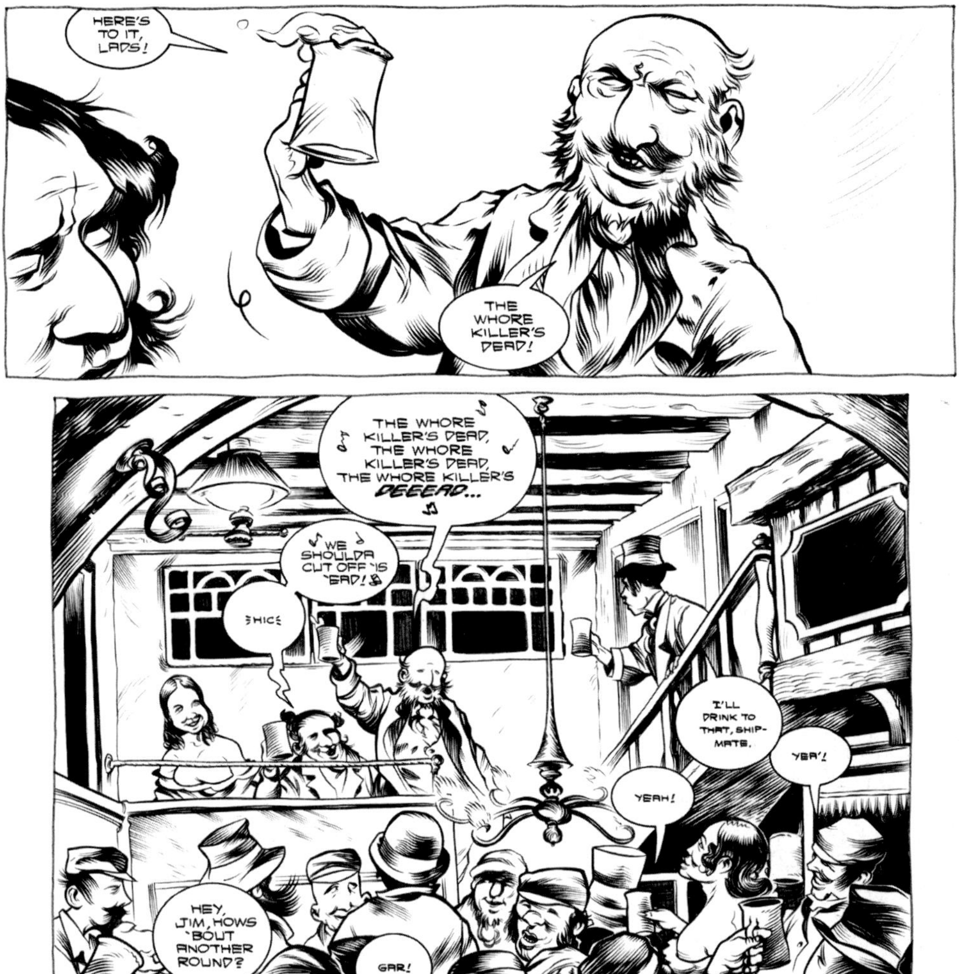
HERE'S TO IT, LADS!
THE WHORE KILLER'S DEAD!
THE WHORE KILLER'S DEAD, THE WHORE KILLER'S DEAD, THE WHORE KILLER'S DEEEAD...
WE SHOULDA CUT OFF 'IS 'EAD!
HIC
I'LL DRINK TO THAT, SHIP-MATE.
YEA'!
YEAH!
HEY, JIM, HOWS 'BOUT ANOTHER ROUND?
GAR!
YES, SIR, WE TOOK GOOD GOD-DAMN CARE OF THE MURDERIN' BUGGER!
...DONE 'IM UP RIGHT AN' PROPER...
DOOM.

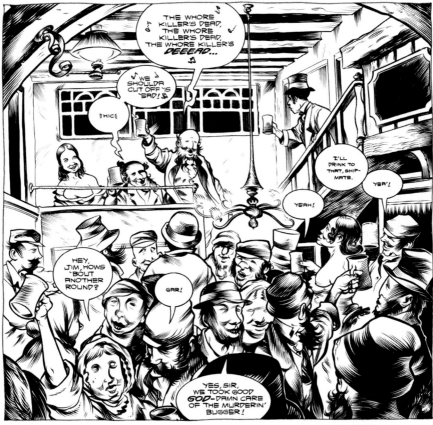

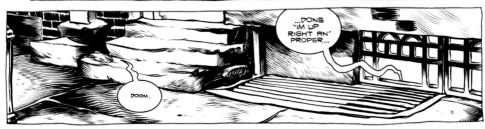

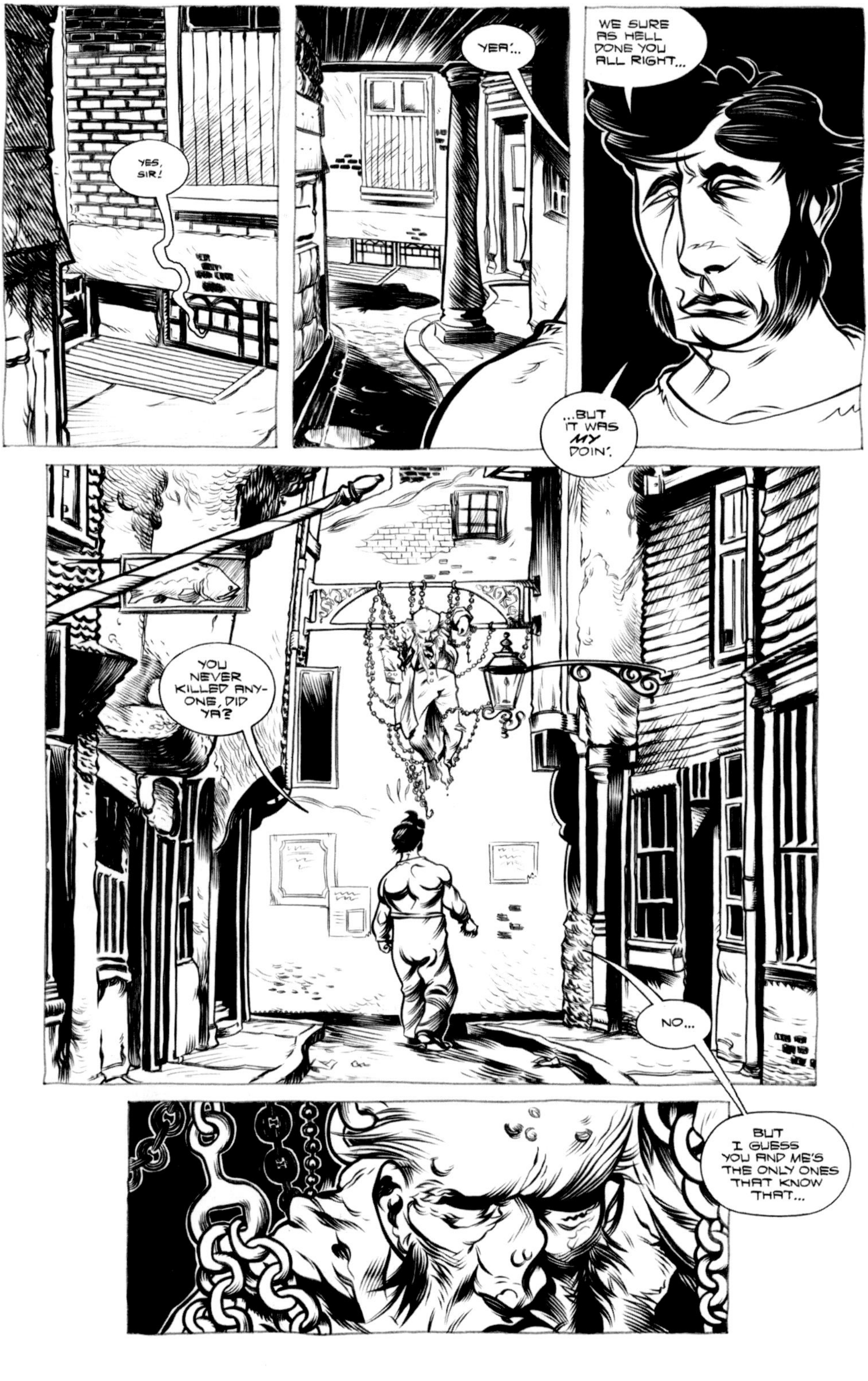
YES, SIR!
YEA'...
WE SURE AS HELL DONE YOU ALL RIGHT...
...BUT IT WAS MY DOIN'.
YOU NEVER KILLED ANY-ONE, DID YA?
NO...
BUT I GUESS YOU AND ME'S THE ONLY ONES THAT KNOW THAT...

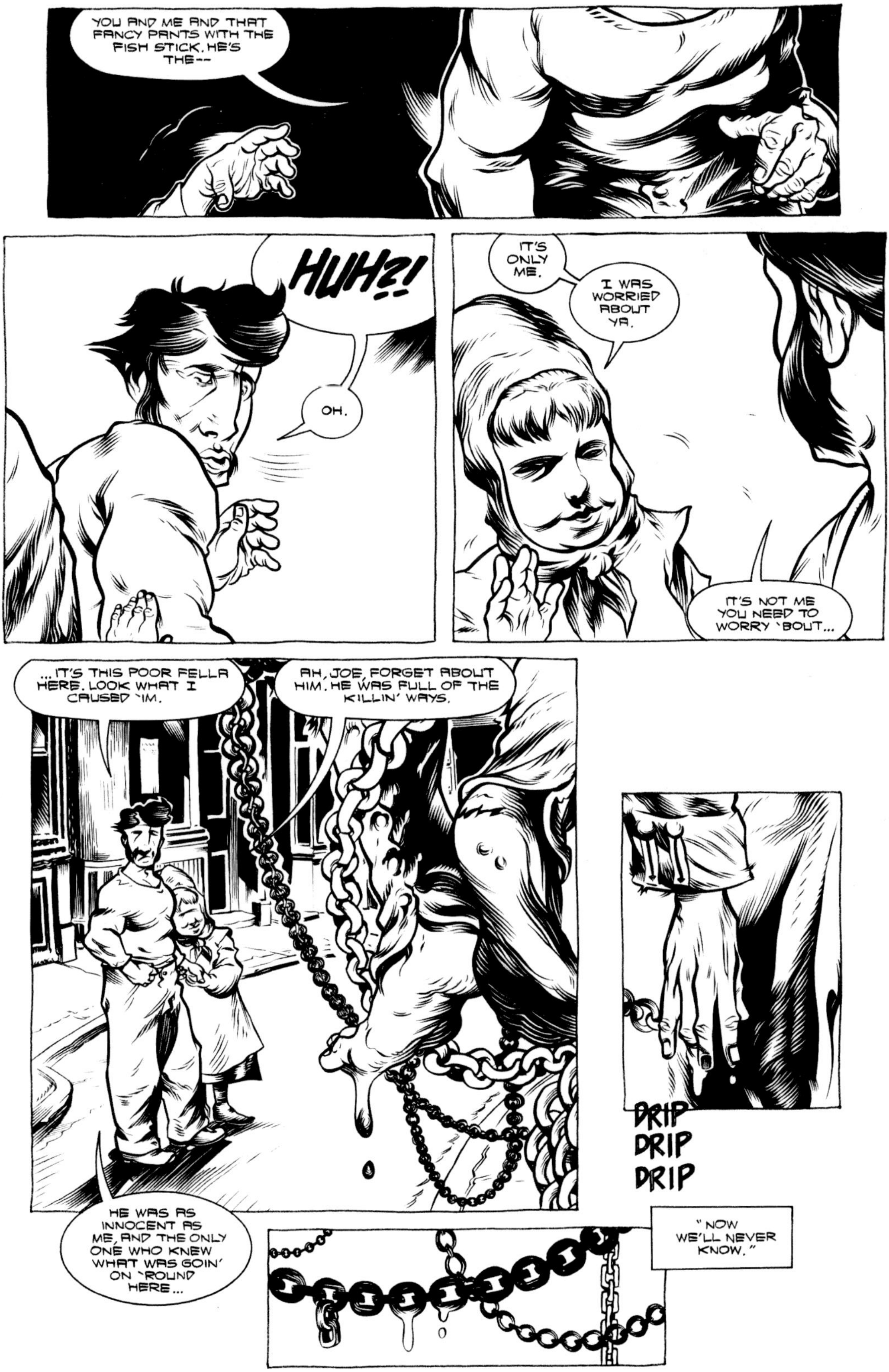
YOU AND ME AND THAT FANCY PANTS WITH THE FISH STICK. HE'S THE--
HUH?!
OH.
IT'S ONLY ME.
I WAS WORRIED ABOUT YA.
IT'S NOT ME YOU NEED TO WORRY 'BOUT...
...IT'S THIS POOR FELLA HERE. LOOK WHAT I CAUSED 'IM.
AH, JOE, FORGET ABOUT HIM. HE WAS FULL OF THE KILLIN' WAYS.
HE WAS AS INNOCENT AS ME, AND THE ONLY ONE WHO KNEW WHAT WAS GOIN' ON 'ROUND HERE...
DRIP
DRIP
DRIP
"NOW WE'LL NEVER KNOW."

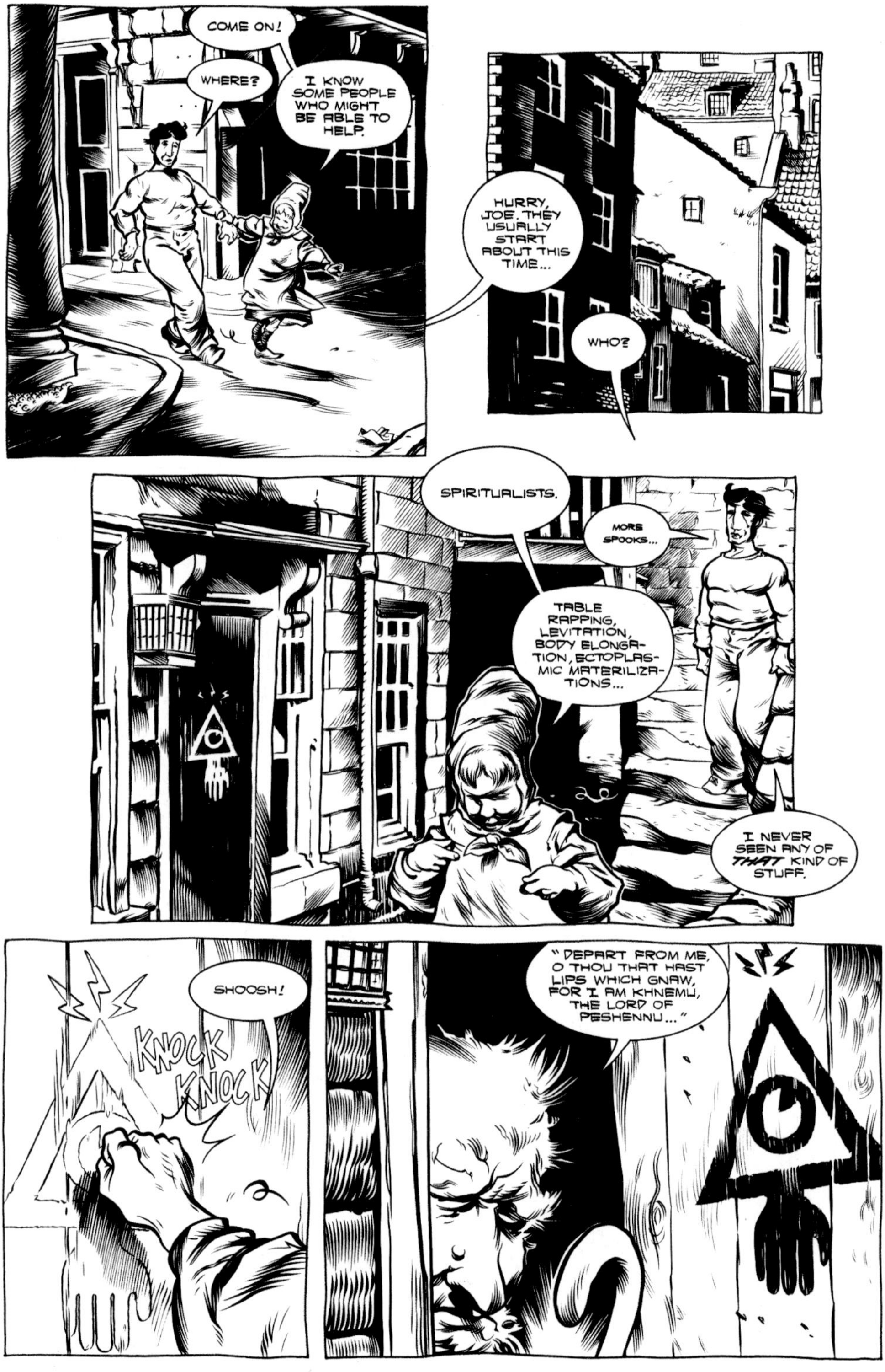
COME ON!
WHERE?
I KNOW SOME PEOPLE WHO MIGHT BE ABLE TO HELP.
HURRY, JOE. THEY USUALLY START ABOUT THIS TIME...
WHO?
SPIRITUALISTS.
MORE SPOOKS...
TABLE RAPPING, LEVITATION, BODY ELONGATION, ECTOPLASMIC MATERILIZATIONS...
I NEVER SEEN ANY OF THAT KIND OF STUFF.
SHOOSH!
KNOCK KNOCK
"DEPART FROM ME, O THOU THAT HAST LIPS WHICH GNAW, FOR I AM KHNEMU, THE LORD OF PESHENNU..."

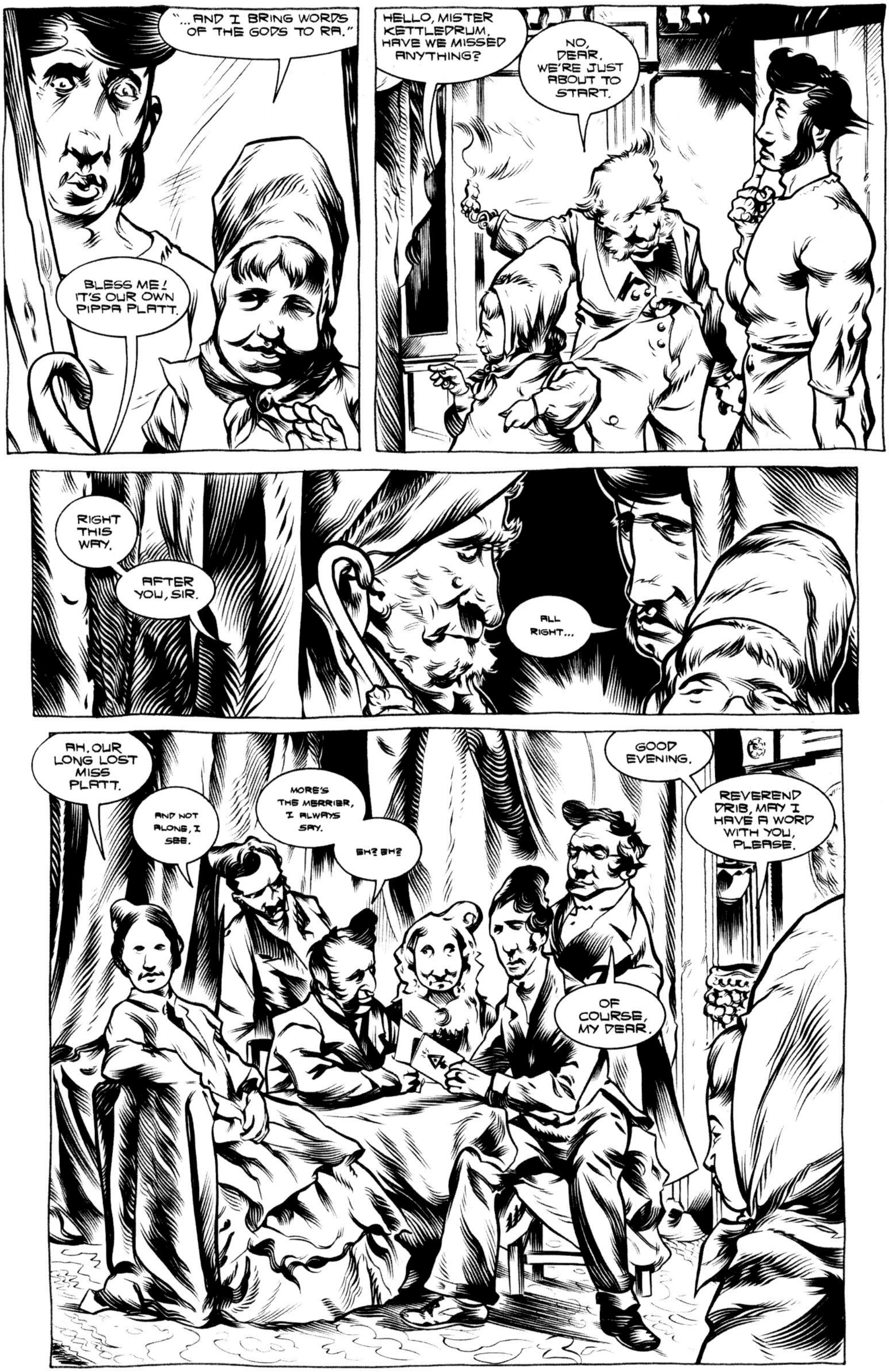
"...AND I BRING WORDS OF THE GODS TO RA."
BLESS ME! IT'S OUR OWN PIPPA PLATT.
HELLO, MISTER KETTLEDRUM. HAVE WE MISSED ANYTHING?
NO, DEAR, WE'RE JUST ABOUT TO START.
RIGHT THIS WAY.
AFTER YOU, SIR.
ALL RIGHT...
AH, OUR LONG LOST MISS PLATT.
AND NOT ALONE, I SEE.
MORE'S THE MERRIER, I ALWAYS SAY.
EH? EH?
GOOD EVENING.
REVEREND DRIB, MAY I HAVE A WORD WITH YOU, PLEASE.
OF COURSE, MY DEAR.

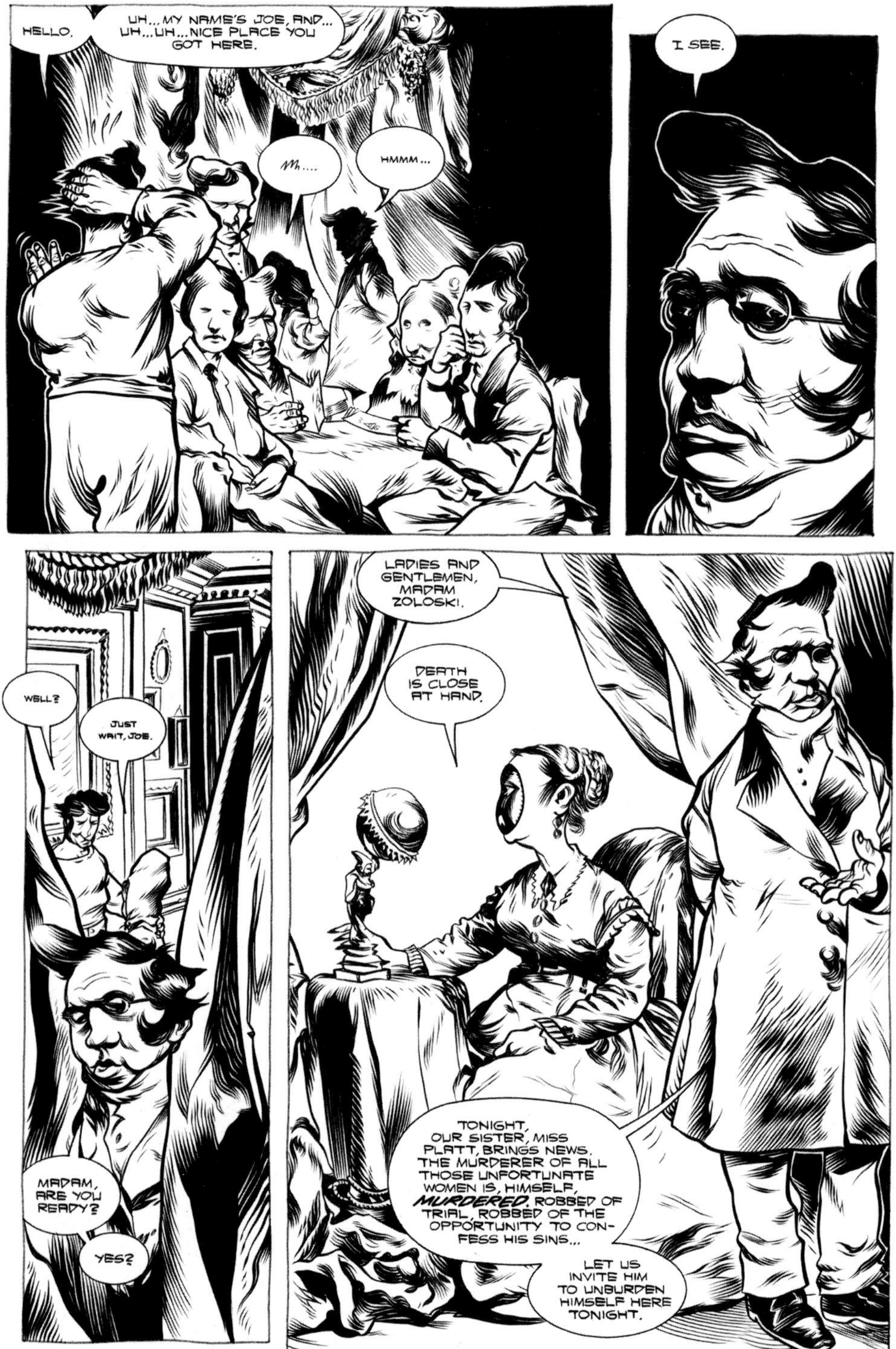
HELLO.
UH... MY NAME'S JOE, AND... UH... UH... NICE PLACE YOU GOT HERE.
M....
HMMM...
I SEE.
WELL?
JUST WAIT, JOE.
MADAM, ARE YOU READY?
YES?
LADIES AND GENTLEMEN, MADAM ZOLOSKI.
DEATH IS CLOSE AT HAND.
TONIGHT, OUR SISTER, MISS PLATT, BRINGS NEWS. THE MURDERER OF ALL THOSE UNFORTUNATE WOMEN IS, HIMSELF, MURDERED. ROBBED OF TRIAL, ROBBED OF THE OPPORTUNITY TO CONFESS HIS SINS...
LET US INVITE HIM TO UNBURDEN HIMSELF HERE TONIGHT.

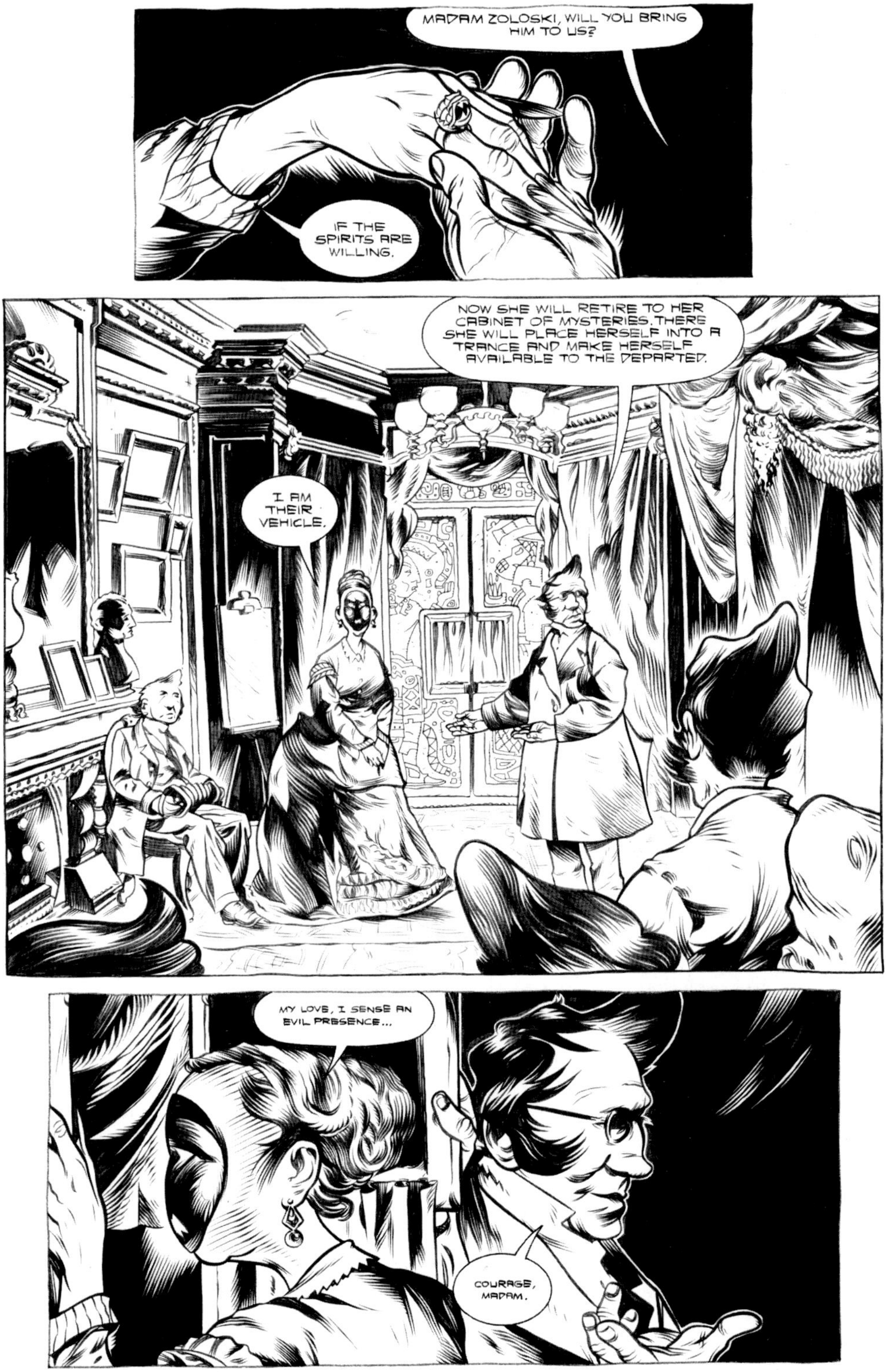
MADAM ZOLOSKI, WILL YOU BRING HIM TO US?
IF THE SPIRITS ARE WILLING.
NOW SHE WILL RETIRE TO HER CABINET OF MYSTERIES. THERE SHE WILL PLACE HERSELF INTO A TRANCE AND MAKE HERSELF AVAILABLE TO THE DEPARTED.
I AM THEIR VEHICLE.
MY LOVE, I SENSE AN EVIL PRESENCE...
COURAGE, MADAM.

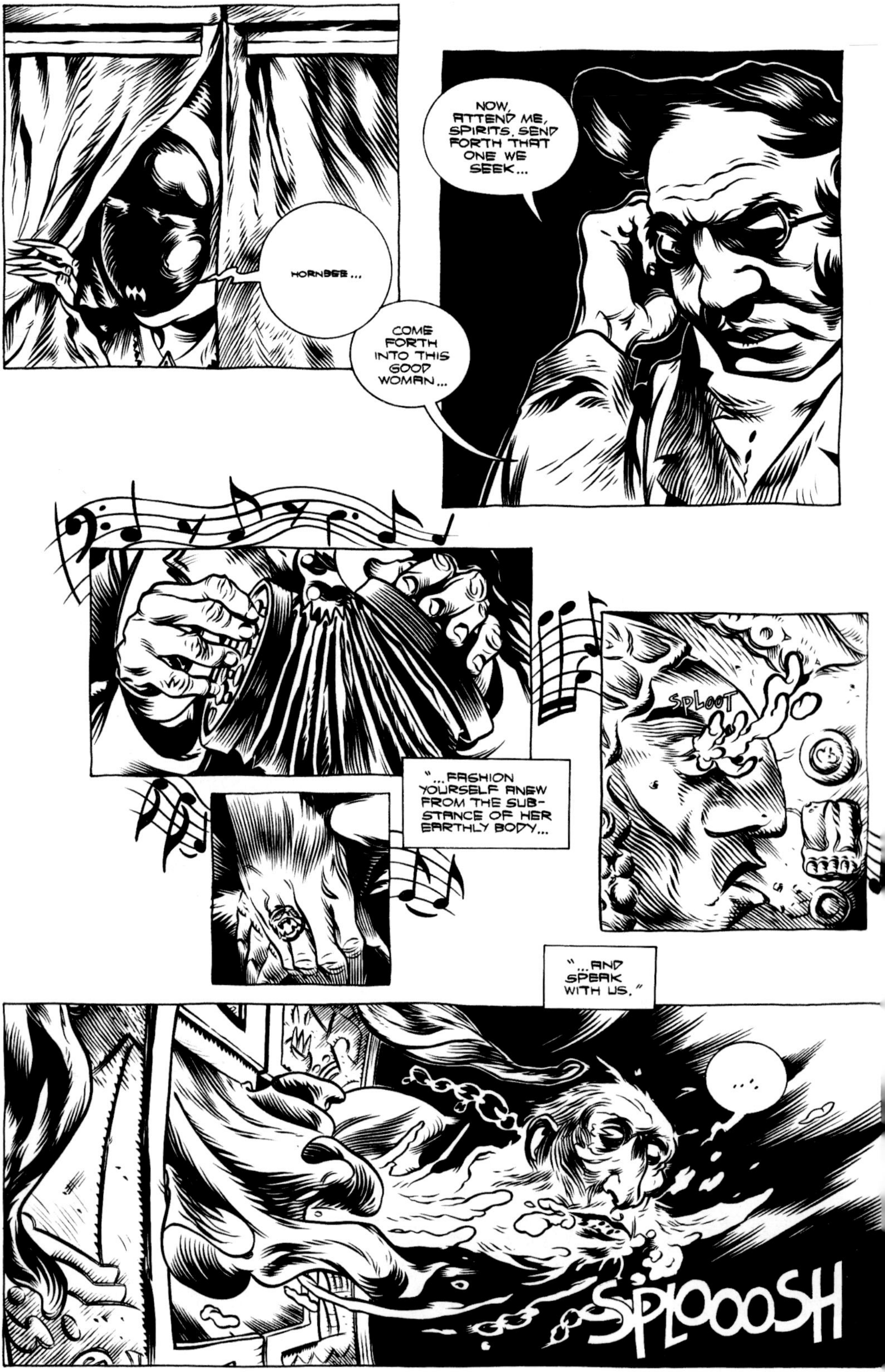
HORNBEE...
NOW, ATTEND ME, SPIRITS, SEND FORTH THAT ONE WE SEEK...
COME FORTH INTO THIS GOOD WOMAN...
"...FASHION YOURSELF ANEW FROM THE SUBSTANCE OF HER EARTHLY BODY...
SPLOOT
"...AND SPEAK WITH US."
...
SPLOOOSH

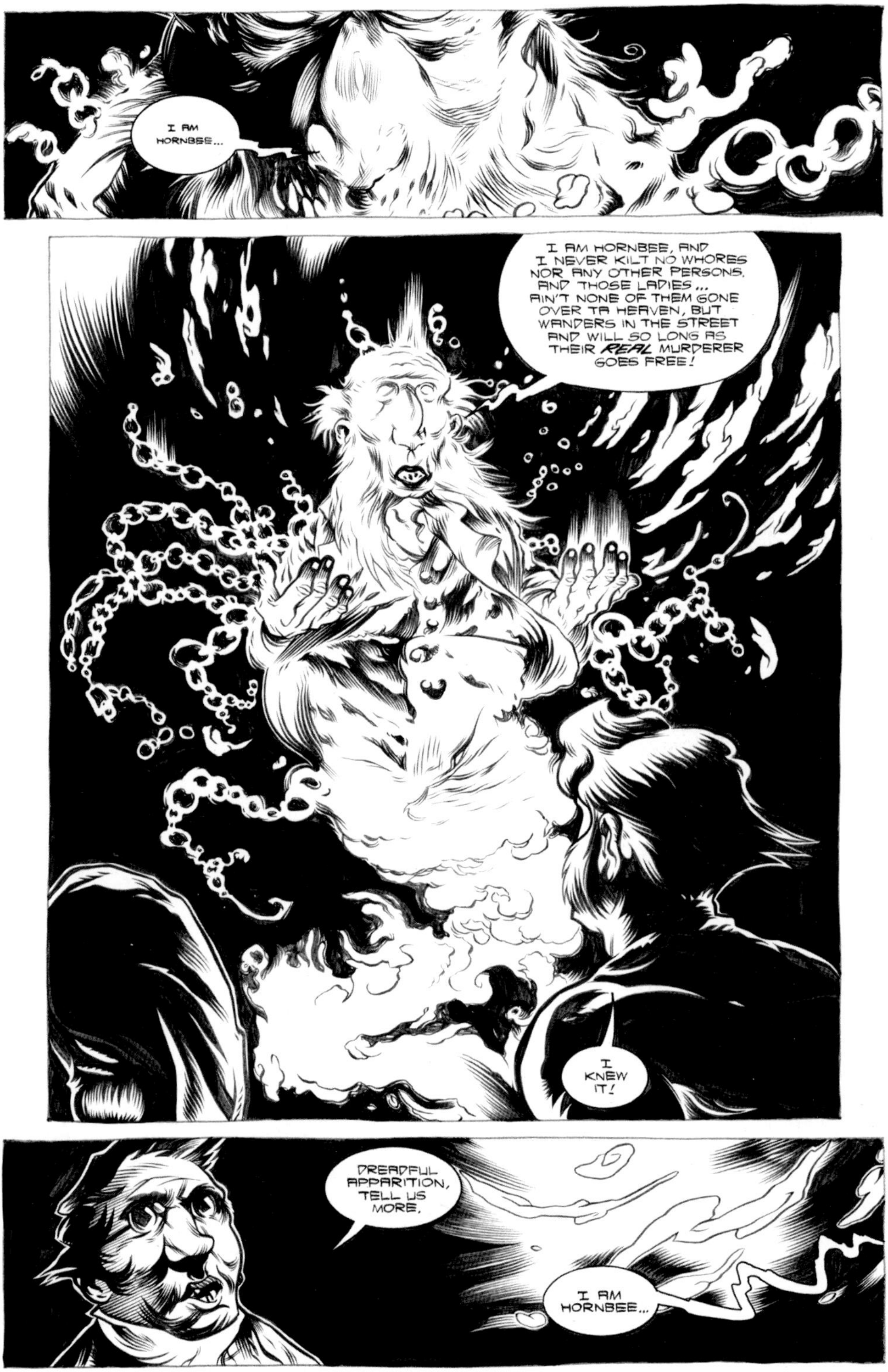
I AM HORNBEE...
I AM HORNBEE, AND I NEVER KILT NO WHORES NOR ANY OTHER PERSONS. AND THOSE LADIES... AIN'T NONE OF THEM GONE OVER TA HEAVEN, BUT WANDERS IN THE STREET AND WILL SO LONG AS THEIR REAL MURDERER GOES FREE!
I KNEW IT!
DREADFUL APPARITION, TELL US MORE.
I AM HORNBEE...

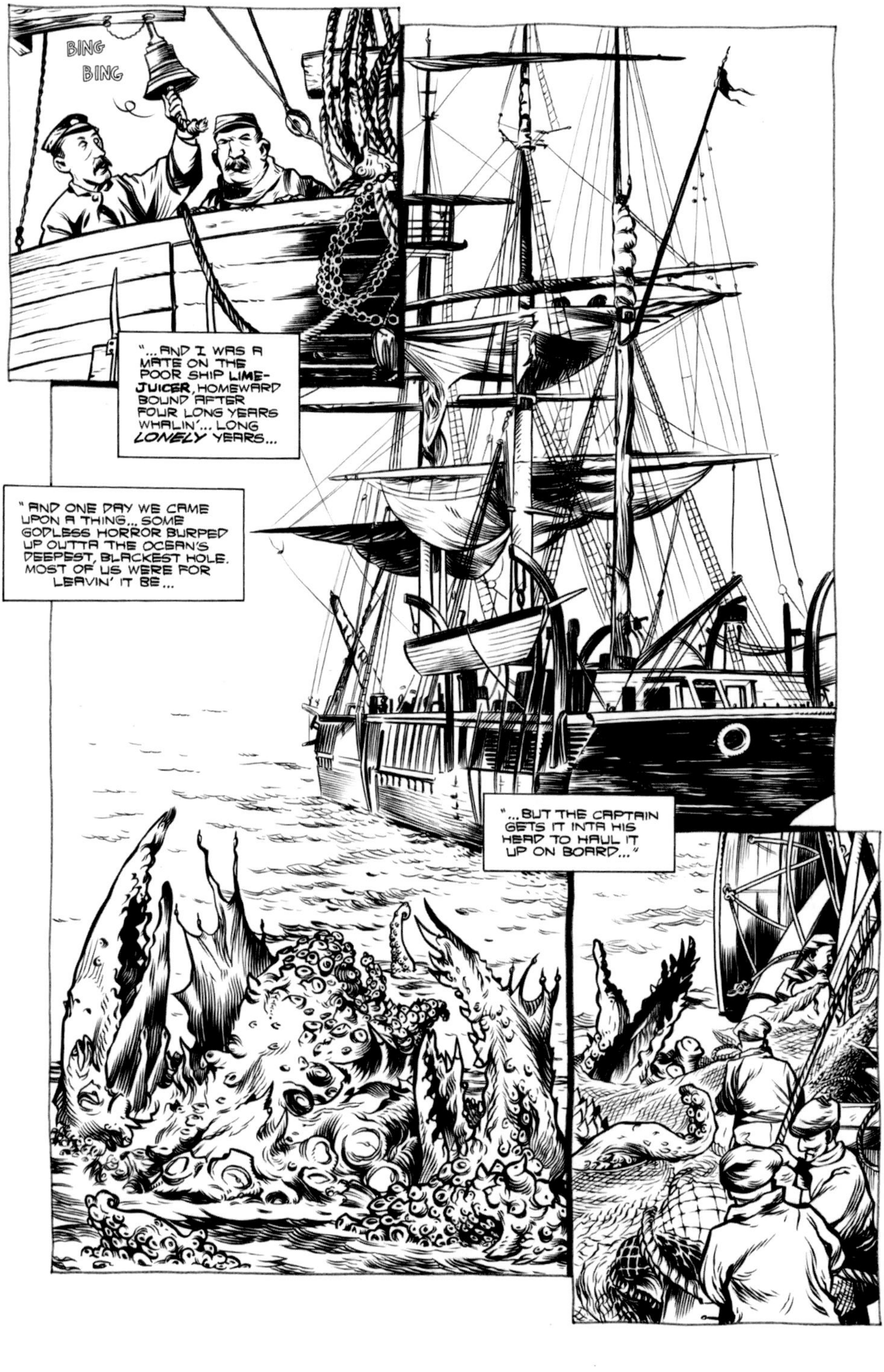
BING
BING
"...AND I WAS A MATE ON THE POOR SHIP **LIME-JUICER**, HOMEWARD BOUND AFTER FOUR LONG YEARS WHALIN'... LONG *LONELY* YEARS...
"AND ONE DAY WE CAME UPON A THING... SOME GODLESS HORROR BURPED UP OUTTA THE OCEAN'S DEEPEST, BLACKEST HOLE. MOST OF US WERE FOR LEAVIN' IT BE...
"...BUT THE CAPTAIN GETS IT INTA HIS HEAD TO HAUL IT UP ON BOARD..."

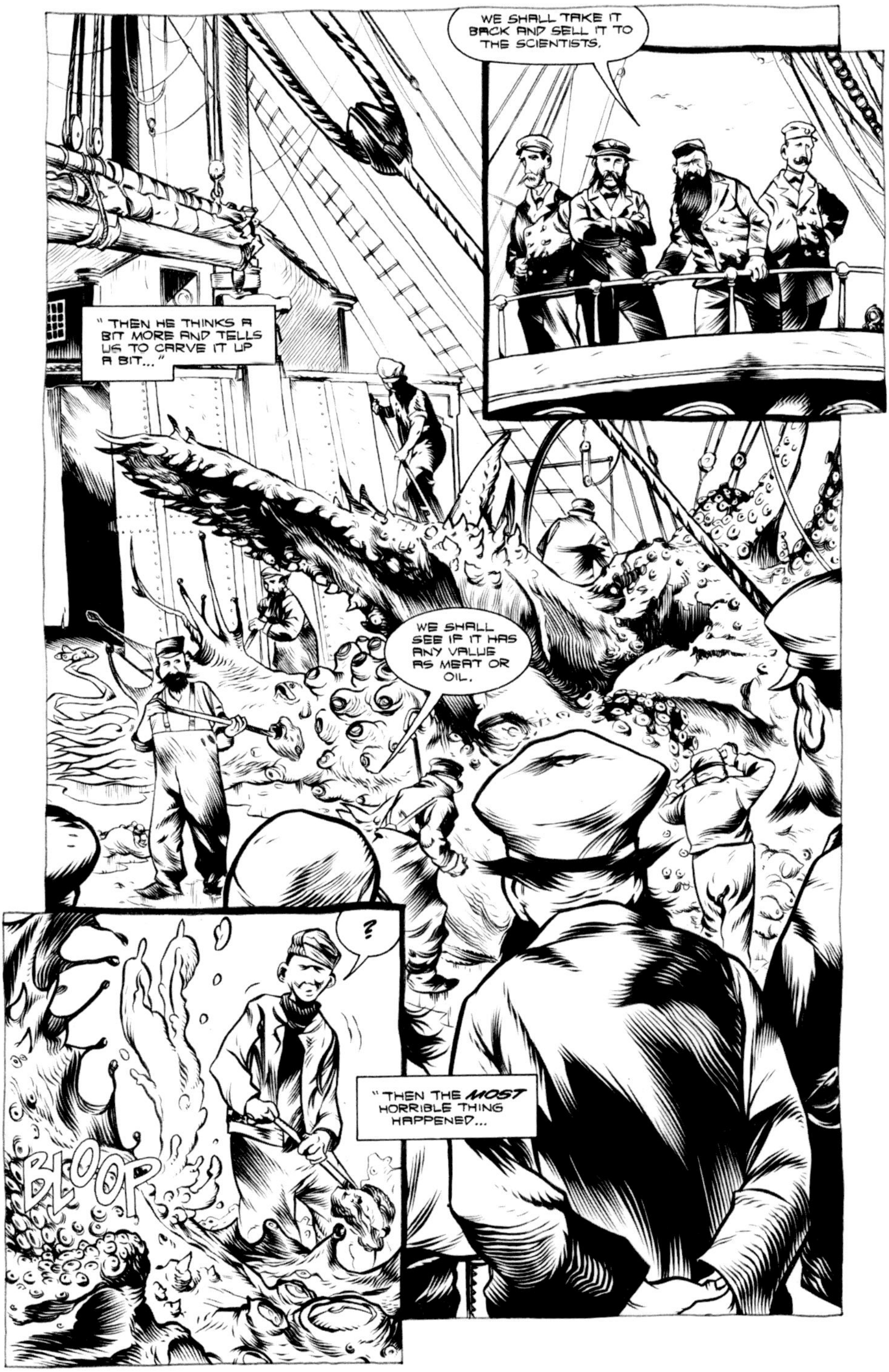

"THEN HE THINKS A BIT MORE AND TELLS US TO CARVE IT UP A BIT..."
WE SHALL TAKE IT BACK AND SELL IT TO THE SCIENTISTS.
WE SHALL SEE IF IT HAS ANY VALUE AS MEAT OR OIL.
?
BLOOP
"THEN THE MOST HORRIBLE THING HAPPENED...

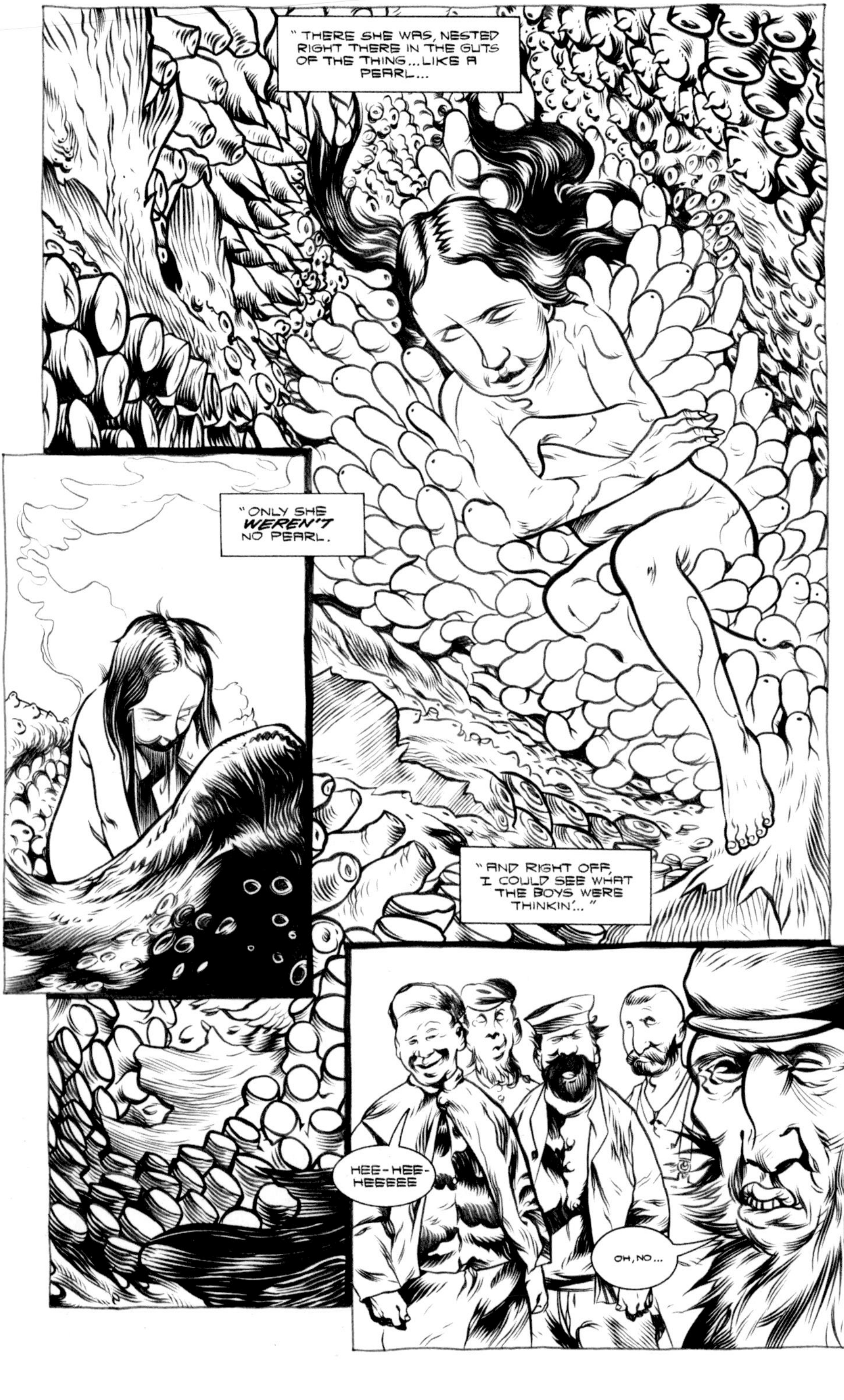
"THERE SHE WAS, NESTED RIGHT THERE IN THE GUTS OF THE THING...LIKE A PEARL...
"ONLY SHE WEREN'T NO PEARL.
"AND RIGHT OFF, I COULD SEE WHAT THE BOYS WERE THINKIN'..."
HEE-HEE-HEEEEEE
OH, NO...

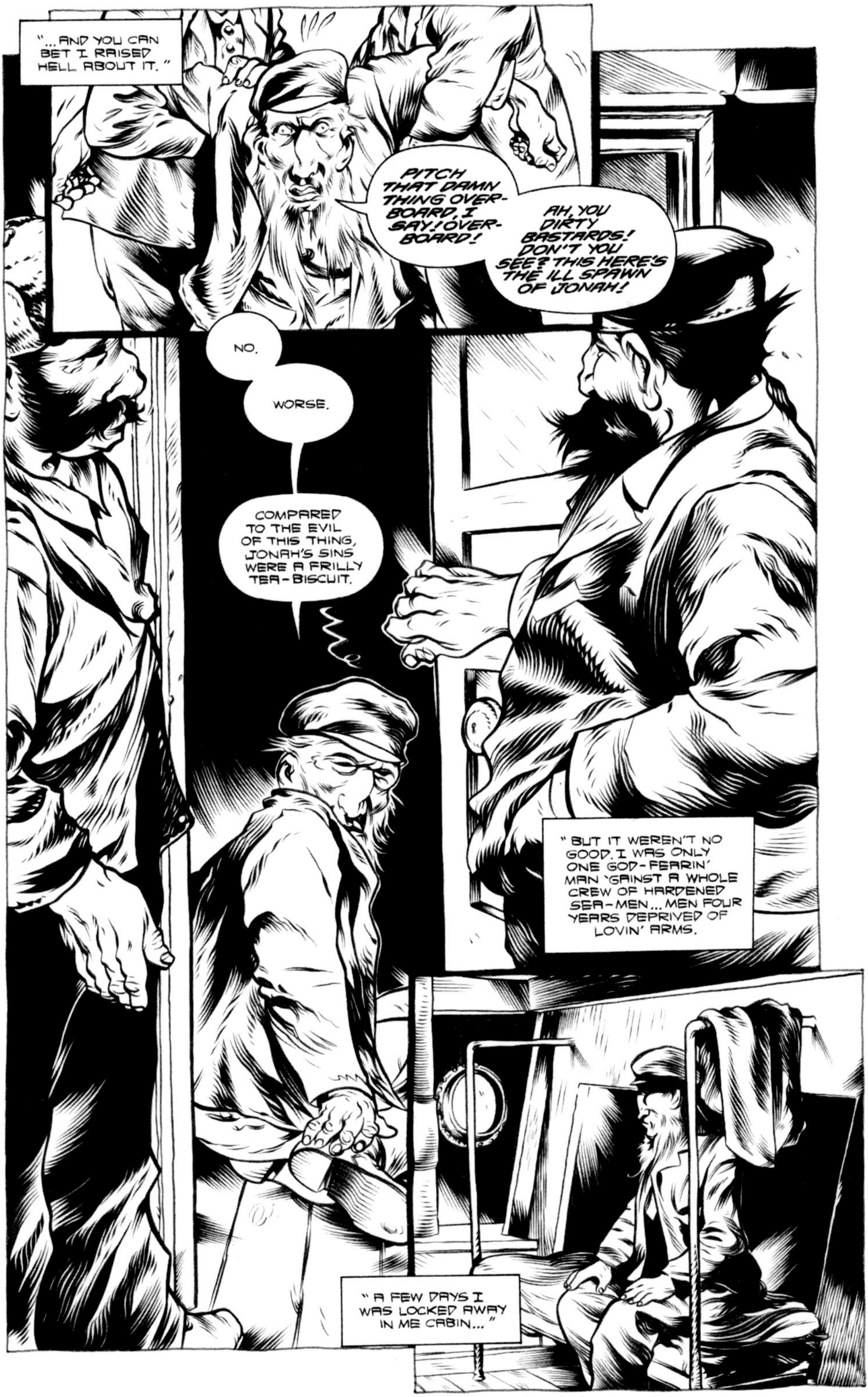
"...AND YOU CAN BET I RAISED HELL ABOUT IT."
PITCH THAT DAMN THING OVER-BOARD, I SAY! OVER-BOARD!
AH, YOU DIRTY BASTARDS! DON'T YOU SEE? THIS HERE'S THE ILL SPAWN OF JONAH!
NO.
WORSE.
COMPARED TO THE EVIL OF THIS THING, JONAH'S SINS WERE A FRILLY TEA-BISCUIT.
"BUT IT WEREN'T NO GOOD. I WAS ONLY ONE GOD-FEARIN' MAN 'GAINST A WHOLE CREW OF HARDENED SEA-MEN... MEN FOUR YEARS DEPRIVED OF LOVIN' ARMS.
"A FEW DAYS I WAS LOCKED AWAY IN ME CABIN..."

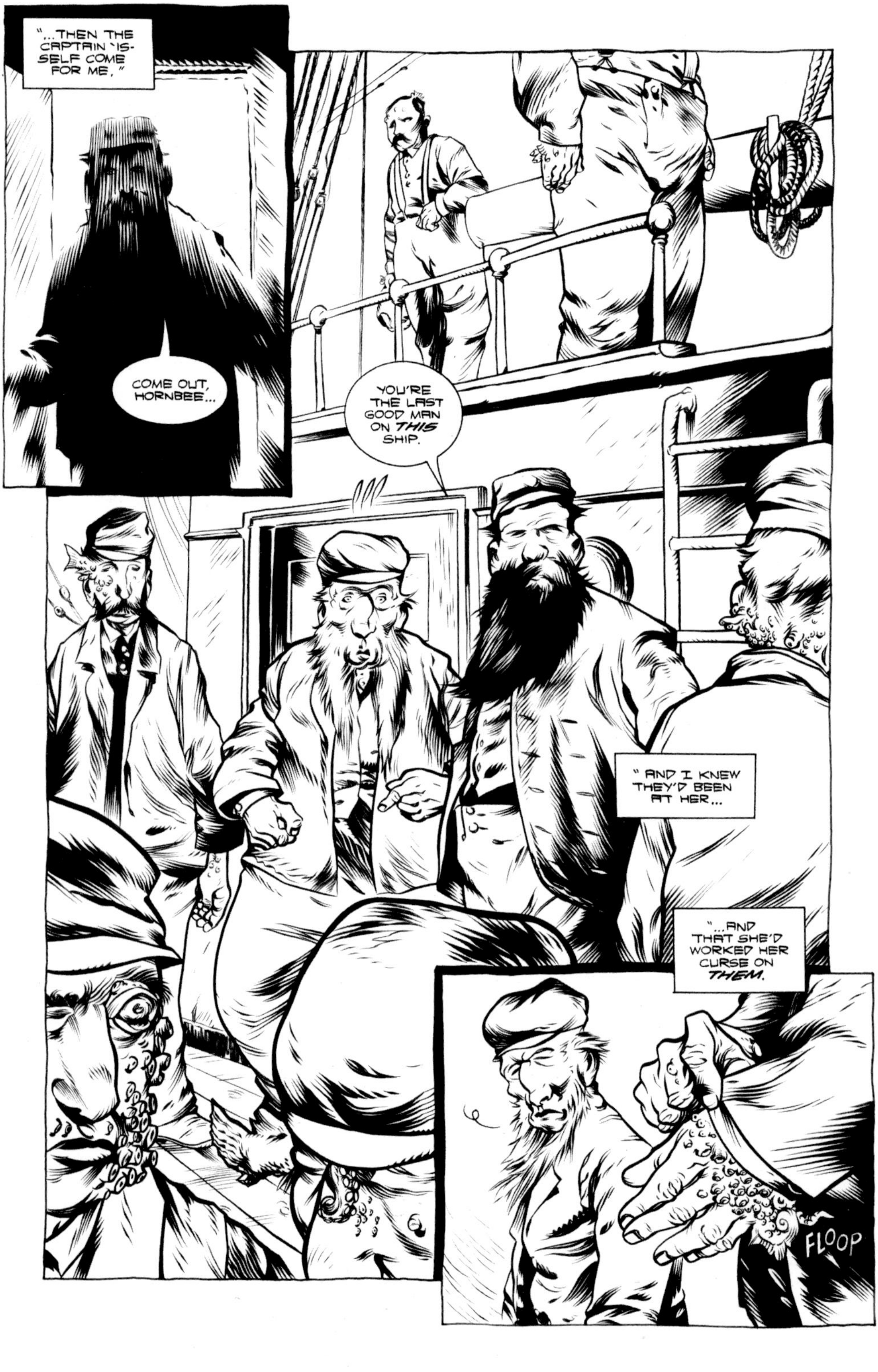
"...THEN THE CAPTAIN 'IS-SELF COME FOR ME."
COME OUT, HORNBEE...
YOU'RE THE LAST GOOD MAN ON *THIS* SHIP.
" AND I KNEW THEY'D BEEN AT HER...
"...AND THAT SHE'D WORKED HER CURSE ON *THEM*.
FLOOP

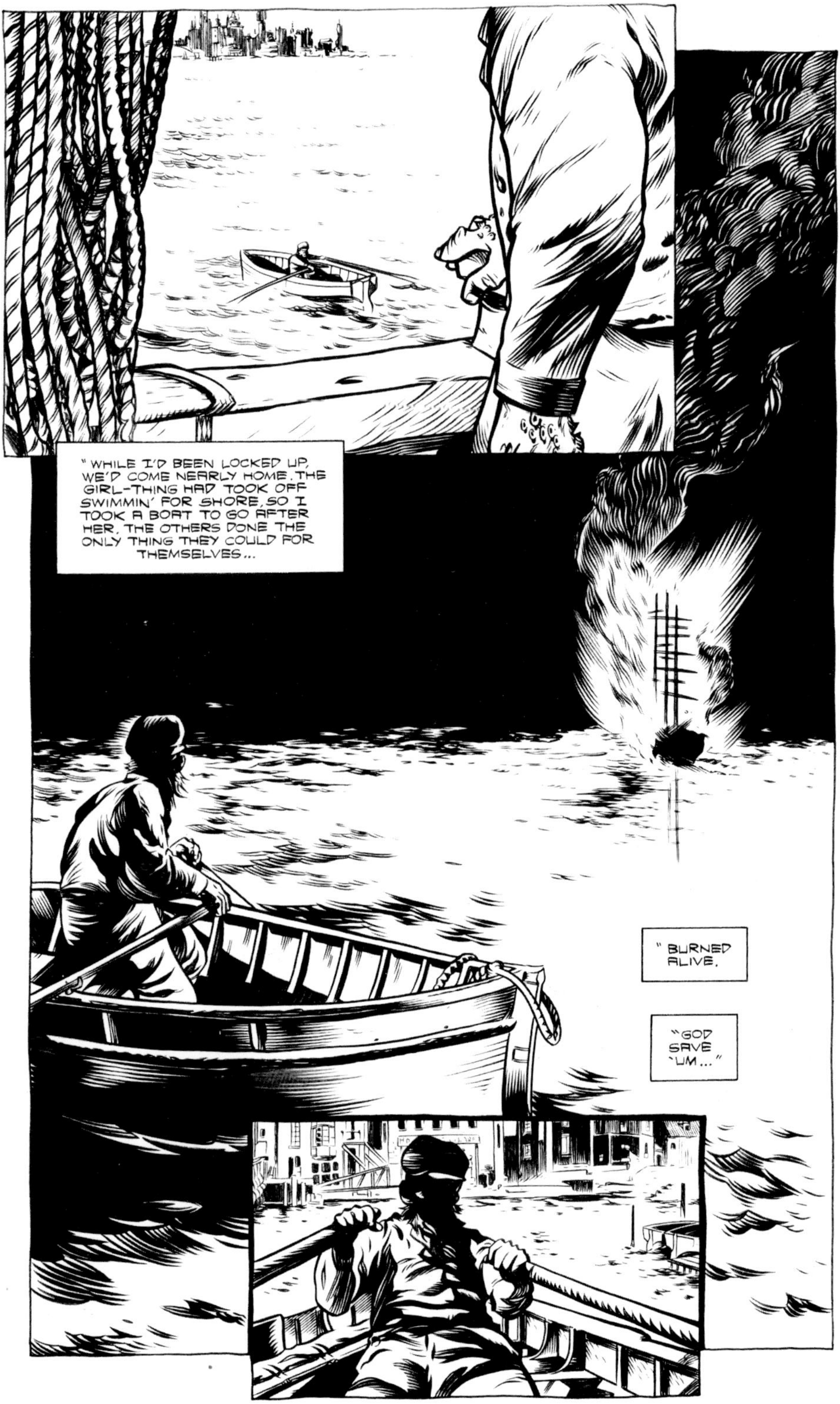
"WHILE I'D BEEN LOCKED UP, WE'D COME NEARLY HOME. THE GIRL-THING HAD TOOK OFF SWIMMIN' FOR SHORE, SO I TOOK A BOAT TO GO AFTER HER. THE OTHERS DONE THE ONLY THING THEY COULD FOR THEMSELVES...
"BURNED ALIVE.
"GOD SAVE 'UM..."

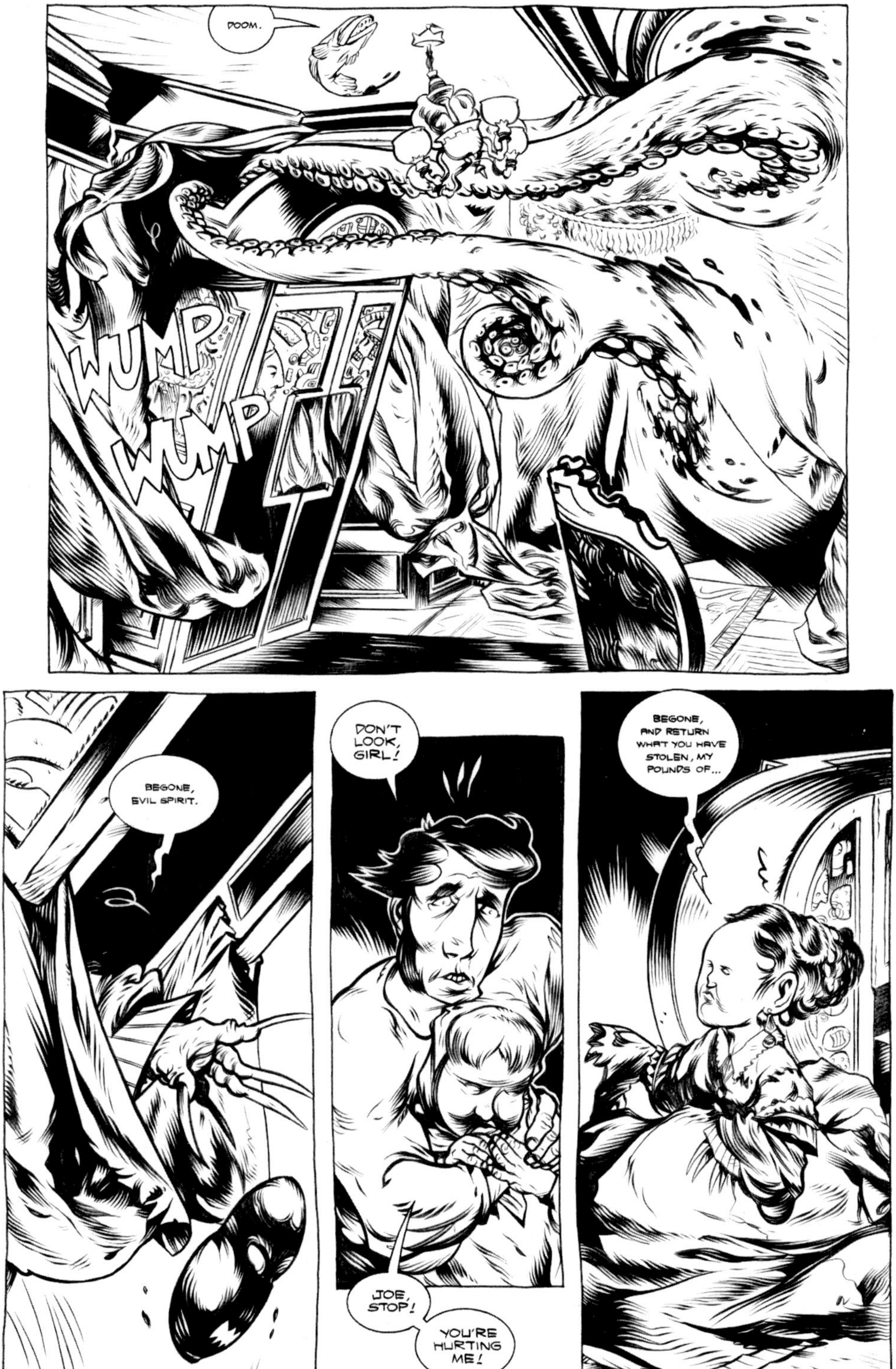
DOOM.
WUMP
WUMP
BEGONE, EVIL SPIRIT.
DON'T LOOK, GIRL!
JOE, STOP!
YOU'RE HURTING ME!
BEGONE, AND RETURN WHAT YOU HAVE STOLEN, MY POUNDS OF...

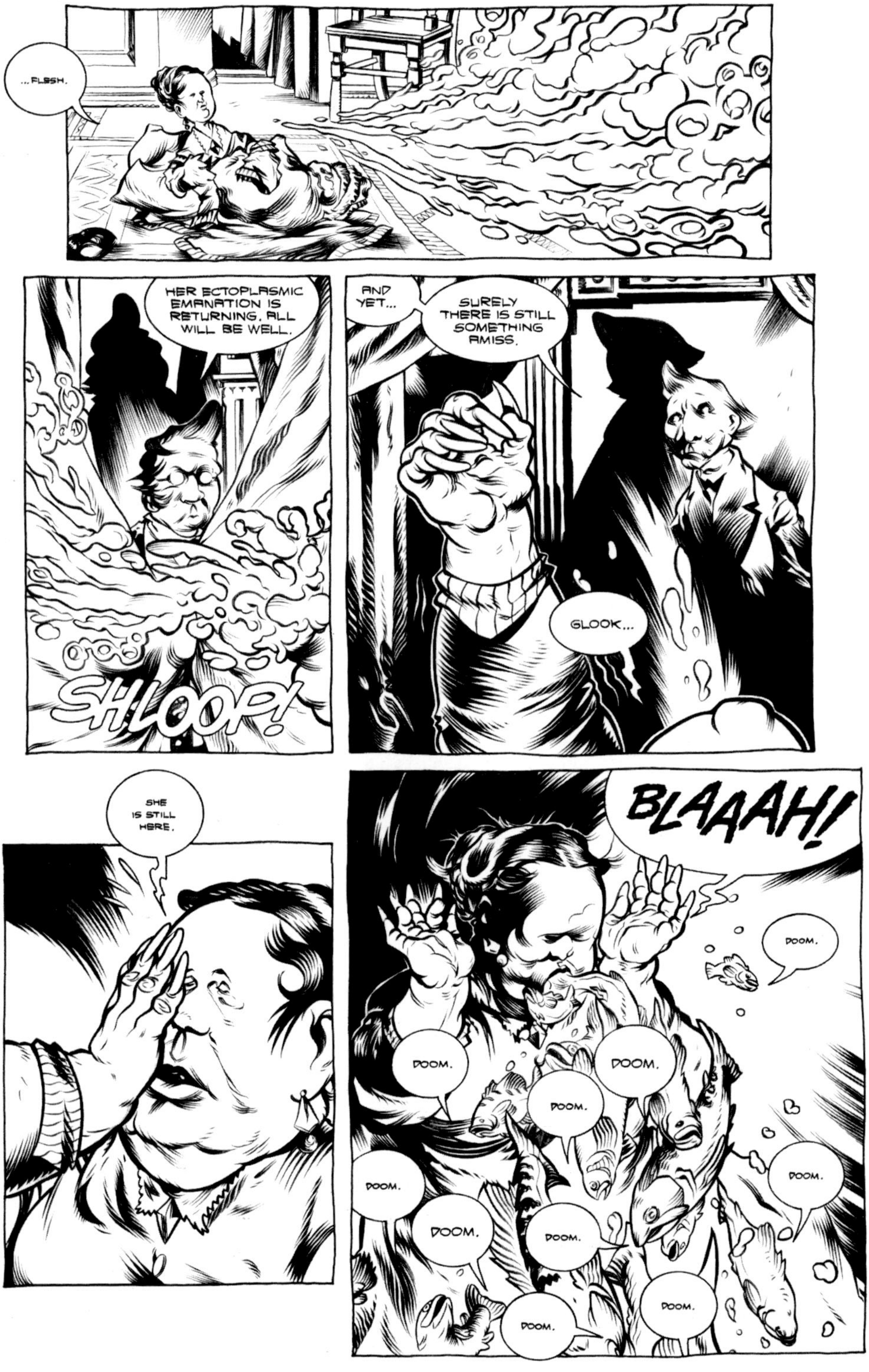
...FLESH.
HER ECTOPLASMIC EMANATION IS RETURNING. ALL WILL BE WELL.
SHLOOP!
AND YET...
SURELY THERE IS STILL SOMETHING AMISS.
GLOOK...
SHE IS STILL HERE.
BLAAAH!
DOOM.
DOOM.
DOOM.
DOOM.
DOOM.
DOOM.
DOOM.
DOOM.
DOOM.
DOOM.

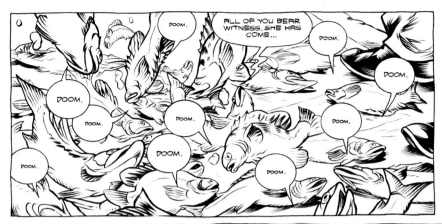

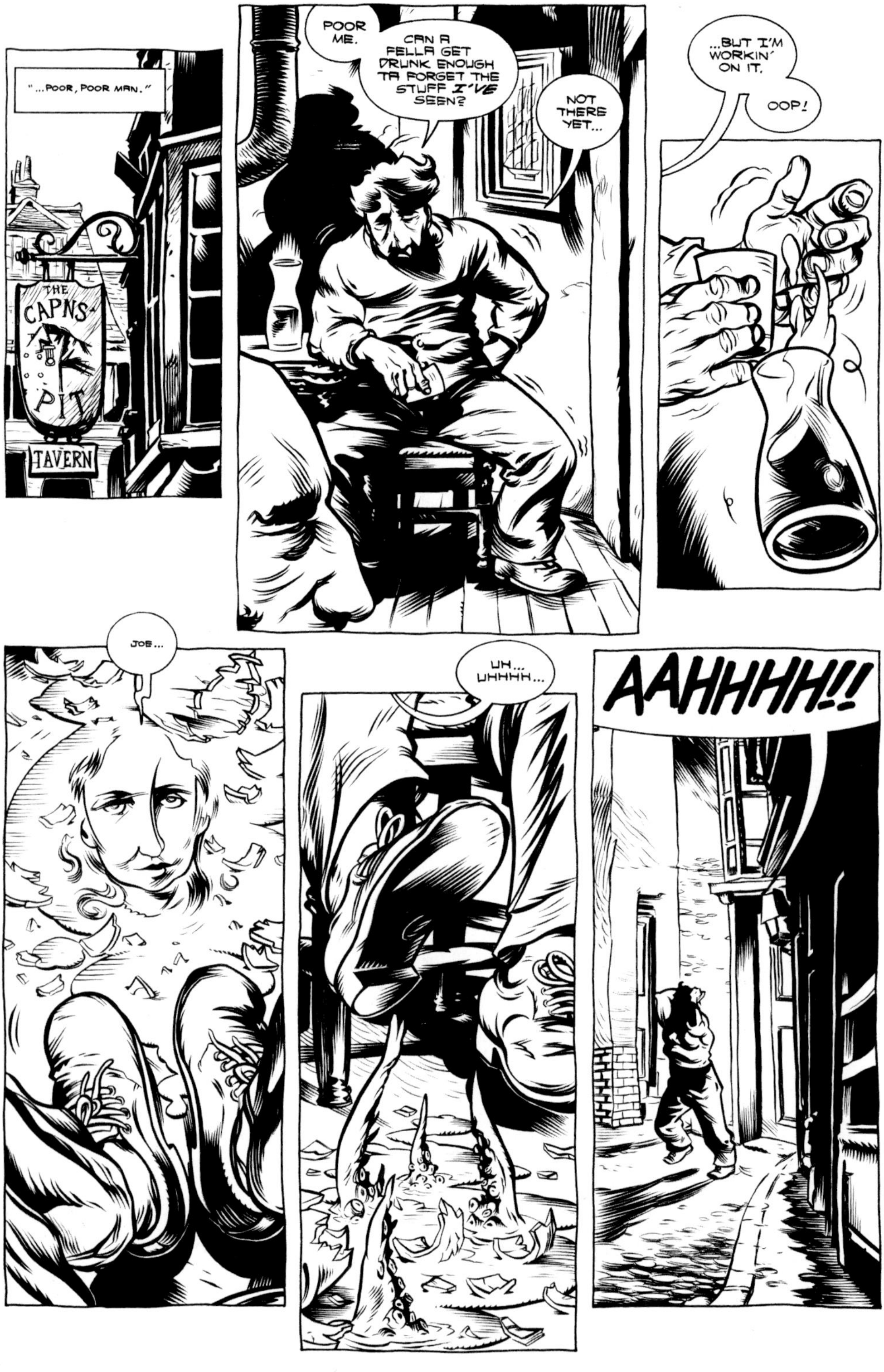
"...POOR, POOR MAN."
THE CAPNS PIT
TAVERN
POOR ME.
CAN A FELLA GET DRUNK ENOUGH TA FORGET THE STUFF *I'VE* SEEN?
NOT THERE YET...
...BUT I'M WORKIN' ON IT.
OOP!
JOE...
UH... UHHHH...
AAHHHH!!

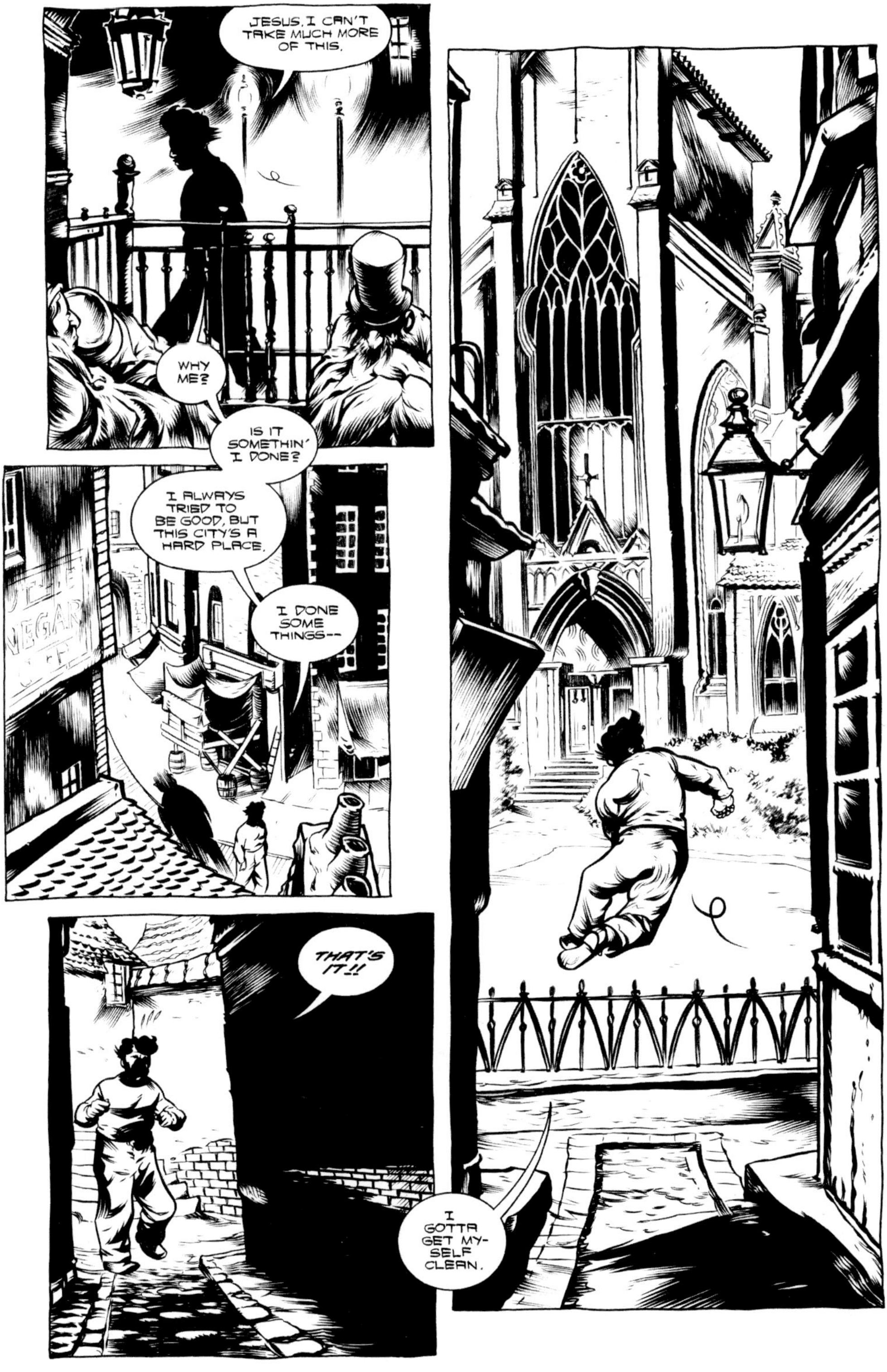
JESUS, I CAN'T TAKE MUCH MORE OF THIS.
WHY ME?
IS IT SOMETHIN' I DONE?
I ALWAYS TRIED TO BE GOOD, BUT THIS CITY'S A HARD PLACE.
I DONE SOME THINGS--
THAT'S IT!!
I GOTTA GET MY-SELF CLEAN.

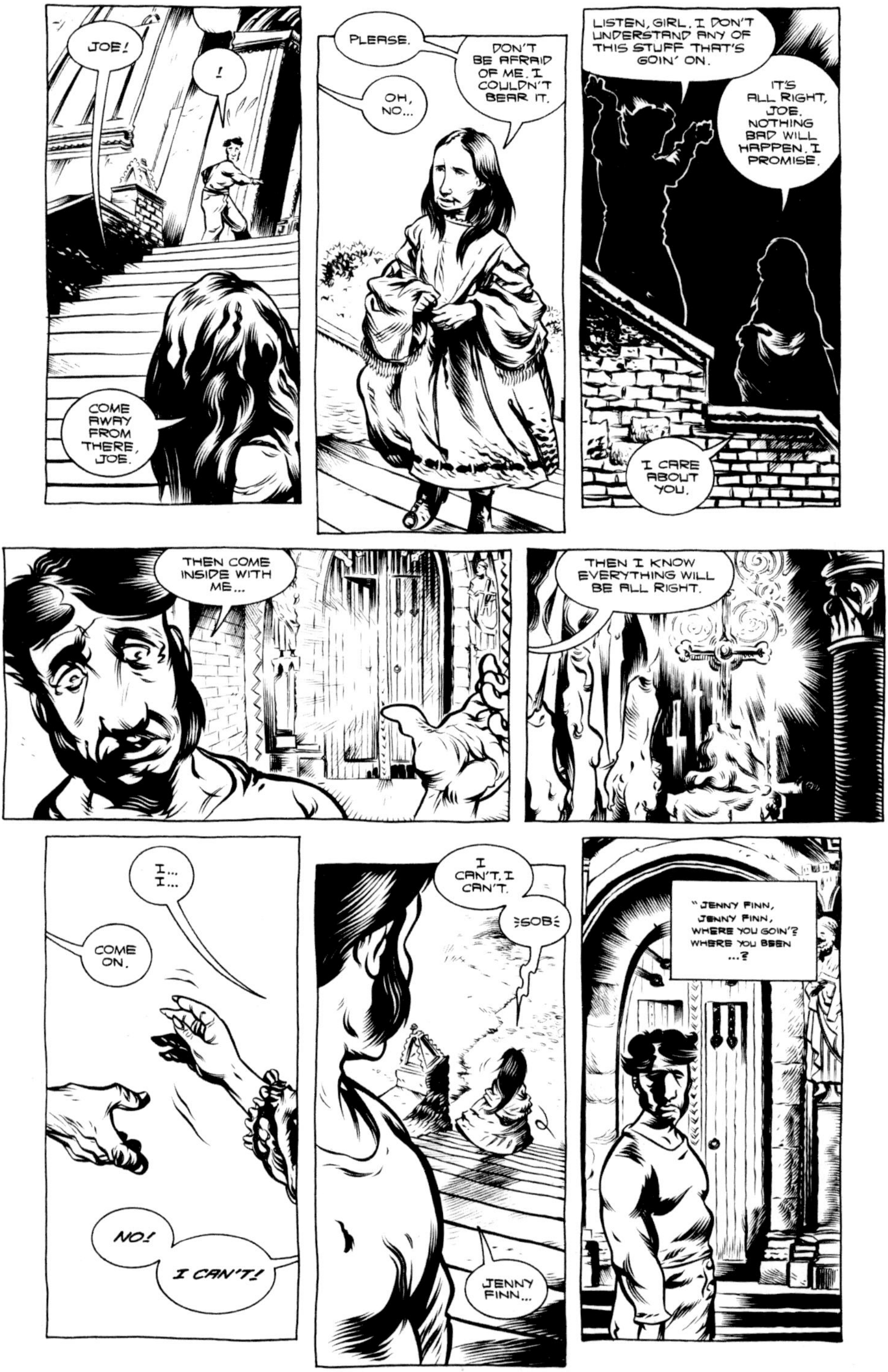
JOE!
!
COME AWAY FROM THERE, JOE.
PLEASE.
DON'T BE AFRAID OF ME. I COULDN'T BEAR IT.
OH, NO...
LISTEN, GIRL. I DON'T UNDERSTAND ANY OF THIS STUFF THAT'S GOIN' ON.
IT'S ALL RIGHT, JOE. NOTHING BAD WILL HAPPEN. I PROMISE.
I CARE ABOUT YOU.
THEN COME INSIDE WITH ME...
THEN I KNOW EVERYTHING WILL BE ALL RIGHT.
I... I...
COME ON.
NO!
I CAN'T!
I CAN'T. I CAN'T.
SOB
JENNY FINN...
"JENNY FINN, JENNY FINN, WHERE YOU GOIN'? WHERE YOU BEEN ...?

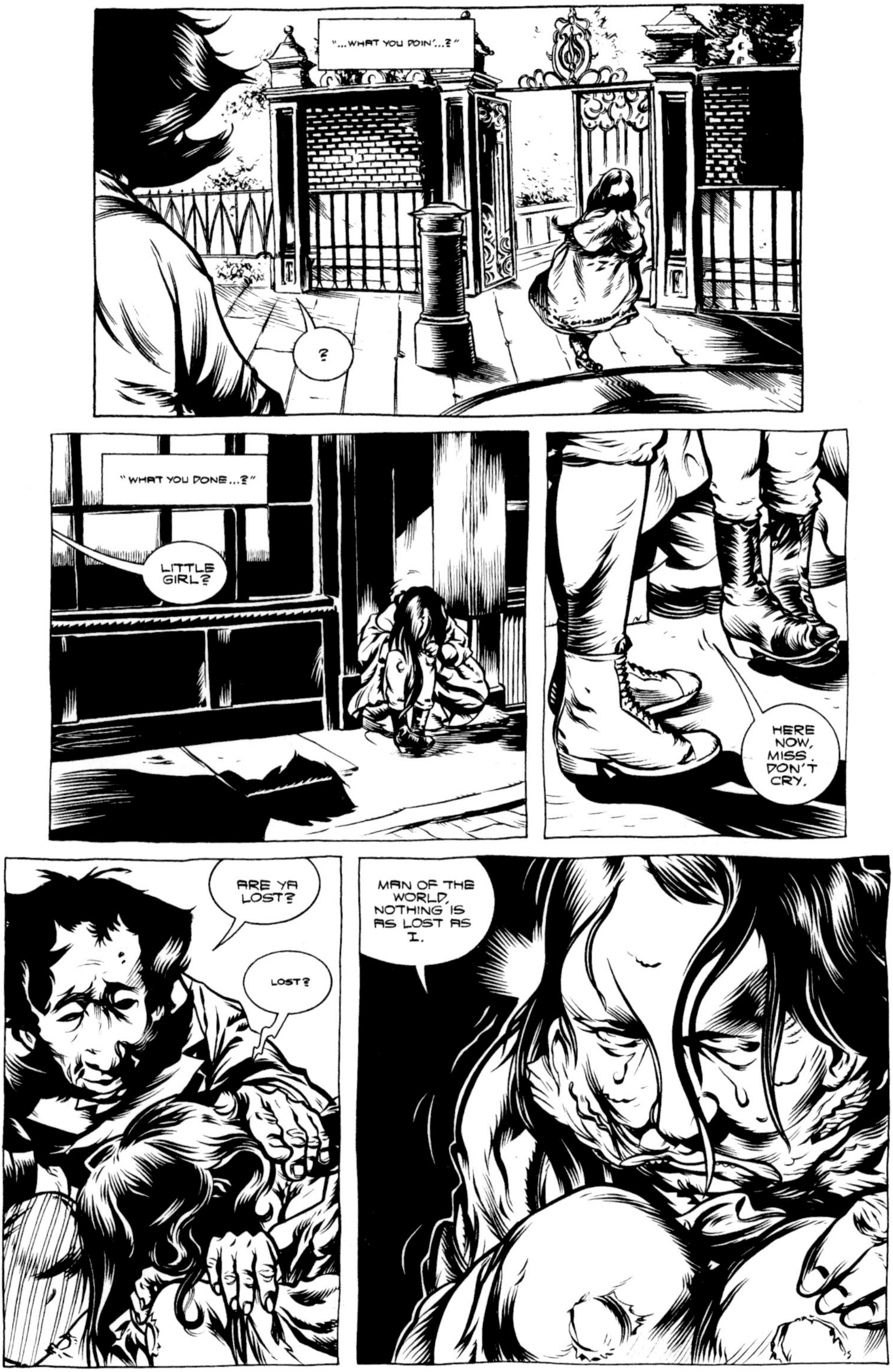
"...WHAT YOU DOIN'...?"
?
"WHAT YOU DONE...?"
LITTLE GIRL?
HERE NOW, MISS. DON'T CRY.
ARE YA LOST?
LOST?
MAN OF THE WORLD, NOTHING IS AS LOST AS I.

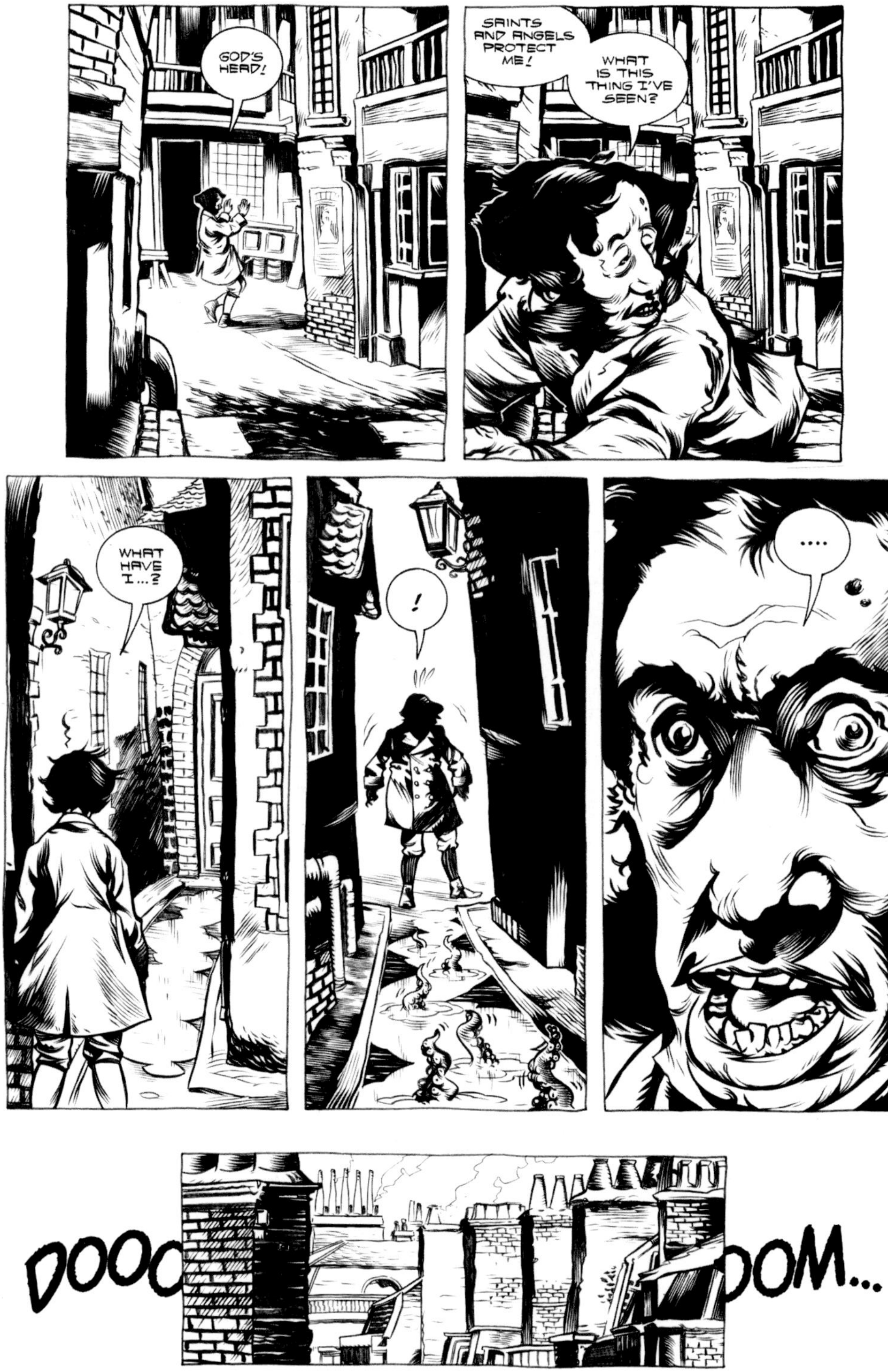
GOD'S HEAD!
SAINTS AND ANGELS PROTECT ME!
WHAT IS THIS THING I'VE SEEN?
WHAT HAVE I...?
!
....
DOOOOOM...

CHAPTER
THREE

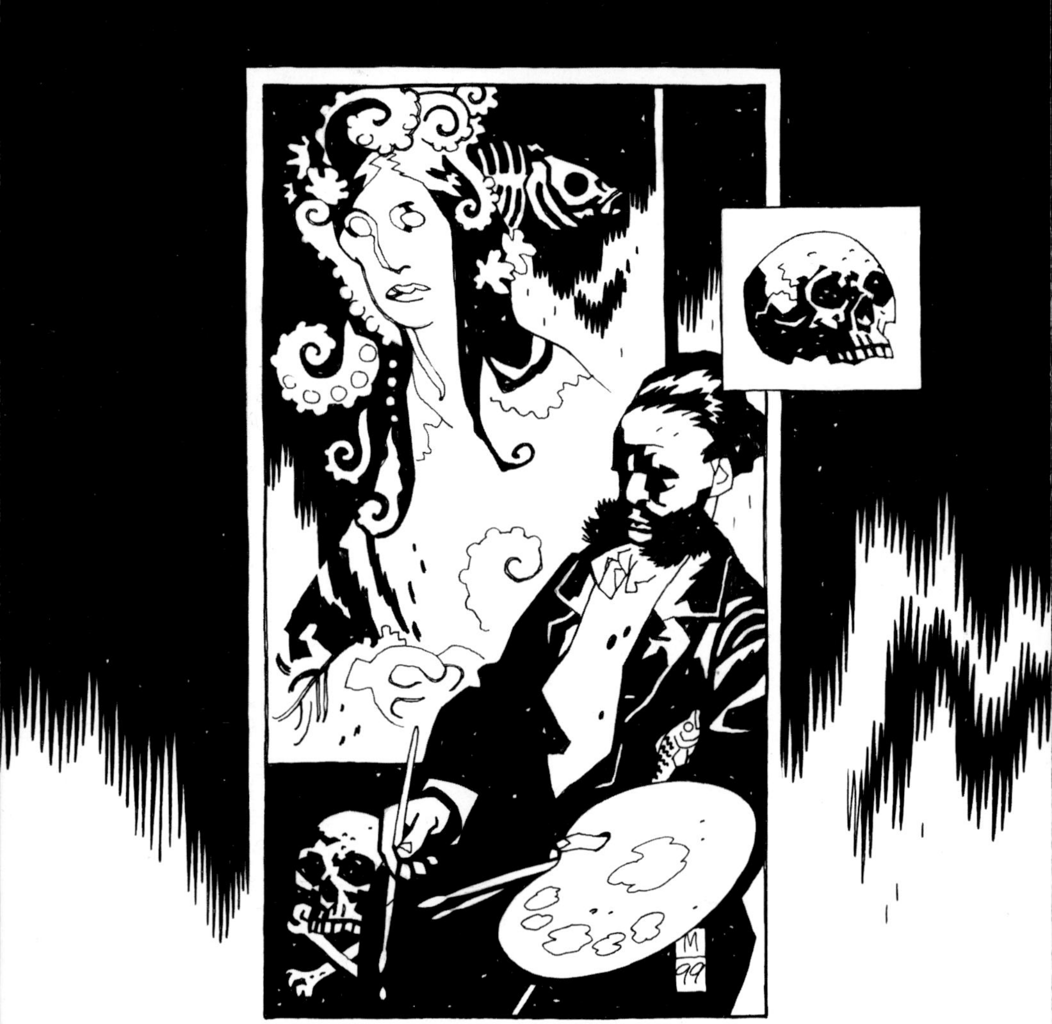

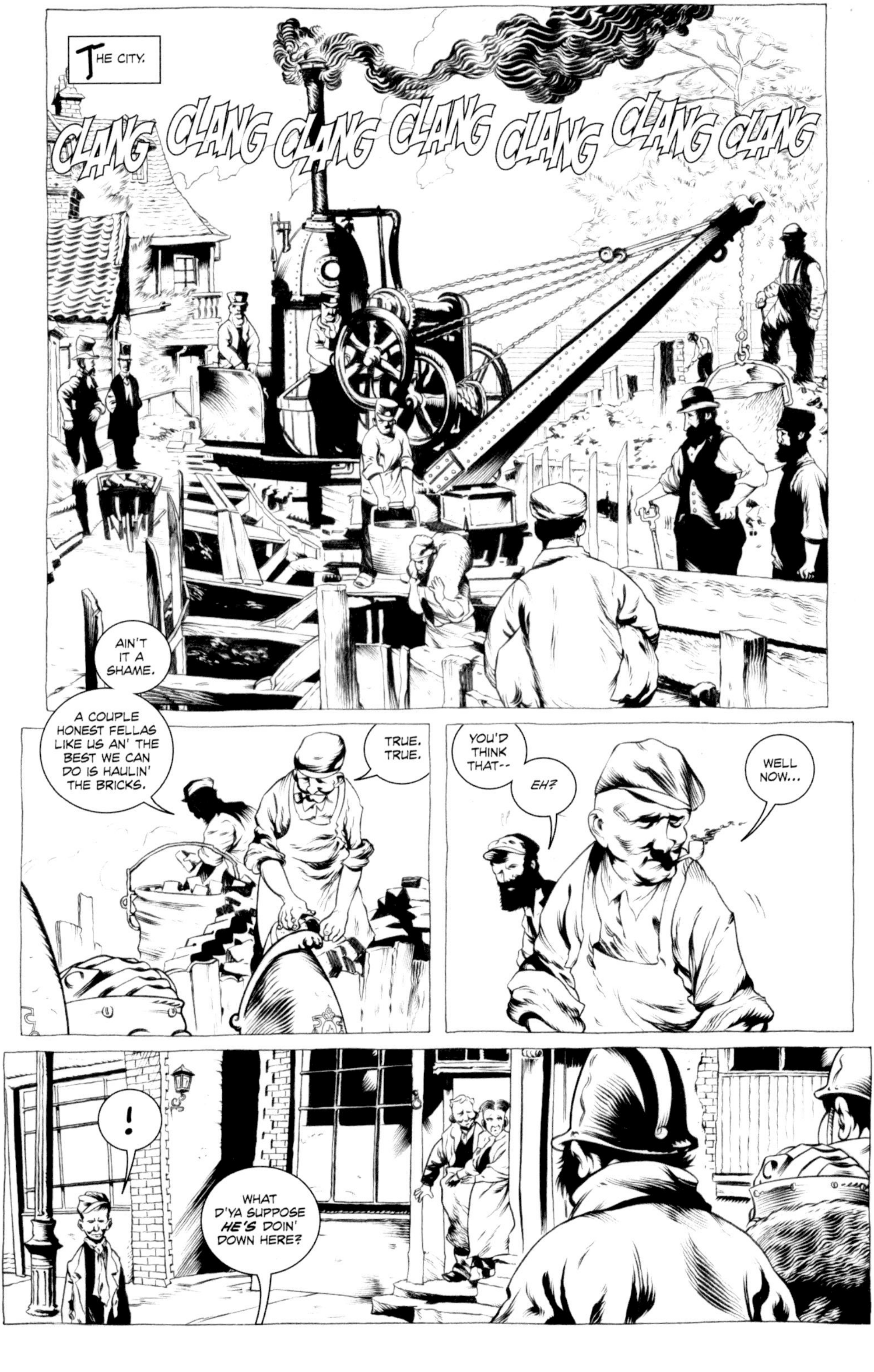
THE CITY.
CLANG CLANG CLANG CLANG CLANG CLANG CLANG
AIN'T IT A SHAME.
A COUPLE HONEST FELLAS LIKE US AN' THE BEST WE CAN DO IS HAULIN' THE BRICKS.
TRUE. TRUE.
YOU'D THINK THAT--
EH?
WELL NOW...
!
WHAT D'YA SUPPOSE HE'S DOIN' DOWN HERE?

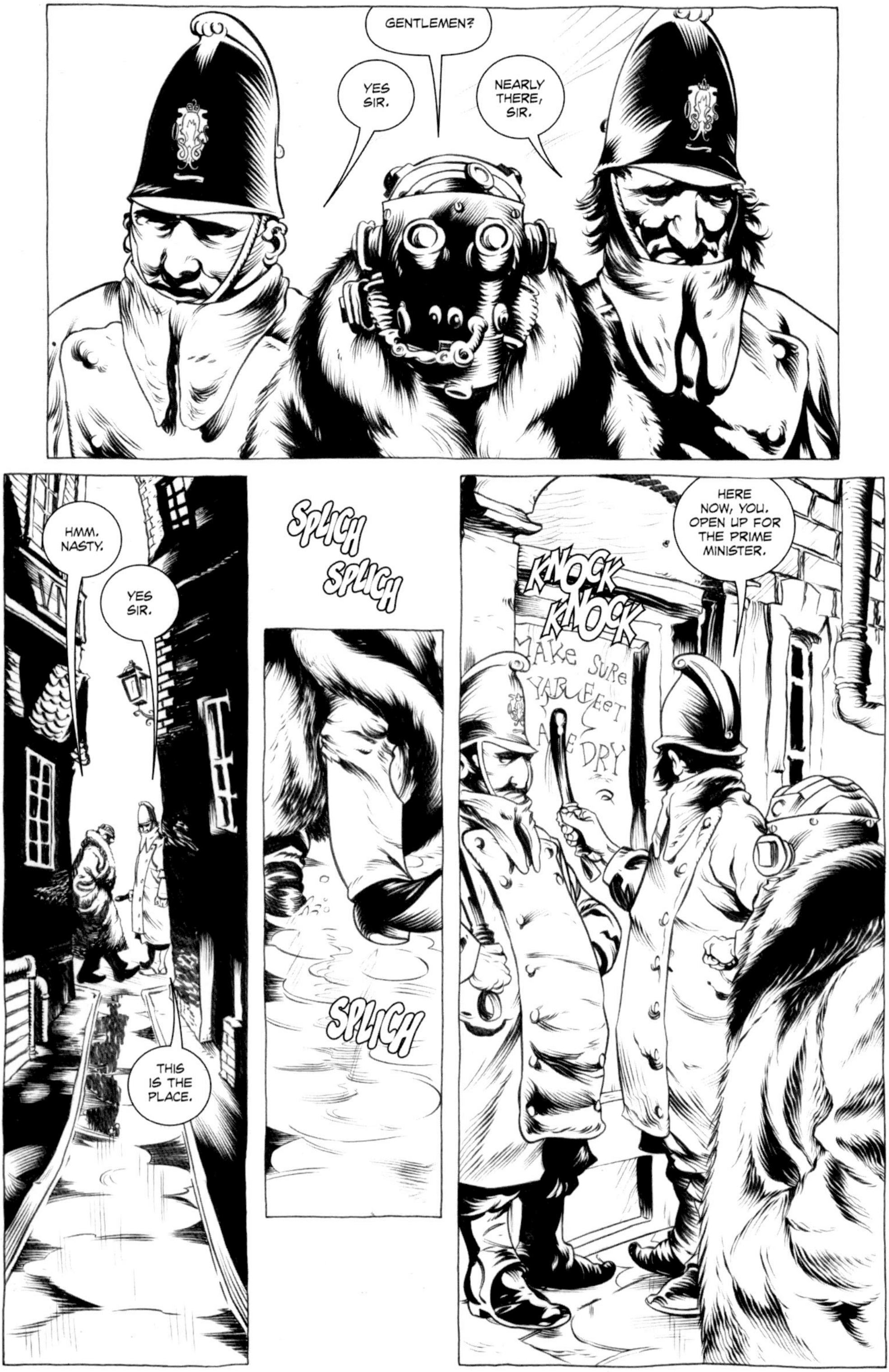
GENTLEMEN?
YES SIR.
NEARLY THERE, SIR.
HMM. NASTY.
YES SIR.
THIS IS THE PLACE.
SPLICH
SPLICH
SPLICH
KNOCK KNOCK
HERE NOW, YOU. OPEN UP FOR THE PRIME MINISTER.

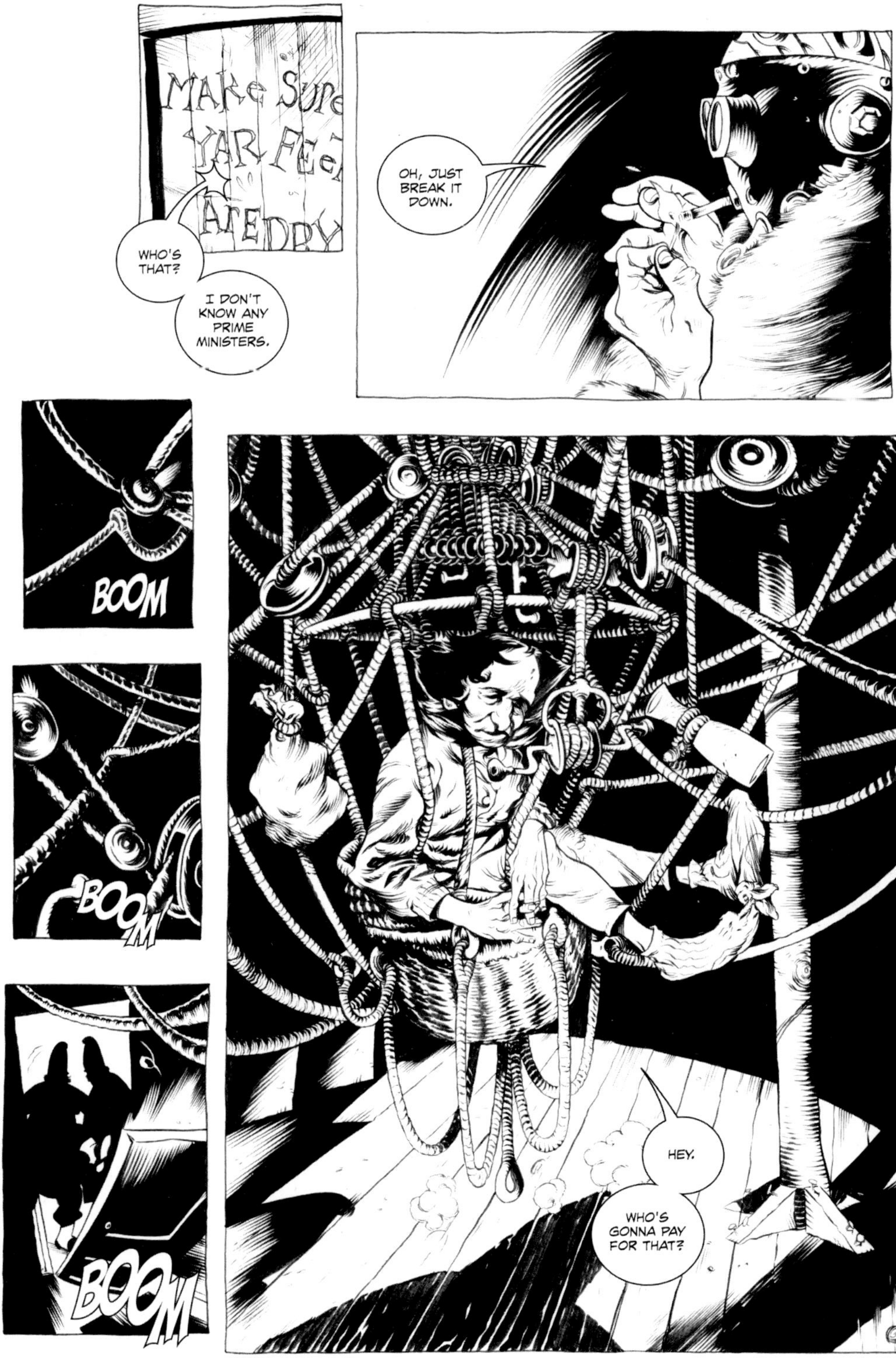
Make Sure
YAR FEE
ArE DRY
WHO'S THAT?
I DON'T KNOW ANY PRIME MINISTERS.
OH, JUST BREAK IT DOWN.
BOOM
BOOM
BOOM
HEY.
WHO'S GONNA PAY FOR THAT?

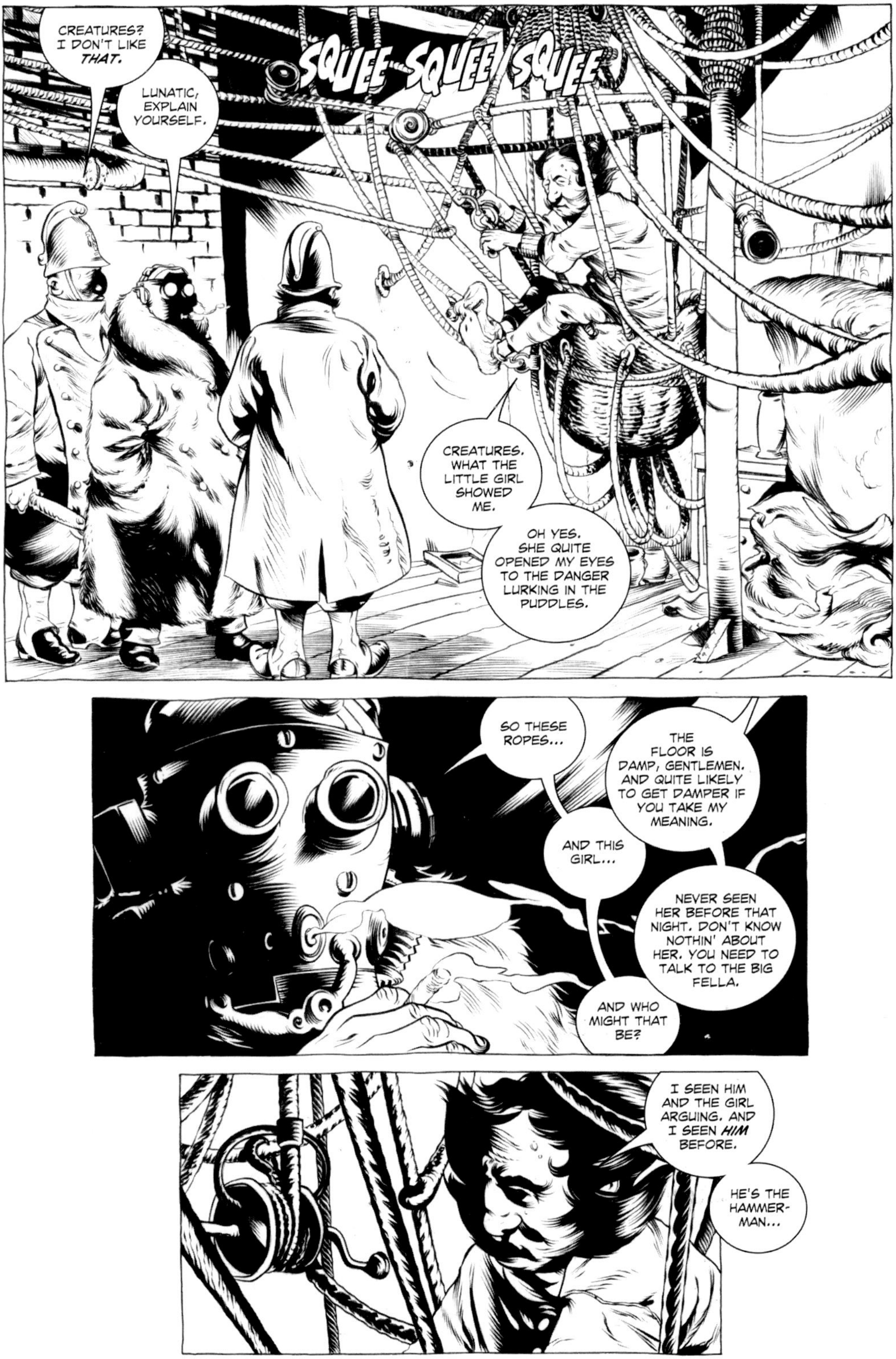
CREATURES? I DON'T LIKE *THAT.*
LUNATIC, EXPLAIN YOURSELF.
SQUEE SQUEE SQUEE
CREATURES. WHAT THE LITTLE GIRL SHOWED ME.
OH YES. SHE QUITE OPENED MY EYES TO THE DANGER LURKING IN THE PUDDLES.
SO THESE ROPES...
THE FLOOR IS DAMP, GENTLEMEN. AND QUITE LIKELY TO GET DAMPER IF YOU TAKE MY MEANING.
AND THIS GIRL...
NEVER SEEN HER BEFORE THAT NIGHT. DON'T KNOW NOTHIN' ABOUT HER. YOU NEED TO TALK TO THE BIG FELLA.
AND WHO MIGHT THAT BE?
I SEEN HIM AND THE GIRL ARGUING. AND I SEEN *HIM* BEFORE.
HE'S THE HAMMER-MAN...

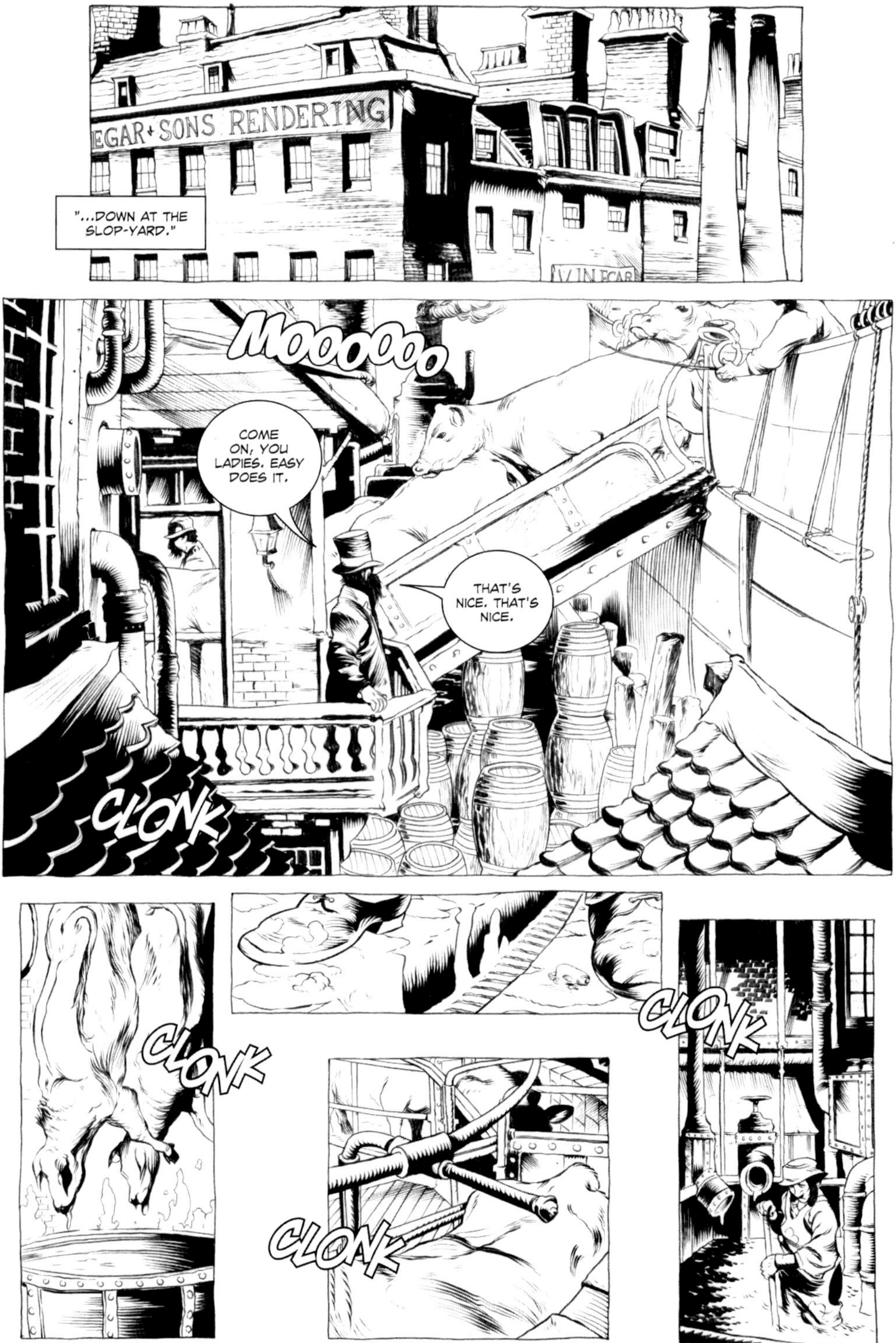
EGAR + SONS RENDERING
"...DOWN AT THE SLOP-YARD."
MOOOOOO
COME ON, YOU LADIES. EASY DOES IT.
THAT'S NICE. THAT'S NICE.
CLONK
CLONK
CLONK
CLONK

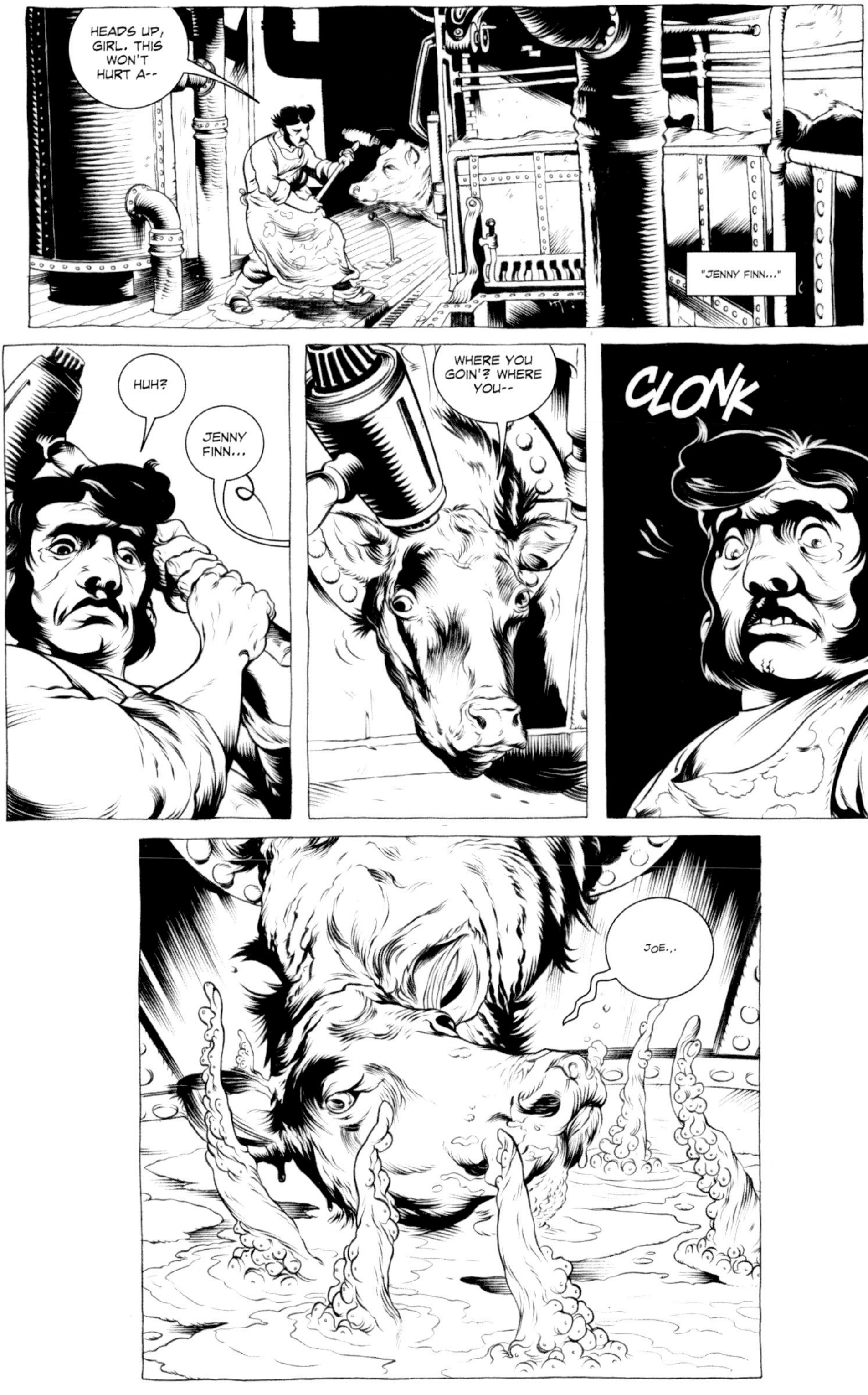
HEADS UP, GIRL. THIS WON'T HURT A--
"JENNY FINN..."
HUH?
JENNY FINN...
WHERE YOU GOIN'? WHERE YOU--
CLONK
JOE...

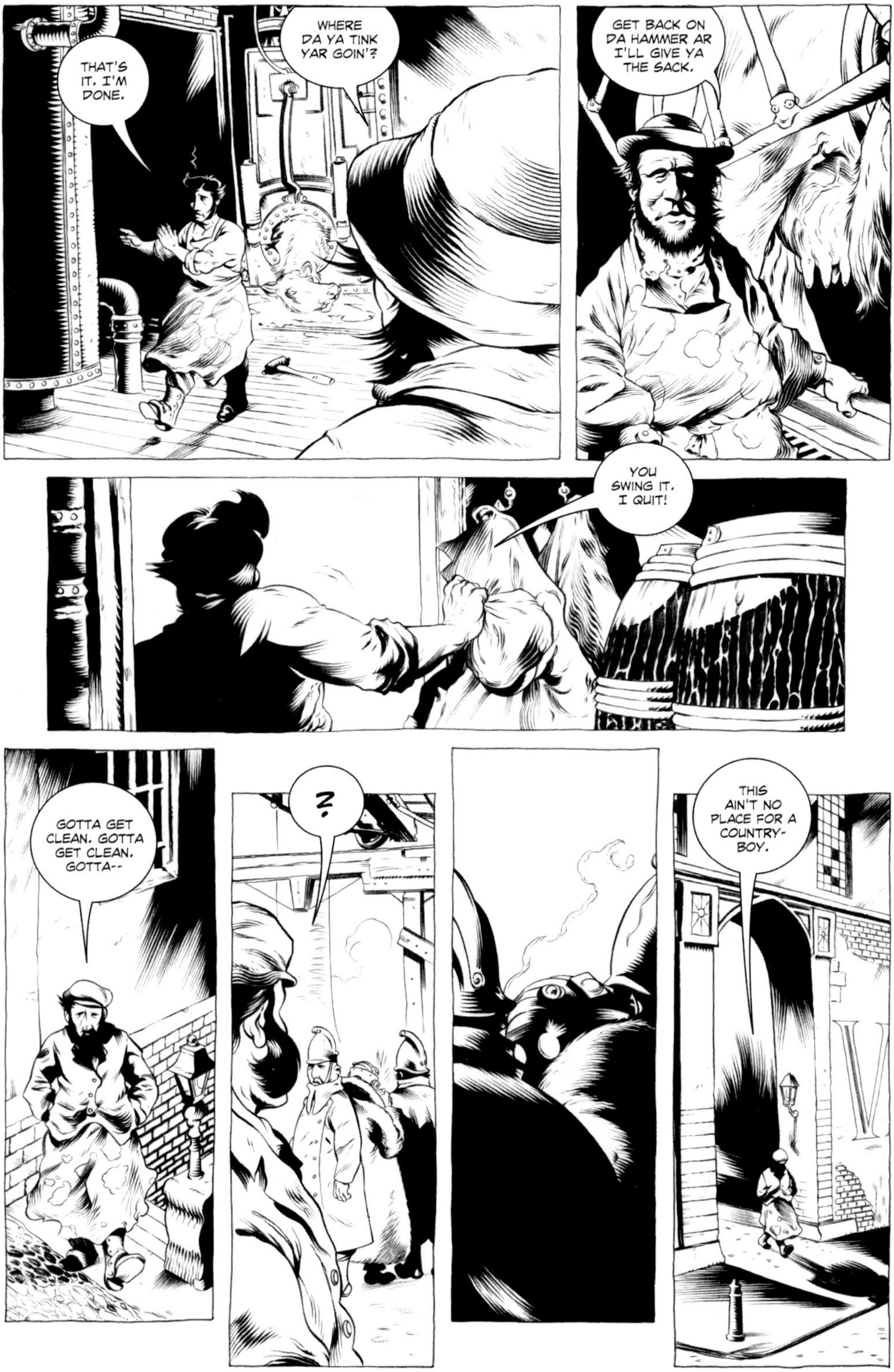
THAT'S IT. I'M DONE.
WHERE DA YA TINK YAR GOIN'?
GET BACK ON DA HAMMER AR I'LL GIVE YA THE SACK.
YOU SWING IT. I QUIT!
GOTTA GET CLEAN. GOTTA GET CLEAN. GOTTA--
?
THIS AIN'T NO PLACE FOR A COUNTRY-BOY.

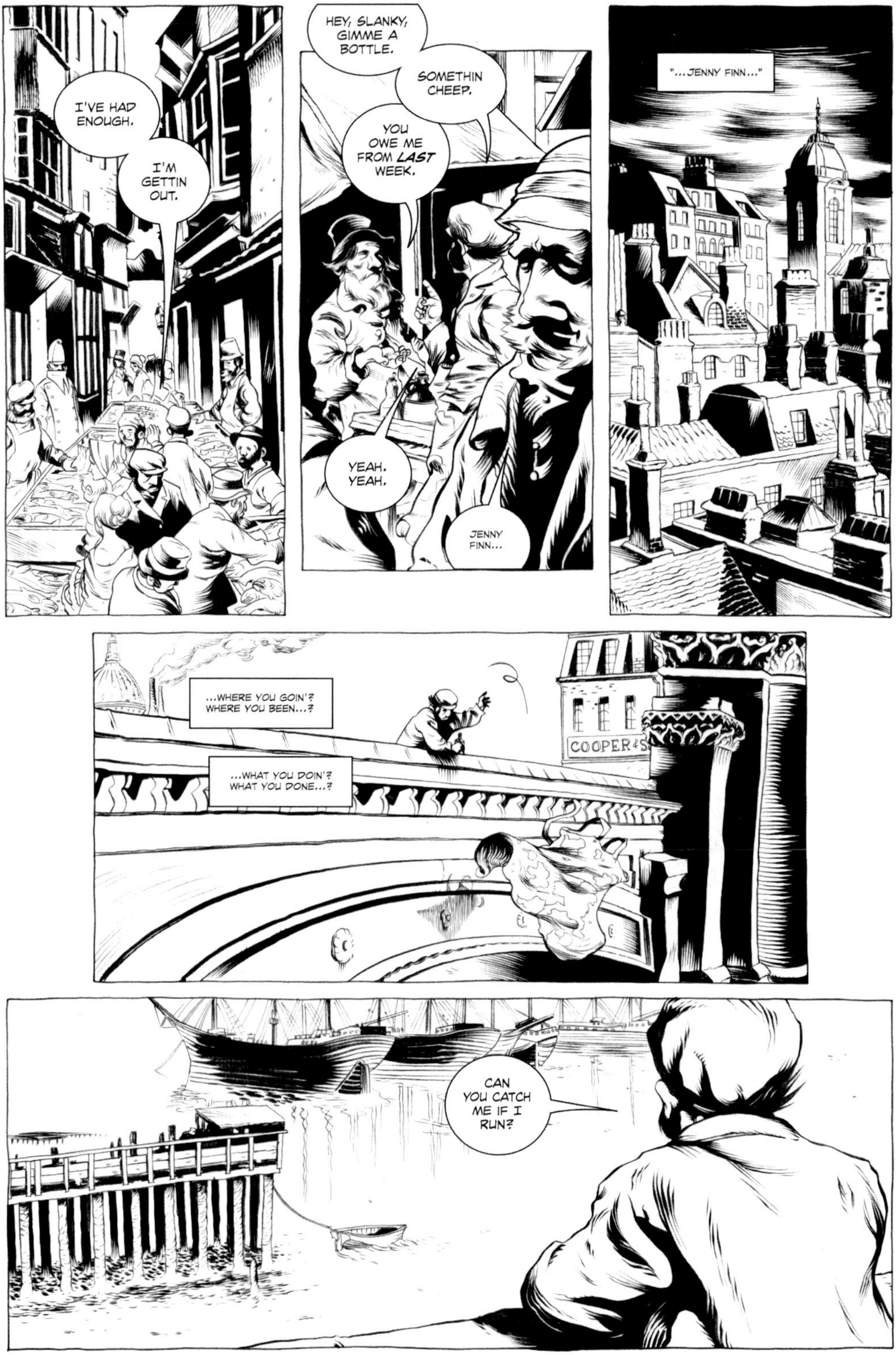
I'VE HAD ENOUGH.
I'M GETTIN OUT.
HEY, SLANKY, GIMME A BOTTLE.
SOMETHIN CHEEP.
YOU OWE ME FROM *LAST* WEEK.
YEAH. YEAH.
JENNY FINN...
"...JENNY FINN..."
...WHERE YOU GOIN'? WHERE YOU BEEN...?
...WHAT YOU DOIN'? WHAT YOU DONE...?
COOPER & S
CAN YOU CATCH ME IF I RUN?

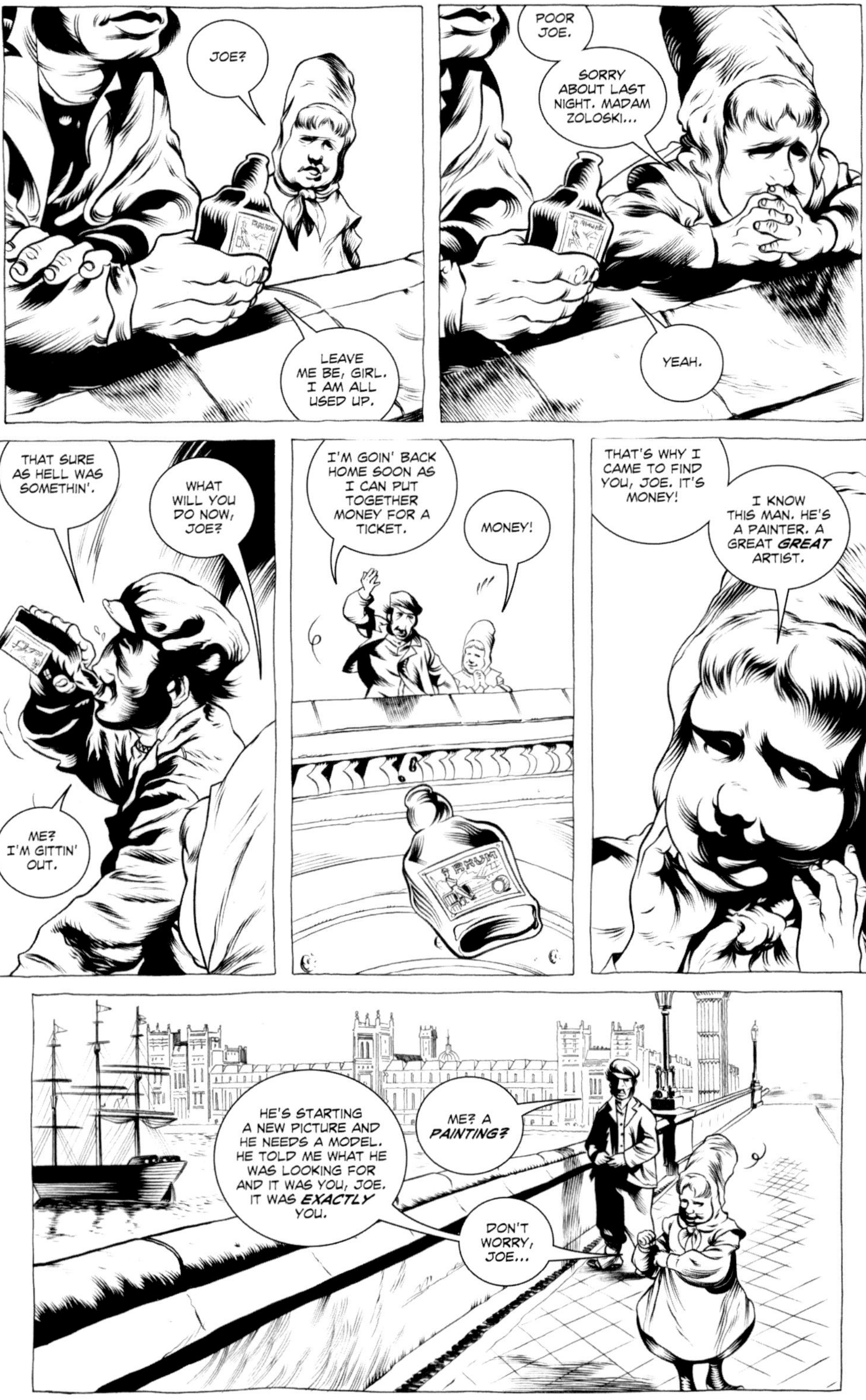
JOE?
LEAVE ME BE, GIRL. I AM ALL USED UP.
POOR JOE.
SORRY ABOUT LAST NIGHT. MADAM ZOLOSKI...
YEAH.
THAT SURE AS HELL WAS SOMETHIN'.
WHAT WILL YOU DO NOW, JOE?
ME? I'M GITTIN' OUT.
I'M GOIN' BACK HOME SOON AS I CAN PUT TOGETHER MONEY FOR A TICKET.
MONEY!
THAT'S WHY I CAME TO FIND YOU, JOE. IT'S MONEY!
I KNOW THIS MAN. HE'S A PAINTER. A GREAT *GREAT* ARTIST.
HE'S STARTING A NEW PICTURE AND HE NEEDS A MODEL. HE TOLD ME WHAT HE WAS LOOKING FOR AND IT WAS YOU, JOE. IT WAS *EXACTLY* YOU.
ME? A *PAINTING?*
DON'T WORRY, JOE...

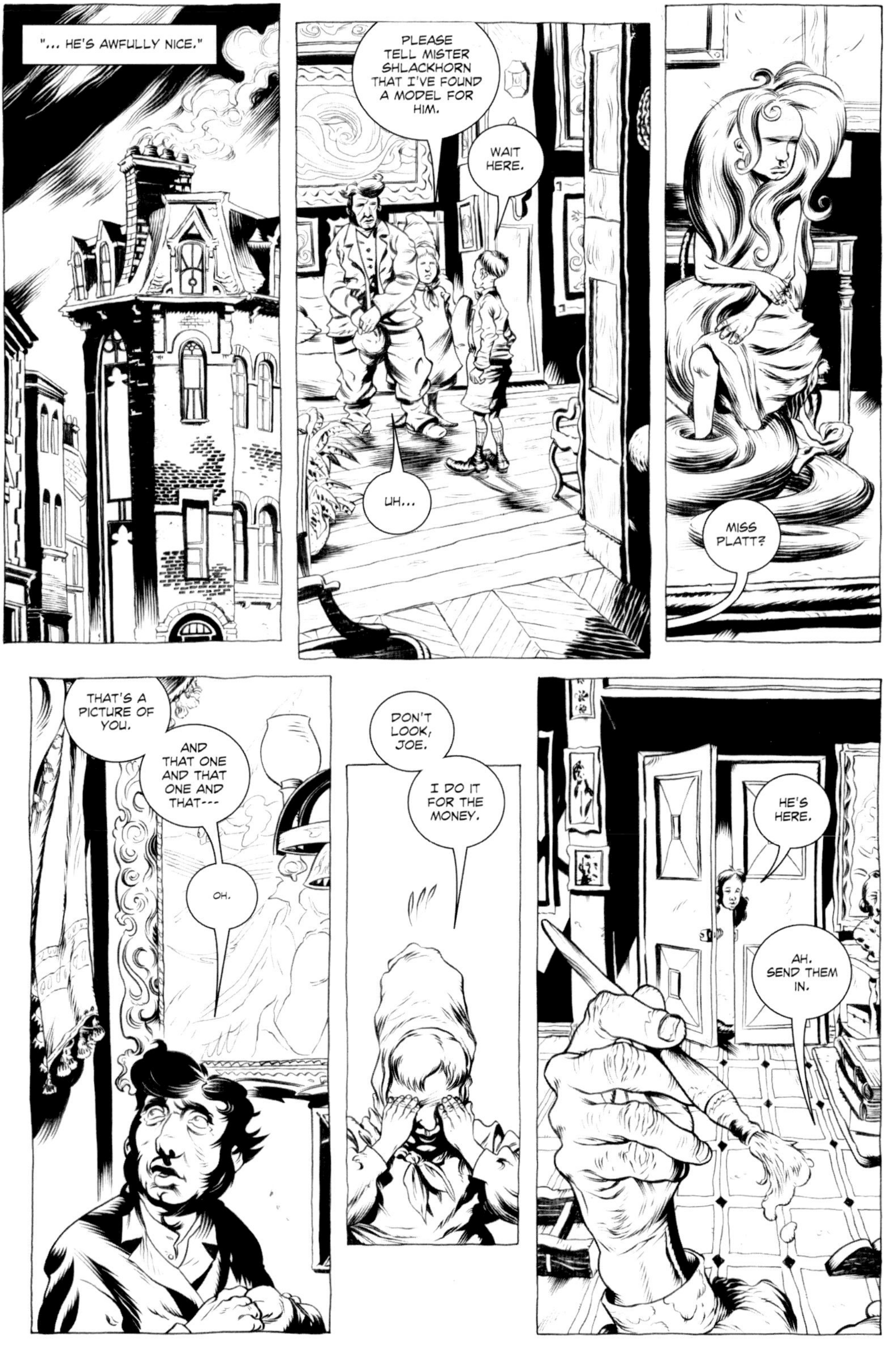
"... HE'S AWFULLY NICE."
PLEASE TELL MISTER SHLACKHORN THAT I'VE FOUND A MODEL FOR HIM.
WAIT HERE.
UH...
MISS PLATT?
THAT'S A PICTURE OF YOU.
AND THAT ONE AND THAT ONE AND THAT---
OH.
DON'T LOOK, JOE.
I DO IT FOR THE MONEY.
HE'S HERE.
AH. SEND THEM IN.

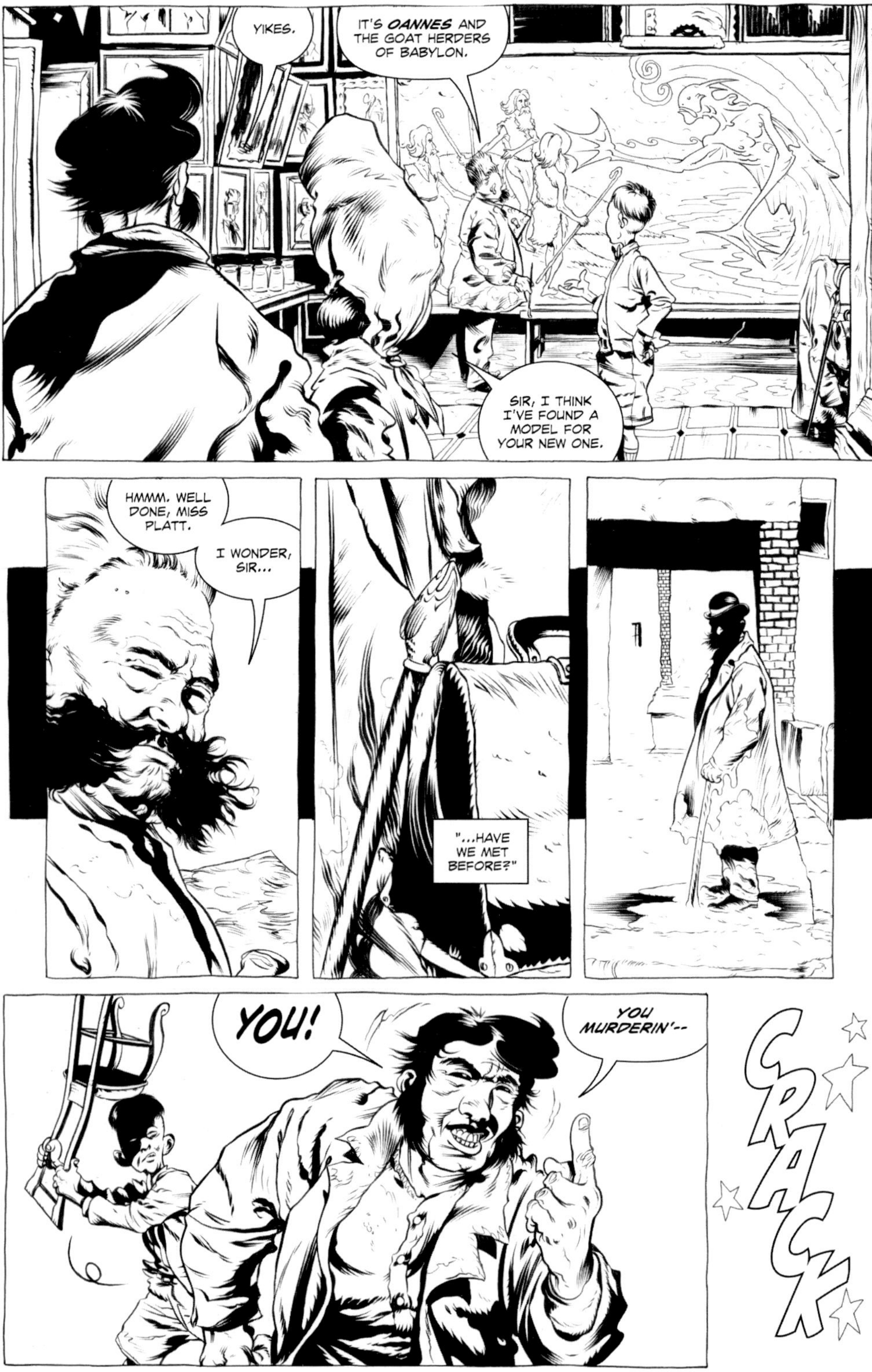
YIKES.
IT'S OANNES AND THE GOAT HERDERS OF BABYLON.
SIR, I THINK I'VE FOUND A MODEL FOR YOUR NEW ONE.
HMMM. WELL DONE, MISS PLATT.
I WONDER, SIR...
"...HAVE WE MET BEFORE?"
YOU!
YOU MURDERIN'--
CRACK

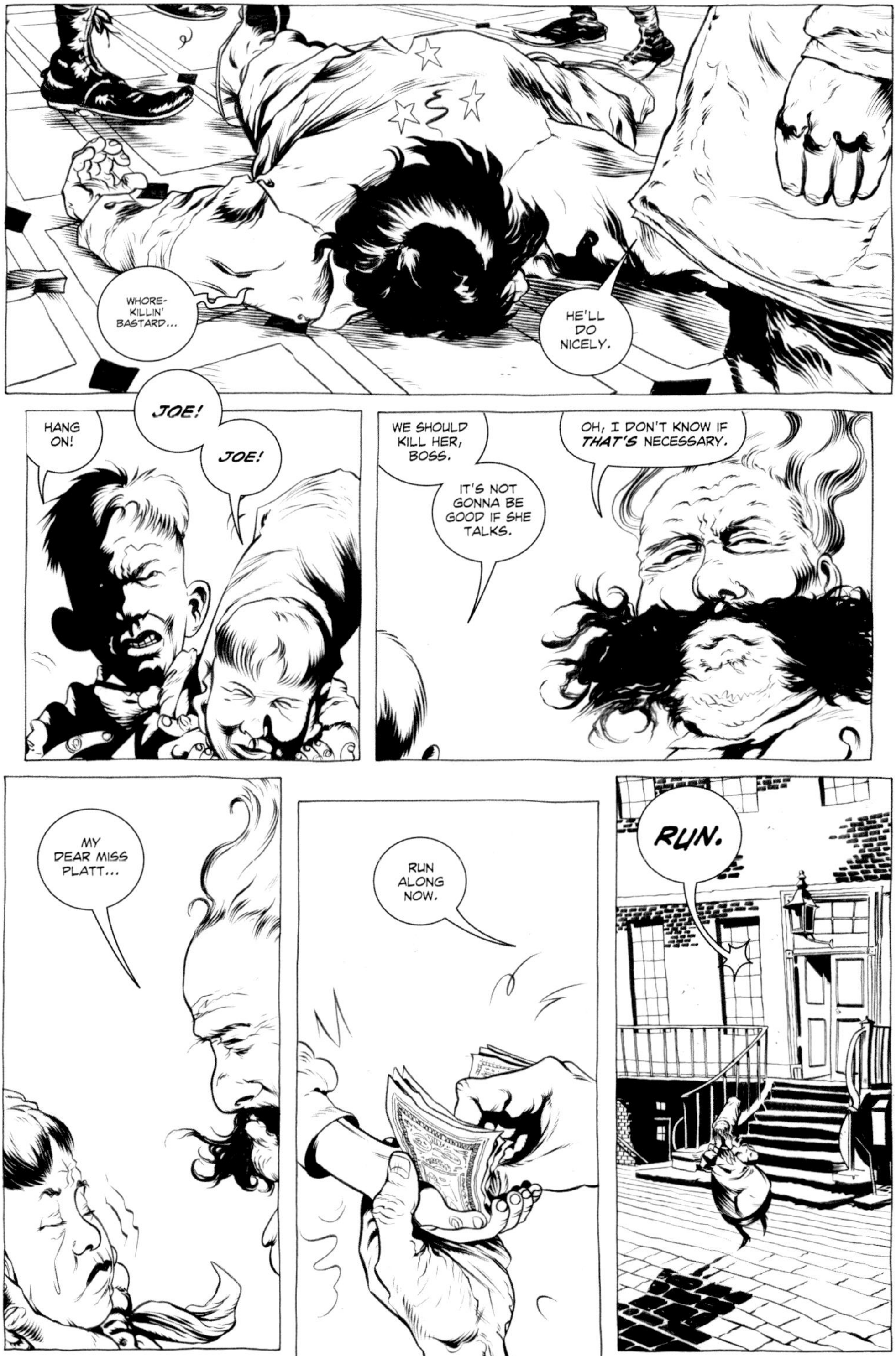
WHORE-KILLIN' BASTARD...
HE'LL DO NICELY.
HANG ON!
JOE!
JOE!
WE SHOULD KILL HER, BOSS.
IT'S NOT GONNA BE GOOD IF SHE TALKS.
OH, I DON'T KNOW IF *THAT'S* NECESSARY.
MY DEAR MISS PLATT...
RUN ALONG NOW.
RUN.

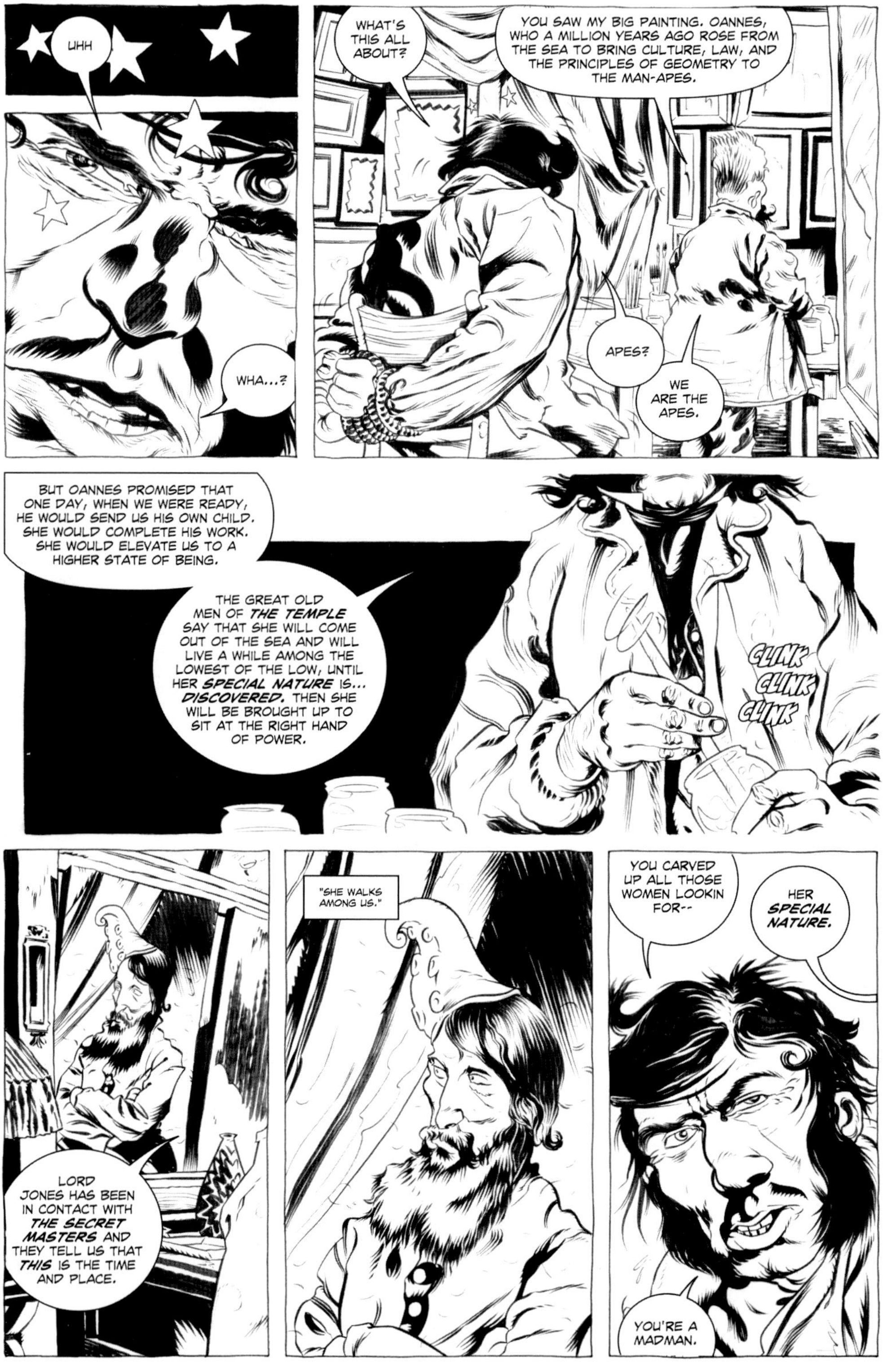
UHH
WHA...?
WHAT'S THIS ALL ABOUT?
YOU SAW MY BIG PAINTING. OANNES, WHO A MILLION YEARS AGO ROSE FROM THE SEA TO BRING CULTURE, LAW, AND THE PRINCIPLES OF GEOMETRY TO THE MAN-APES.
APES?
WE ARE THE APES.
BUT OANNES PROMISED THAT ONE DAY, WHEN WE WERE READY, HE WOULD SEND US HIS OWN CHILD. SHE WOULD COMPLETE HIS WORK. SHE WOULD ELEVATE US TO A HIGHER STATE OF BEING.
THE GREAT OLD MEN OF THE TEMPLE SAY THAT SHE WILL COME OUT OF THE SEA AND WILL LIVE A WHILE AMONG THE LOWEST OF THE LOW, UNTIL HER SPECIAL NATURE IS... DISCOVERED. THEN SHE WILL BE BROUGHT UP TO SIT AT THE RIGHT HAND OF POWER.
CLINK
CLINK
CLINK
LORD JONES HAS BEEN IN CONTACT WITH THE SECRET MASTERS AND THEY TELL US THAT THIS IS THE TIME AND PLACE.
"SHE WALKS AMONG US."
YOU CARVED UP ALL THOSE WOMEN LOOKIN FOR--
HER SPECIAL NATURE.
YOU'RE A MADMAN.

THAT WELL MAY BE.

THERE WERE THOSE WHO FELT THE JOB SHOULD BE DONE BY A MEDICAL MAN, BUT *I* TELL YOU IT WILL TAKE AN *ARTIST* TO RECOGNIZE THE MESSIAH IN THE GUTS OF A STREET WHORE.

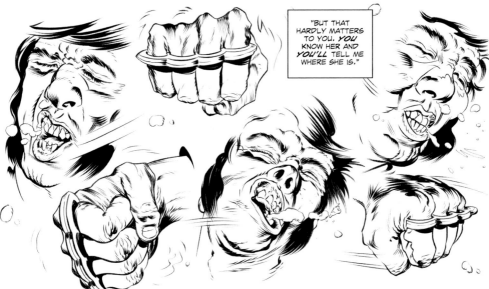

"BUT THAT HARDLY MATTERS TO YOU. *YOU* KNOW HER AND *YOU'LL* TELL ME WHERE SHE IS."

YOU'LL TELL ME OR I'LL BEAT IT--

OH.

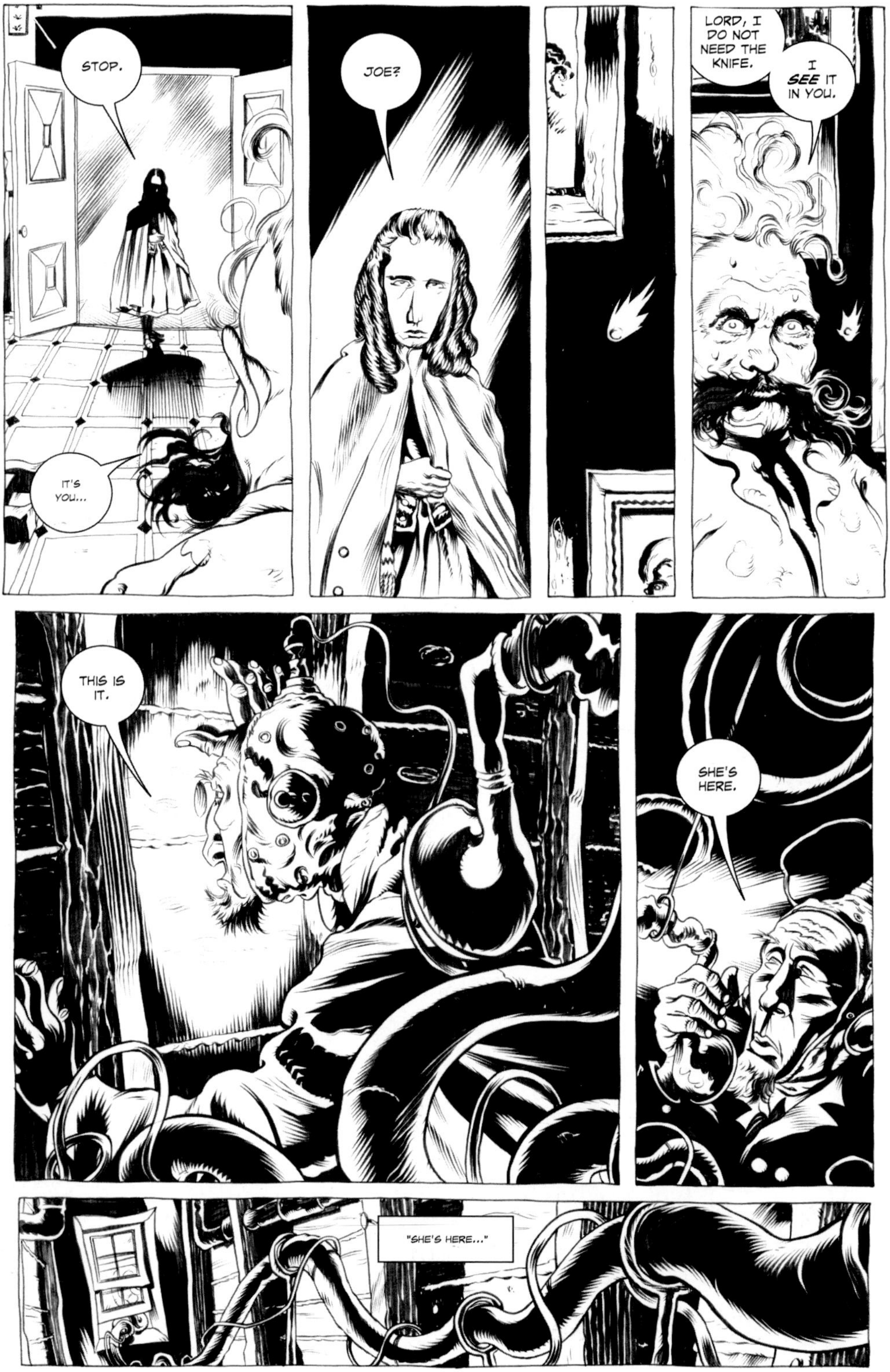
STOP.
IT'S YOU...
JOE?
LORD, I DO NOT NEED THE KNIFE.
I SEE IT IN YOU.
THIS IS IT.
SHE'S HERE.
"SHE'S HERE..."

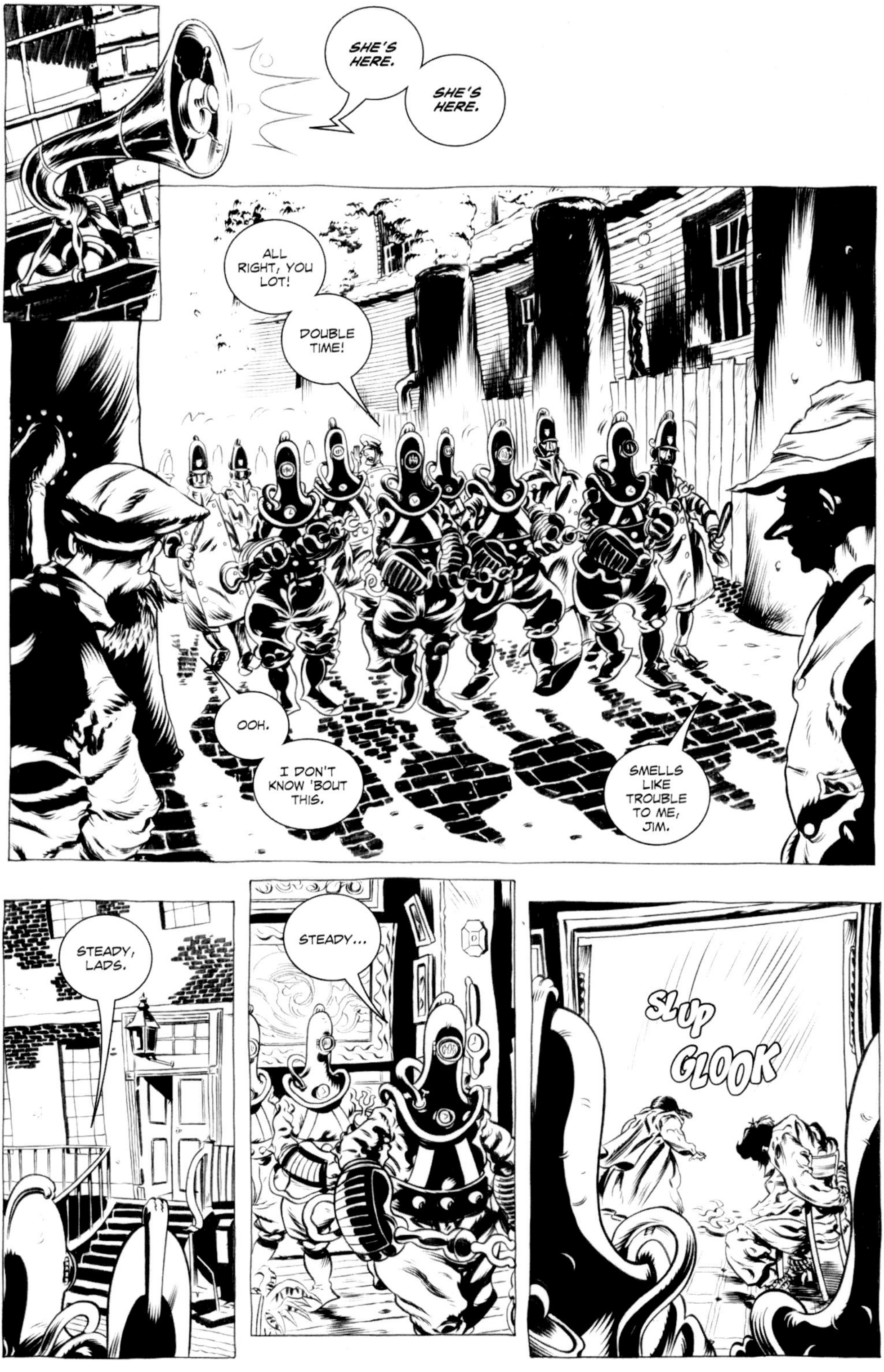
SHE'S HERE.
SHE'S HERE.
ALL RIGHT, YOU LOT!
DOUBLE TIME!
OOH.
I DON'T KNOW 'BOUT THIS.
SMELLS LIKE TROUBLE TO ME, JIM.
STEADY, LADS.
STEADY...
SLUP
GLOOK

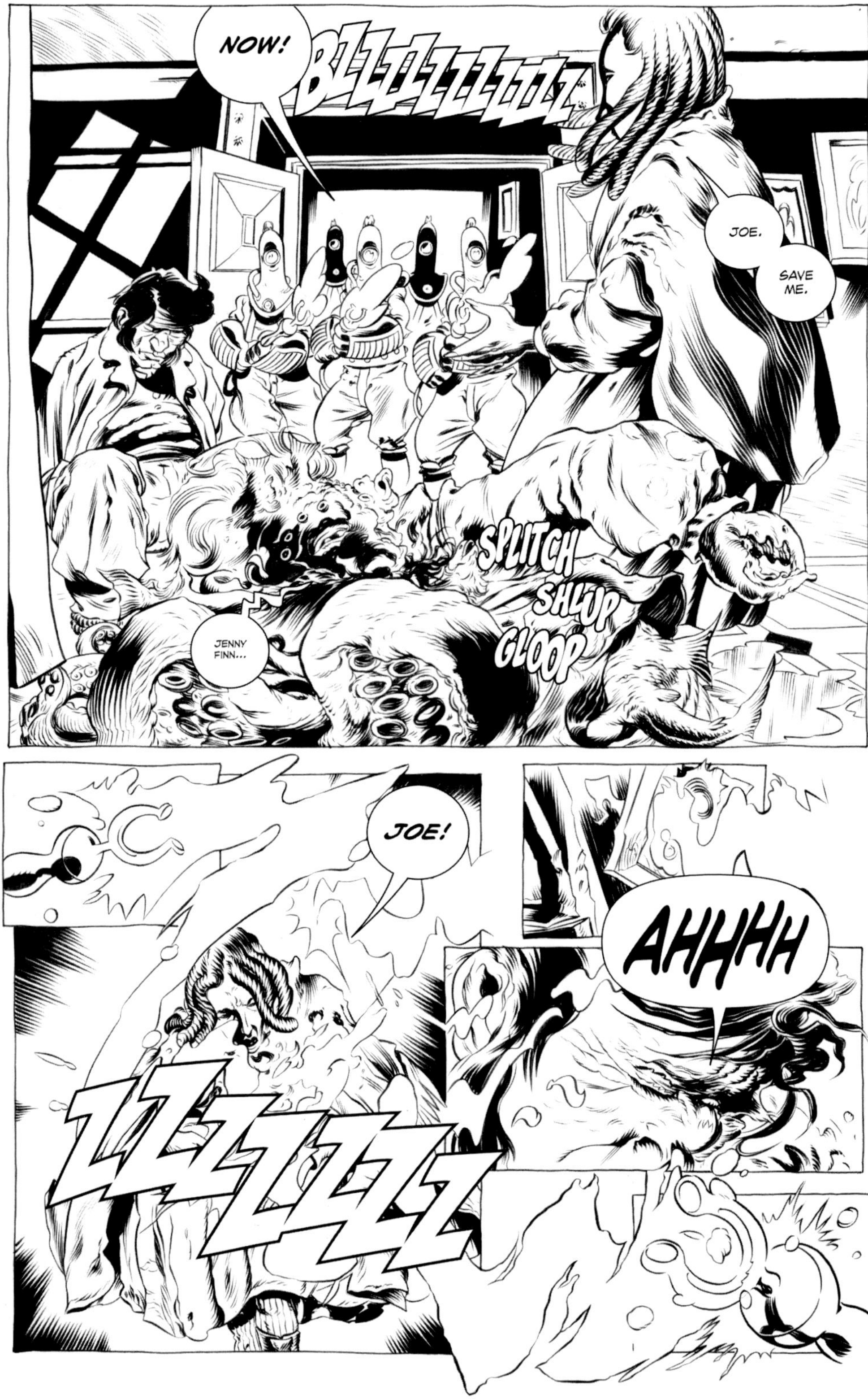
NOW!
BZZZZZZZZZZ
JOE.
SAVE ME.
SPLITCH
SHLUP
GLOOP
JENNY FINN...
JOE!
AHHHH
ZZZZZZ

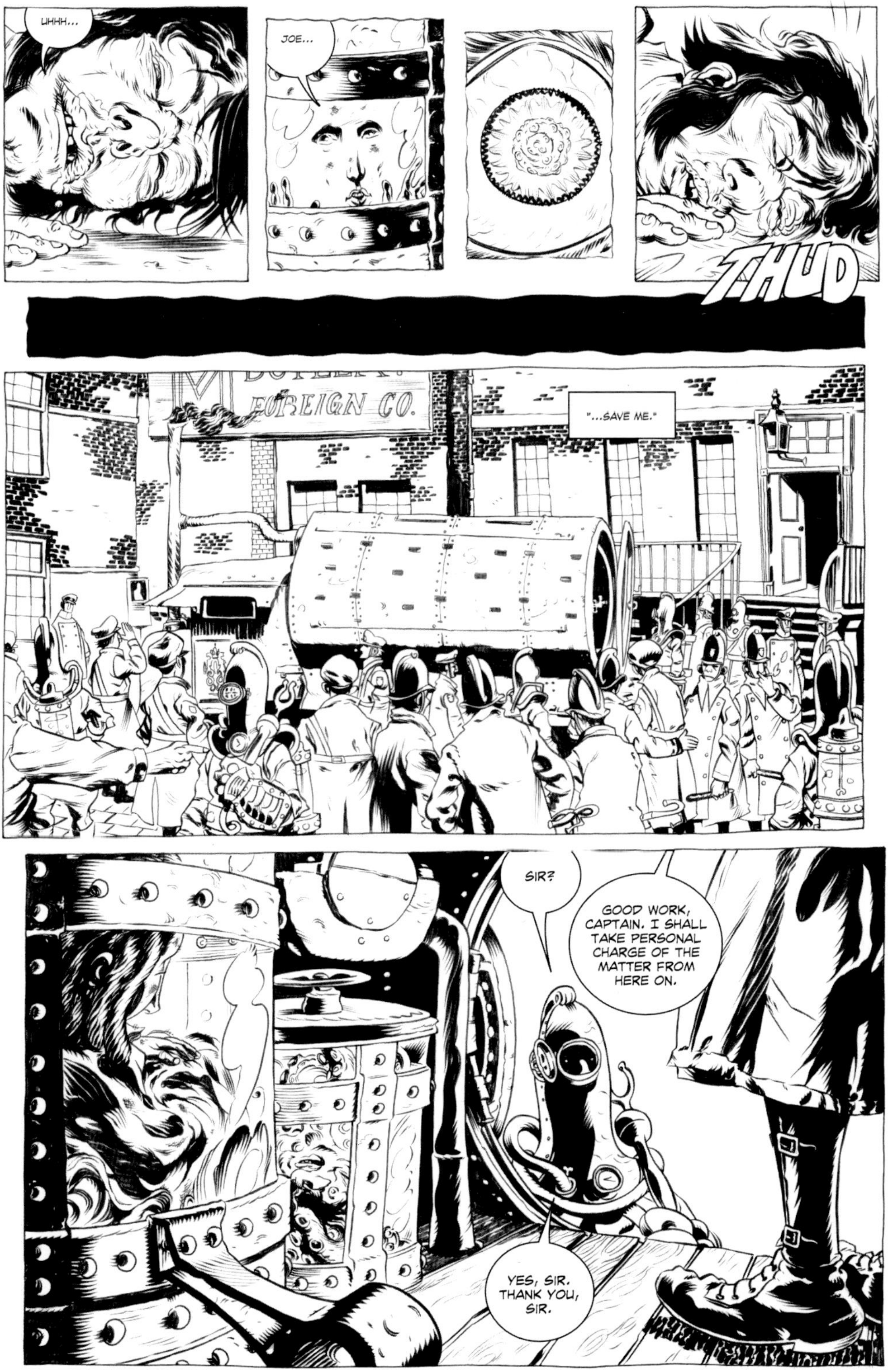
UHHH...
JOE...
THUD
"...SAVE ME."
SIR?
GOOD WORK, CAPTAIN. I SHALL TAKE PERSONAL CHARGE OF THE MATTER FROM HERE ON.
YES, SIR. THANK YOU, SIR.

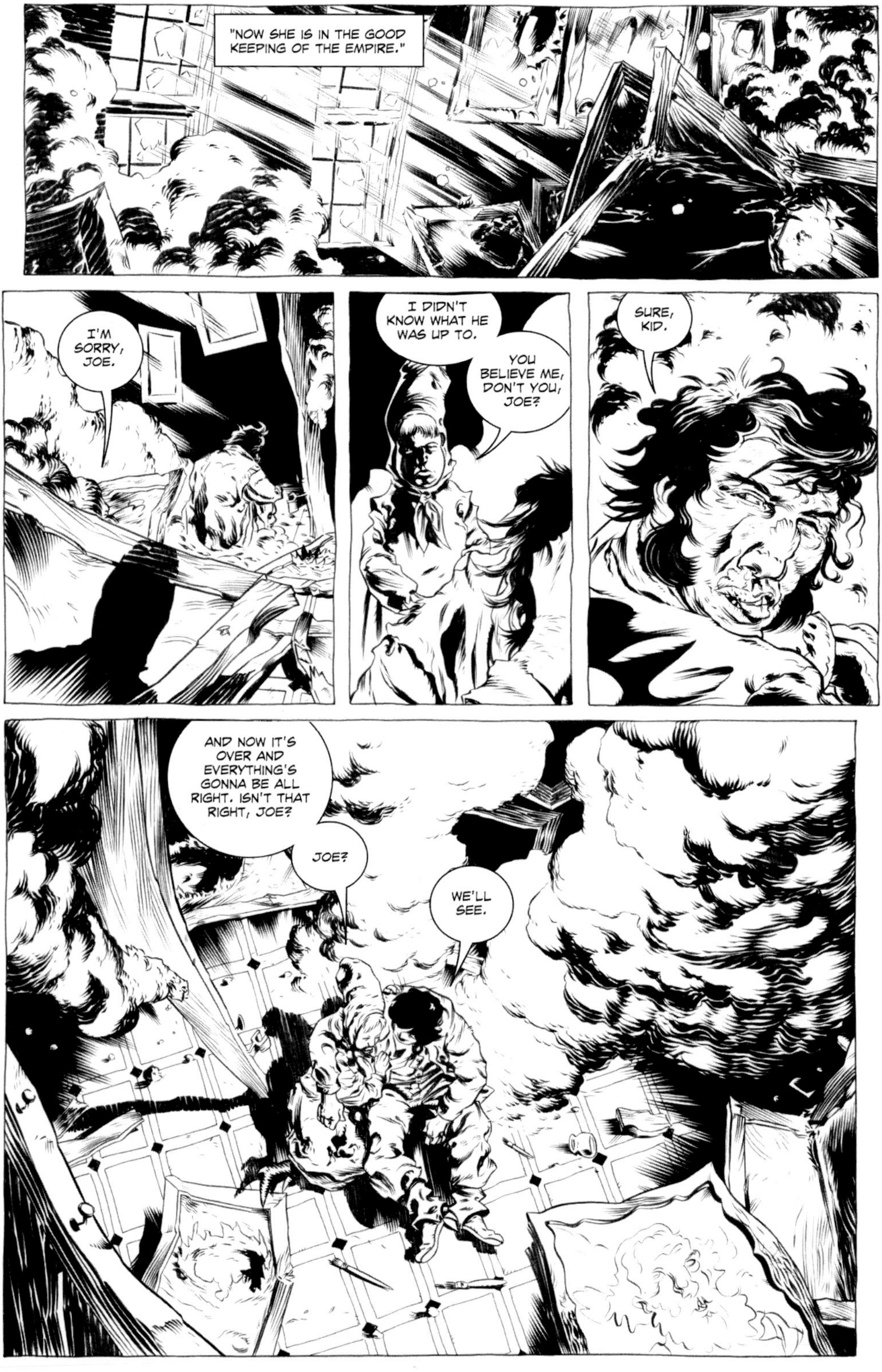
"NOW SHE IS IN THE GOOD KEEPING OF THE EMPIRE."
I'M SORRY, JOE.
I DIDN'T KNOW WHAT HE WAS UP TO.
YOU BELIEVE ME, DON'T YOU, JOE?
SURE, KID.
AND NOW IT'S OVER AND EVERYTHING'S GONNA BE ALL RIGHT. ISN'T THAT RIGHT, JOE?
JOE?
WE'LL SEE.

CHAPTER FOUR

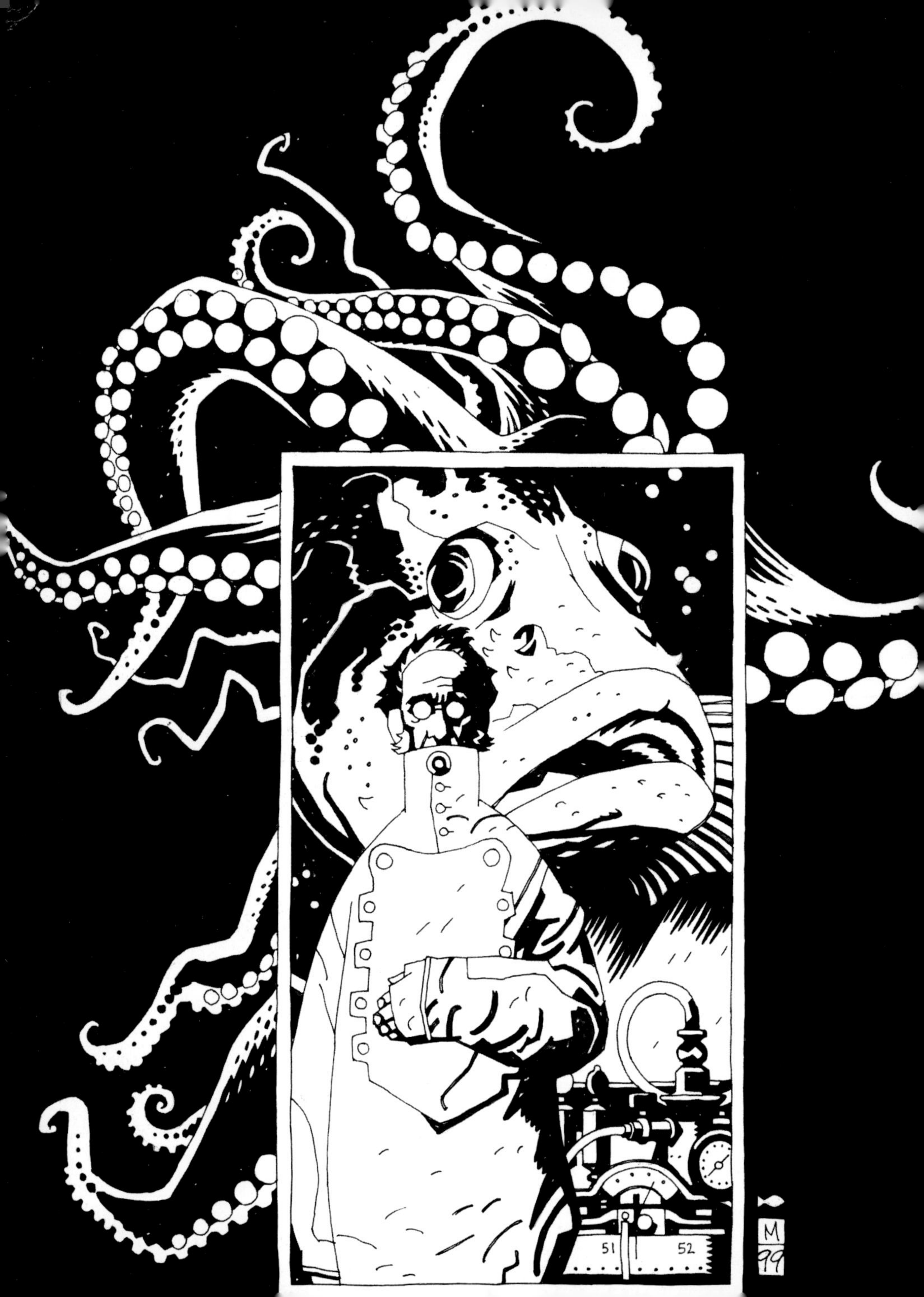
51
52
M
99

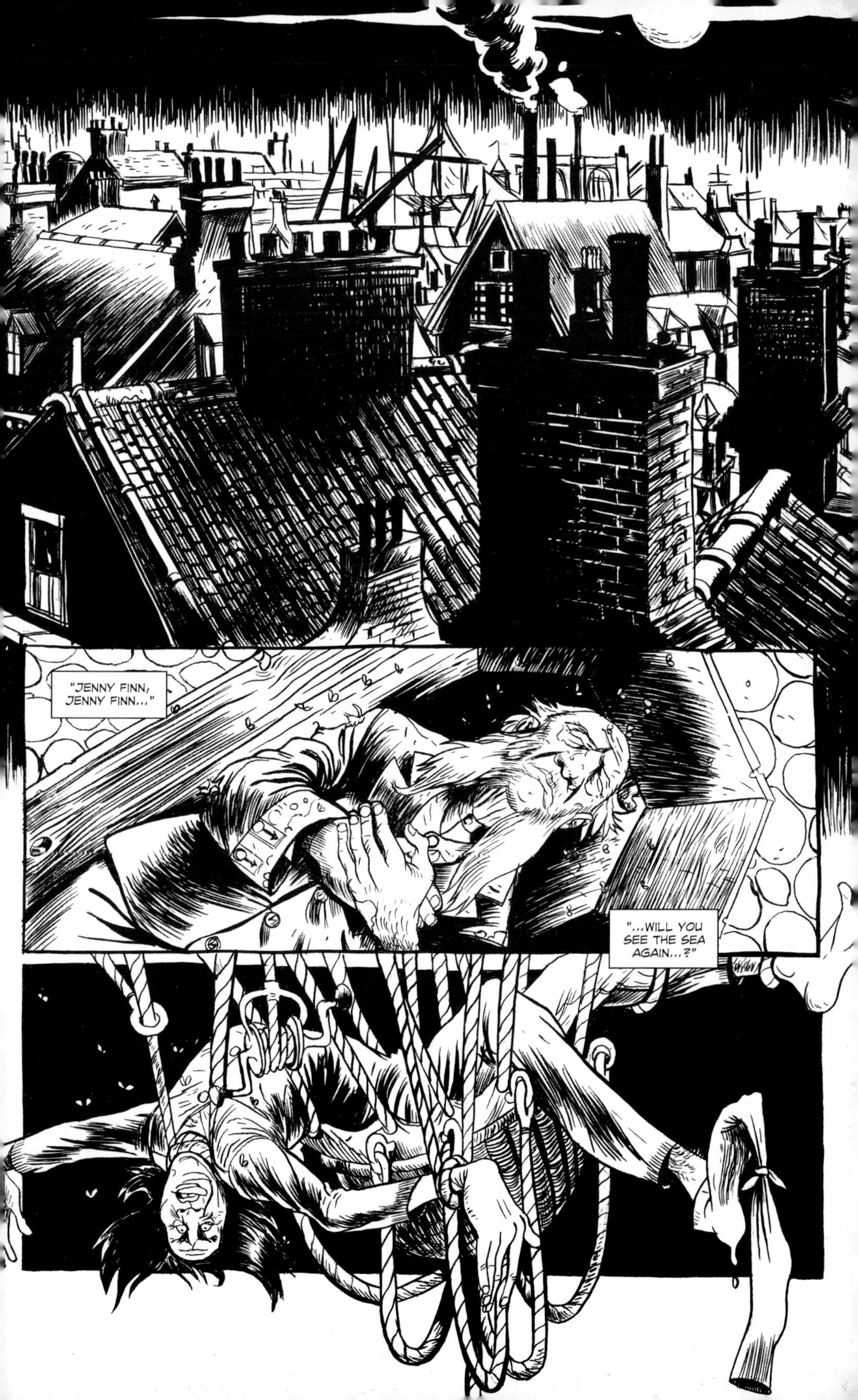
"JENNY FINN,
JENNY FINN..."
"...WILL YOU
SEE THE SEA
AGAIN...?"

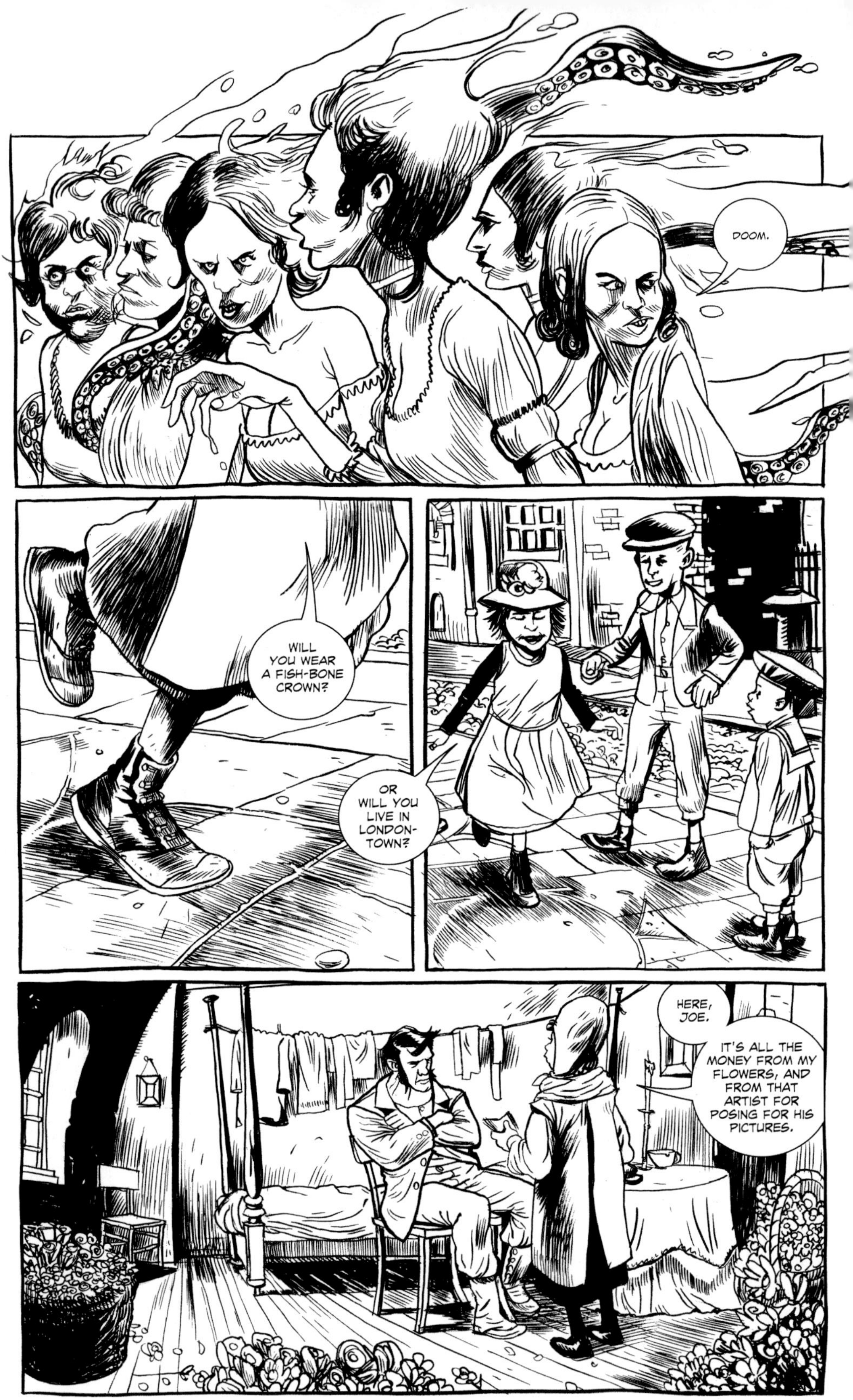
DOOM.
WILL YOU WEAR A FISH-BONE CROWN?
OR WILL YOU LIVE IN LONDON-TOWN?
HERE, JOE.
IT'S ALL THE MONEY FROM MY FLOWERS, AND FROM THAT ARTIST FOR POSING FOR HIS PICTURES.

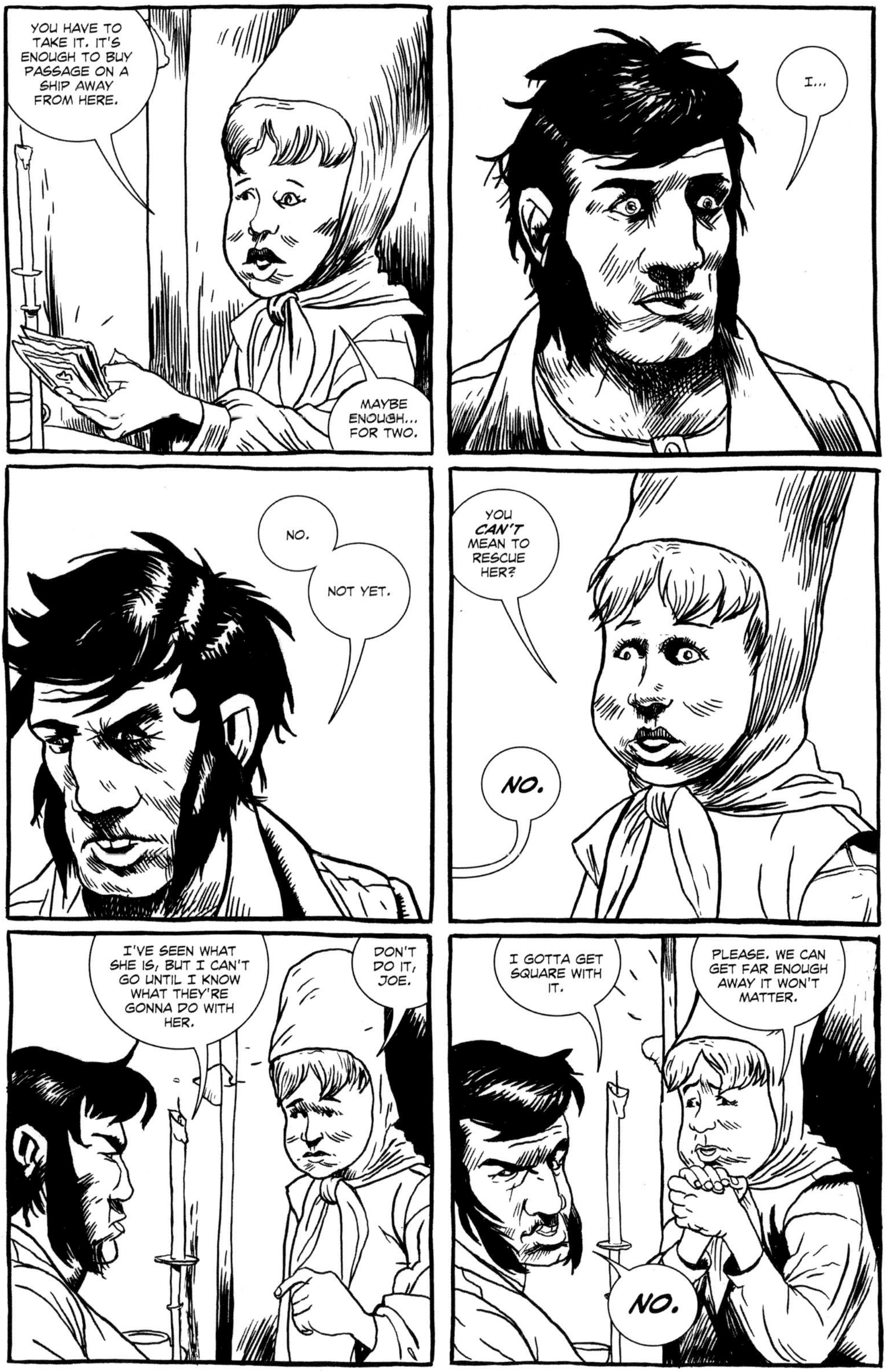

YOU HAVE TO TAKE IT. IT'S ENOUGH TO BUY PASSAGE ON A SHIP AWAY FROM HERE.
MAYBE ENOUGH... FOR TWO.
I...
NO.
NOT YET.
YOU *CAN'T* MEAN TO RESCUE HER?
NO.
I'VE SEEN WHAT SHE IS, BUT I CAN'T GO UNTIL I KNOW WHAT THEY'RE GONNA DO WITH HER.
DON'T DO IT, JOE.
I GOTTA GET SQUARE WITH IT.
PLEASE. WE CAN GET FAR ENOUGH AWAY IT WON'T MATTER.
NO.

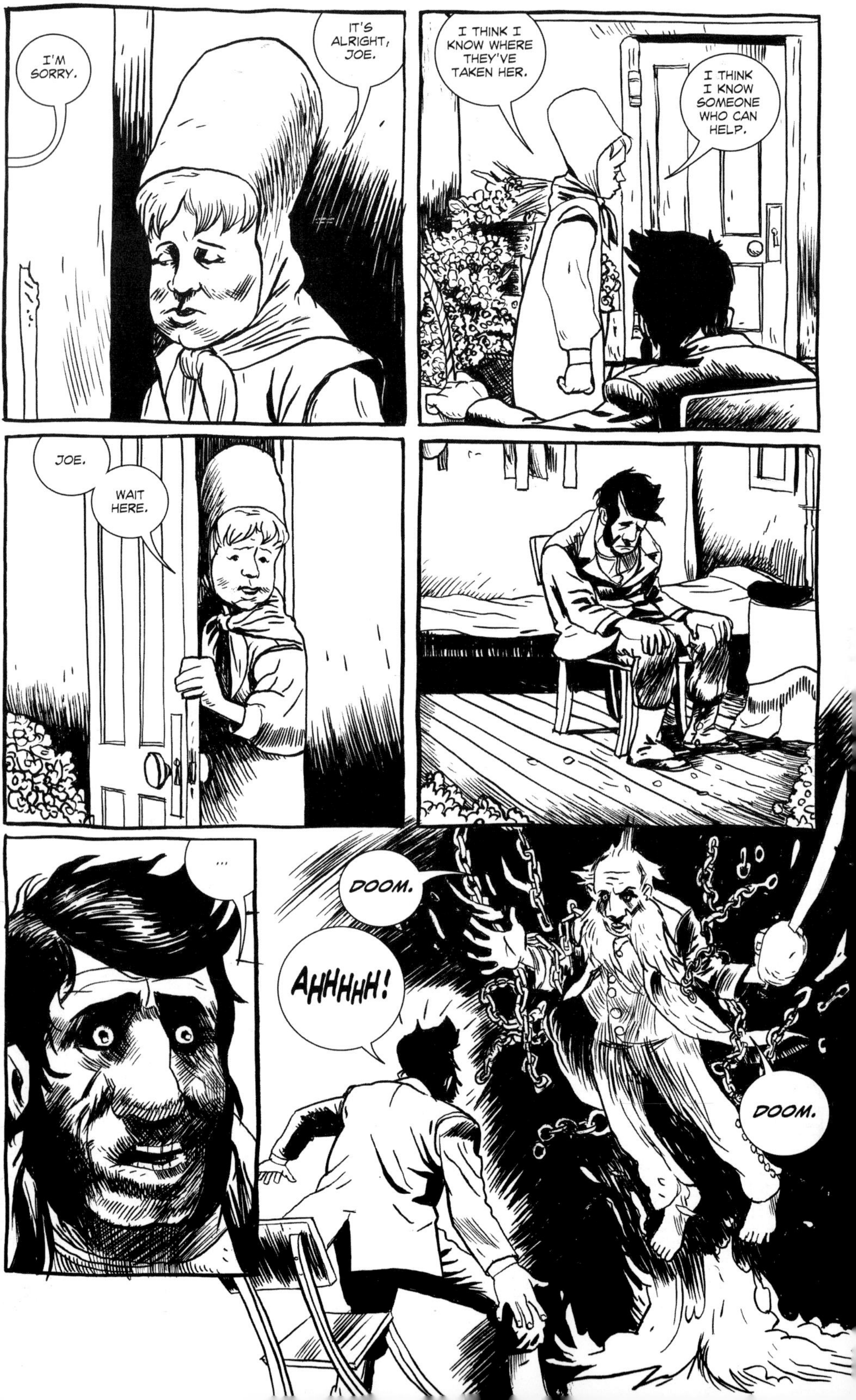
I'M SORRY.
IT'S ALRIGHT, JOE.
I THINK I KNOW WHERE THEY'VE TAKEN HER.
I THINK I KNOW SOMEONE WHO CAN HELP.
JOE.
WAIT HERE.
...
DOOM.
AHHHHH!
DOOM.

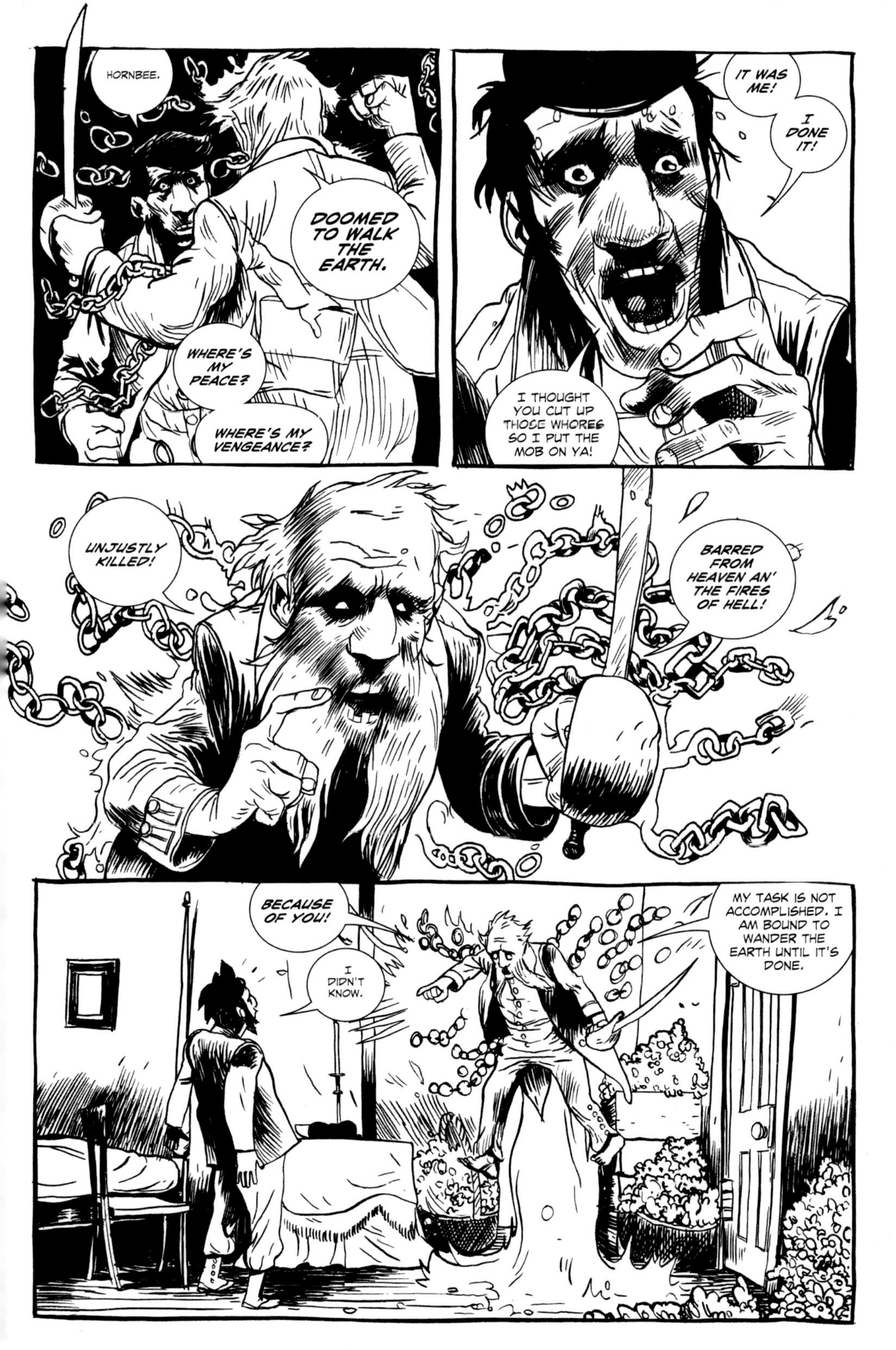
HORNBEE.
DOOMED TO WALK THE EARTH.
WHERE'S MY PEACE?
WHERE'S MY VENGEANCE?
IT WAS ME!
I DONE IT!
I THOUGHT YOU CUT UP THOSE WHORES SO I PUT THE MOB ON YA!
UNJUSTLY KILLED!
BARRED FROM HEAVEN AN' THE FIRES OF HELL!
BECAUSE OF YOU!
I DIDN'T KNOW.
MY TASK IS NOT ACCOMPLISHED. I AM BOUND TO WANDER THE EARTH UNTIL IT'S DONE.

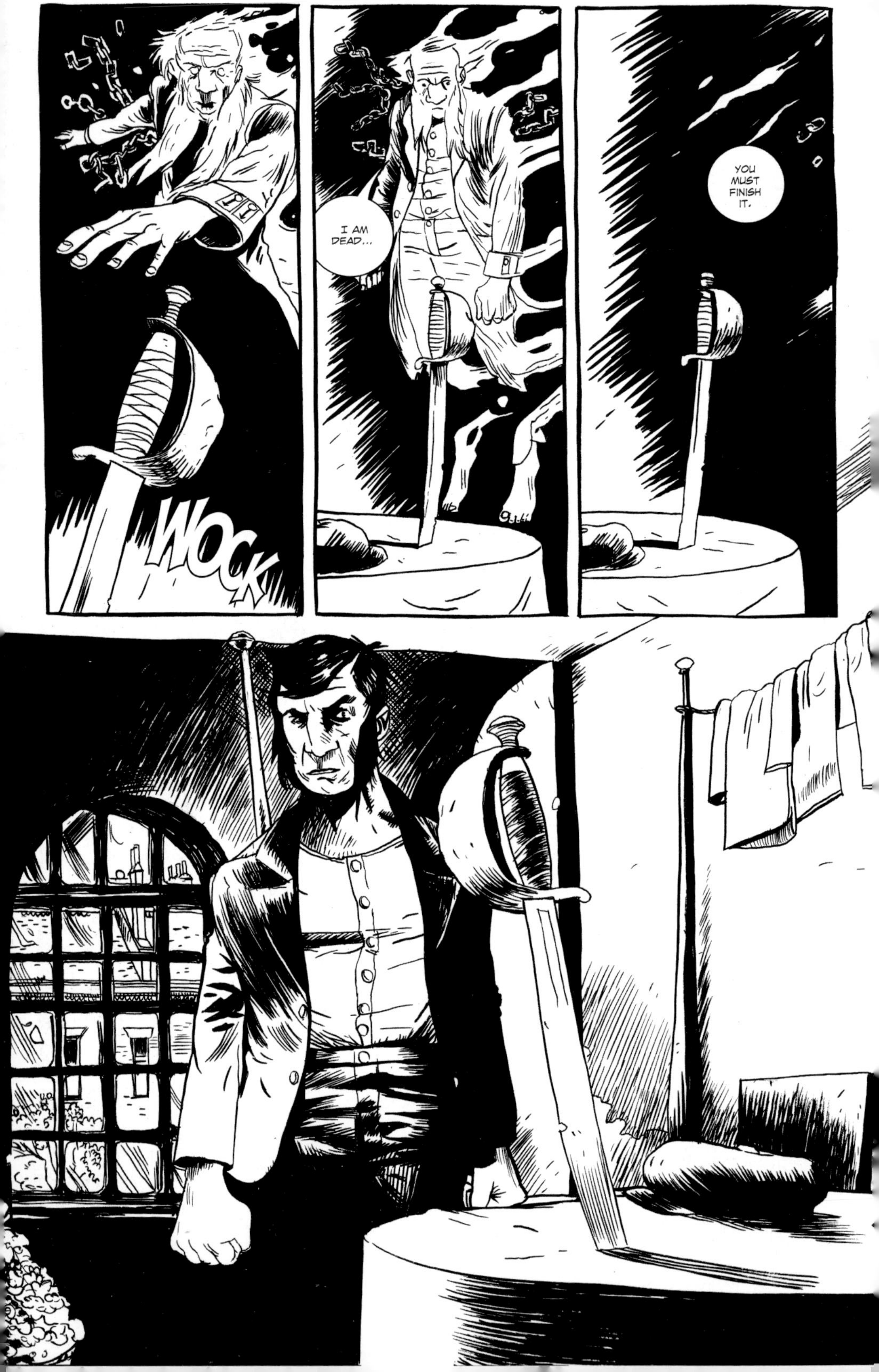
WOCK
I AM DEAD...
YOU MUST FINISH IT.

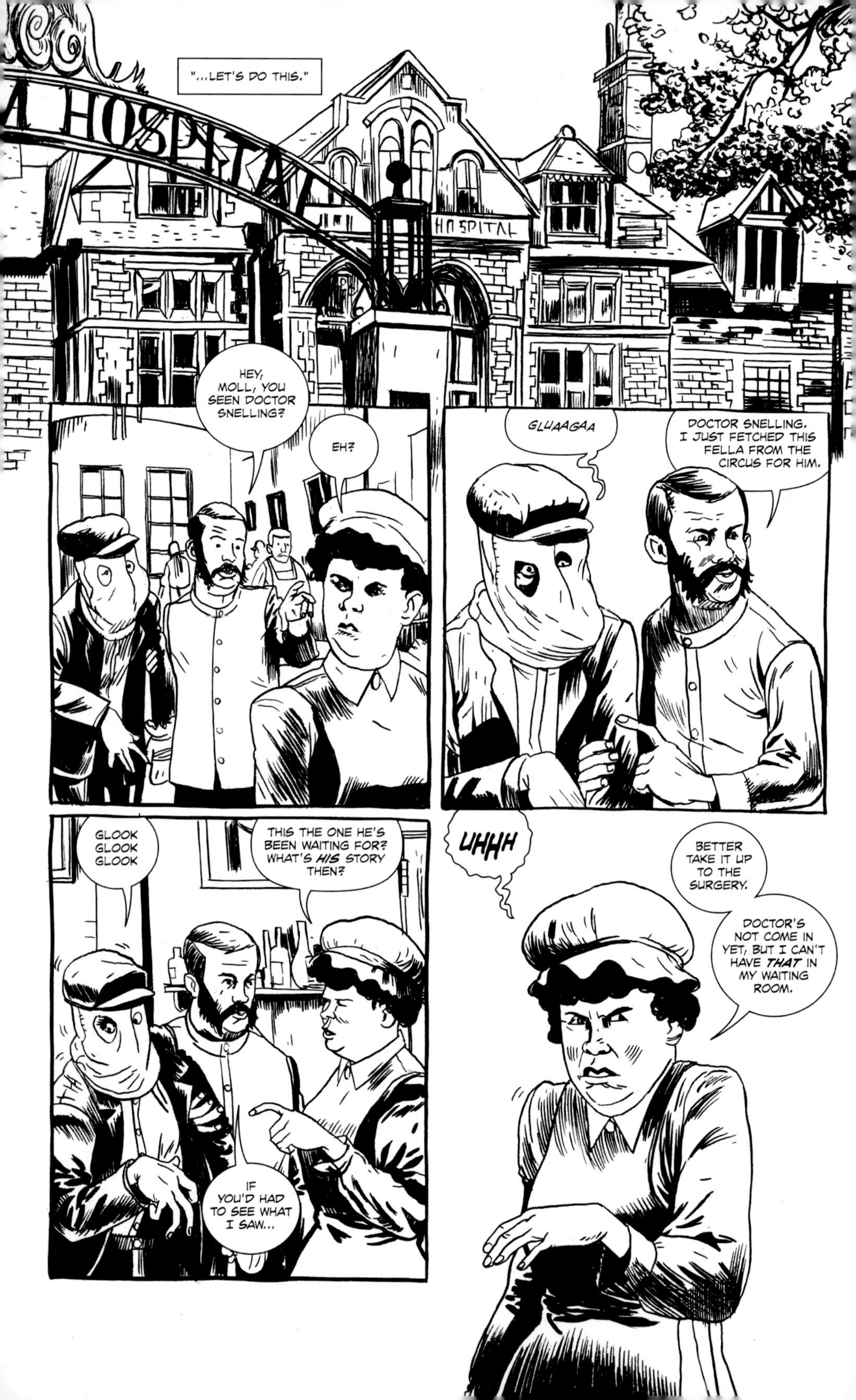
"...LET'S DO THIS."
HOSPITAL
HOSPITAL
HEY, MOLL, YOU SEEN DOCTOR SNELLING?
EH?
GLUAAGAA
DOCTOR SNELLING. I JUST FETCHED THIS FELLA FROM THE CIRCUS FOR HIM.
GLOOK GLOOK GLOOK
THIS THE ONE HE'S BEEN WAITING FOR? WHAT'S *HIS* STORY THEN?
IF YOU'D HAD TO SEE WHAT I SAW...
UHHH
BETTER TAKE IT UP TO THE SURGERY.
DOCTOR'S NOT COME IN YET, BUT I CAN'T HAVE *THAT* IN MY WAITING ROOM.

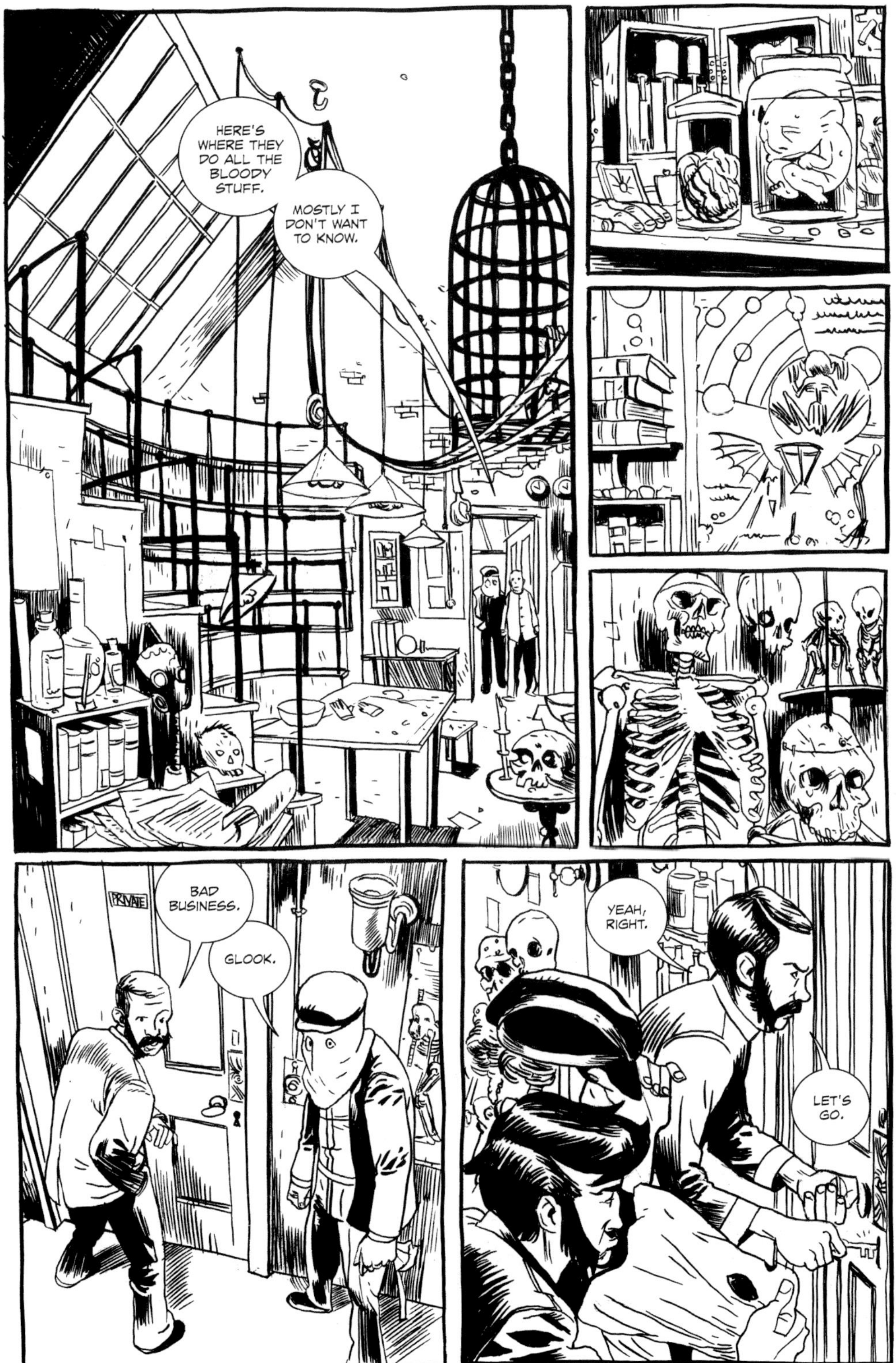
HERE'S WHERE THEY DO ALL THE BLOODY STUFF.
MOSTLY I DON'T WANT TO KNOW.
PRIVATE
BAD BUSINESS.
GLOOK.
YEAH, RIGHT.
LET'S GO.

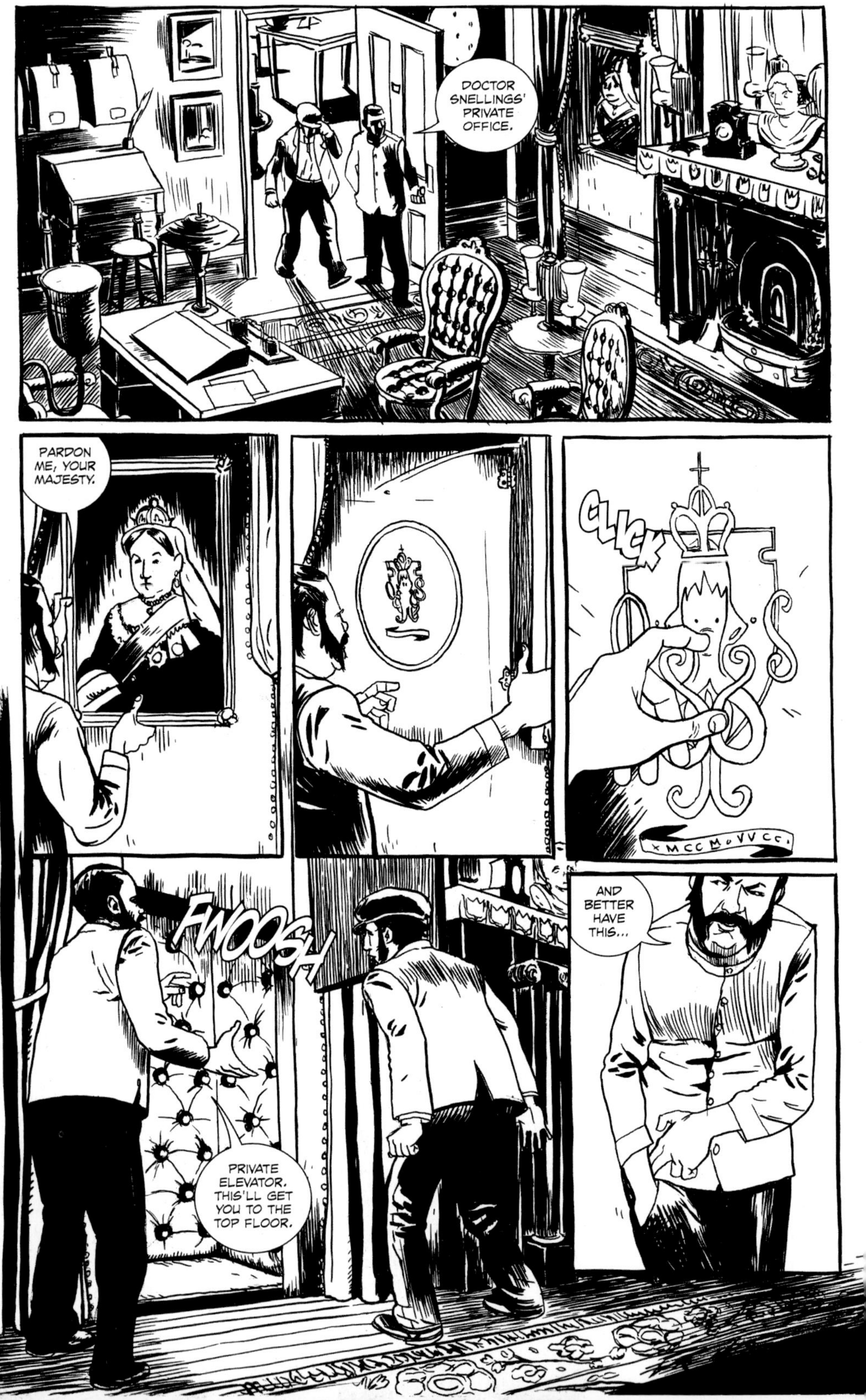
DOCTOR SNELLINGS' PRIVATE OFFICE.
PARDON ME, YOUR MAJESTY.
CLICK
FWOOSH
PRIVATE ELEVATOR. THIS'LL GET YOU TO THE TOP FLOOR.
AND BETTER HAVE THIS...

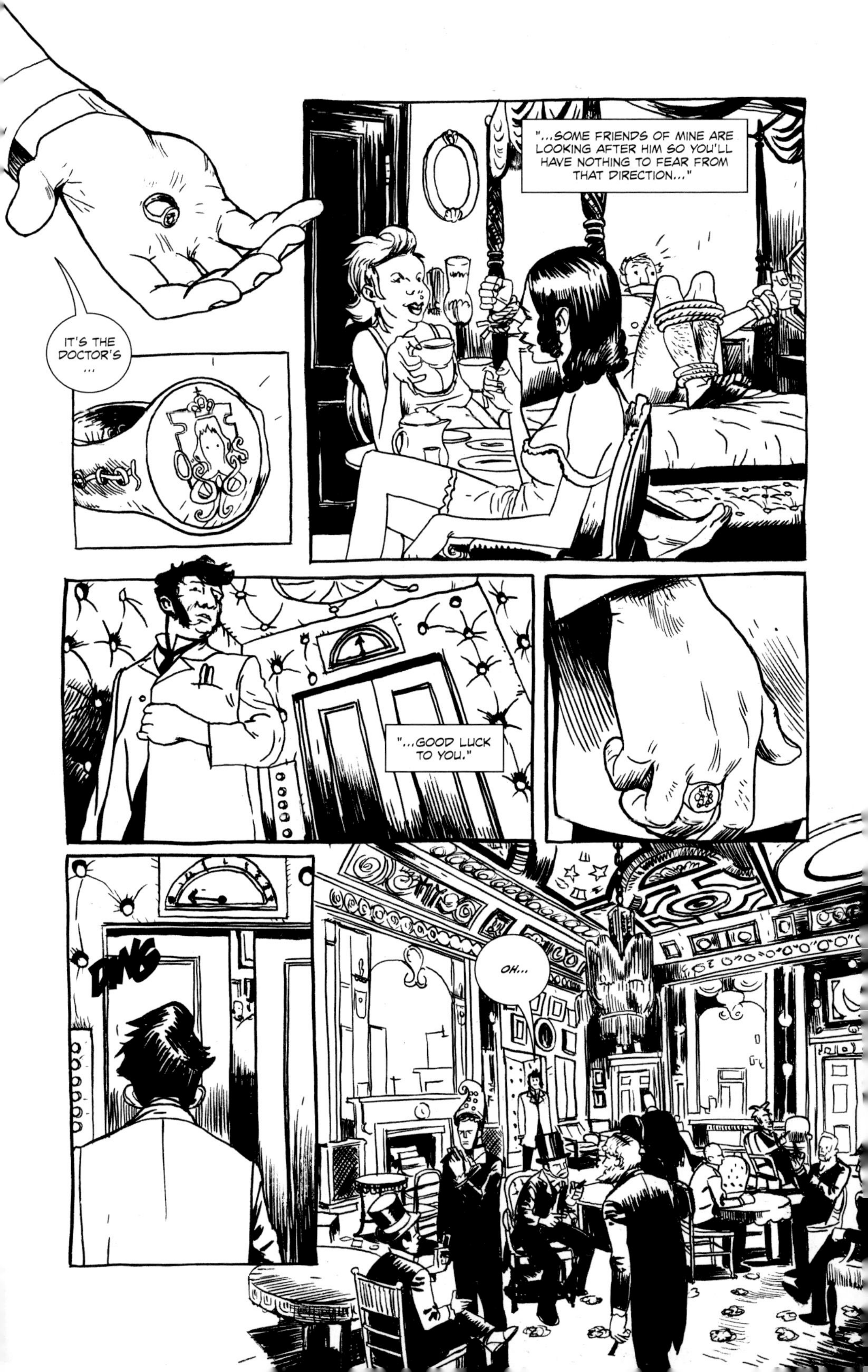
IT'S THE DOCTOR'S ...
"...SOME FRIENDS OF MINE ARE LOOKING AFTER HIM SO YOU'LL HAVE NOTHING TO FEAR FROM THAT DIRECTION..."
"...GOOD LUCK TO YOU."
DING
OH...

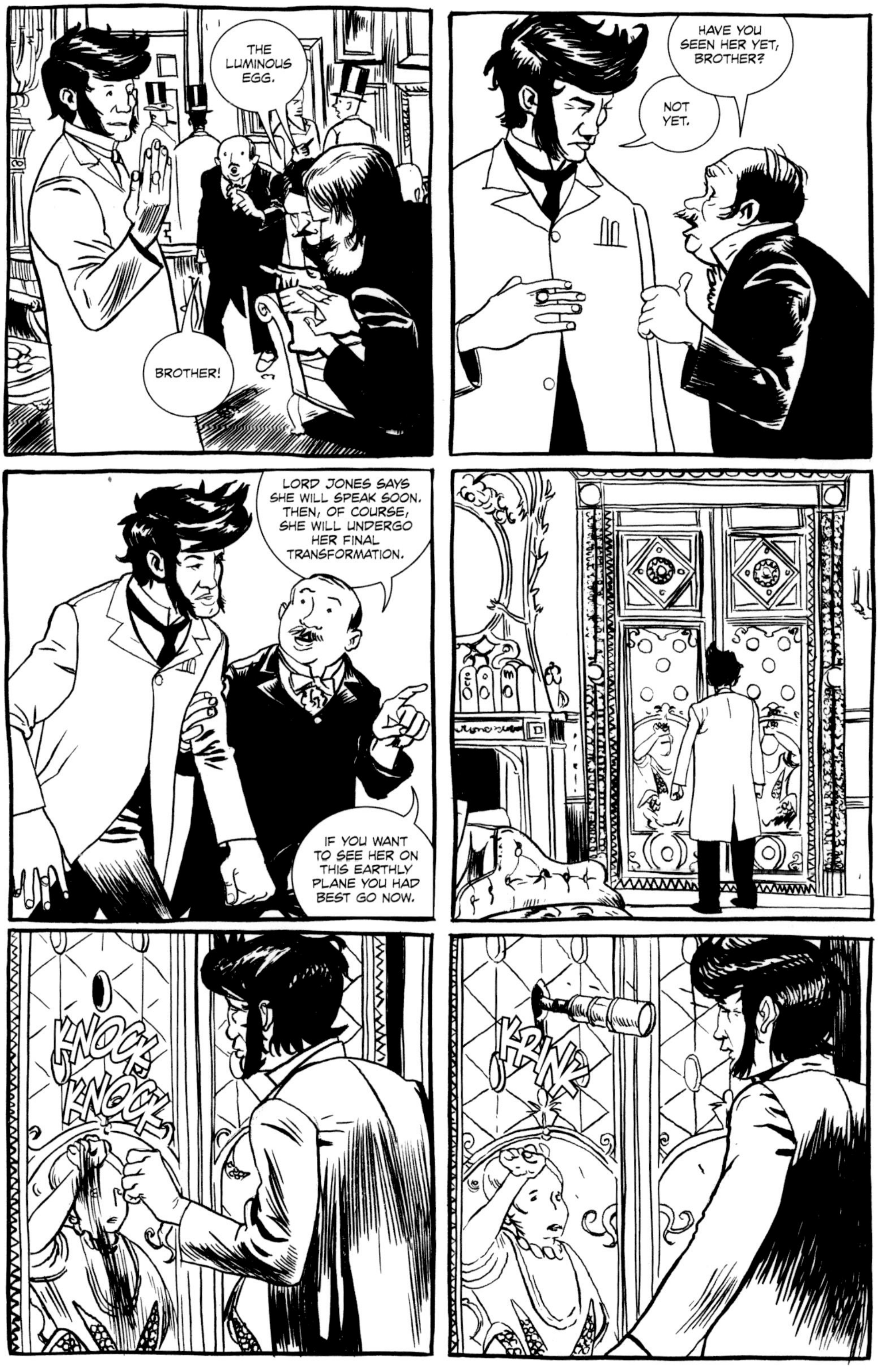

THE LUMINOUS EGG.
BROTHER!
HAVE YOU SEEN HER YET, BROTHER?
NOT YET.
LORD JONES SAYS SHE WILL SPEAK SOON. THEN, OF COURSE, SHE WILL UNDERGO HER FINAL TRANSFORMATION.
IF YOU WANT TO SEE HER ON THIS EARTHLY PLANE YOU HAD BEST GO NOW.
KNOCK KNOCK
KRINK

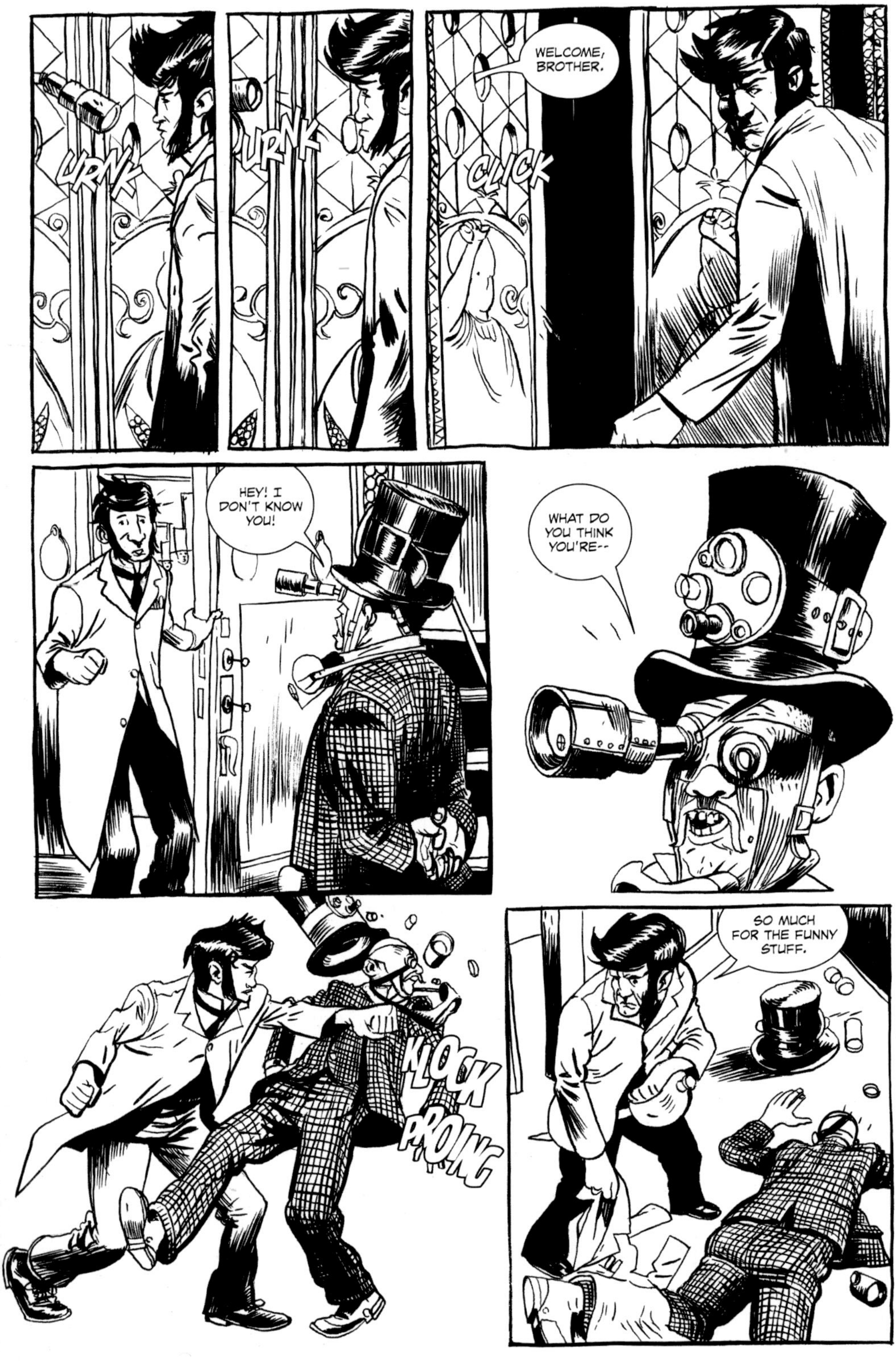
URNK
URNK
CLICK
WELCOME, BROTHER.
HEY! I DON'T KNOW YOU!
WHAT DO YOU THINK YOU'RE--
KLOCK
PROING
SO MUCH FOR THE FUNNY STUFF.

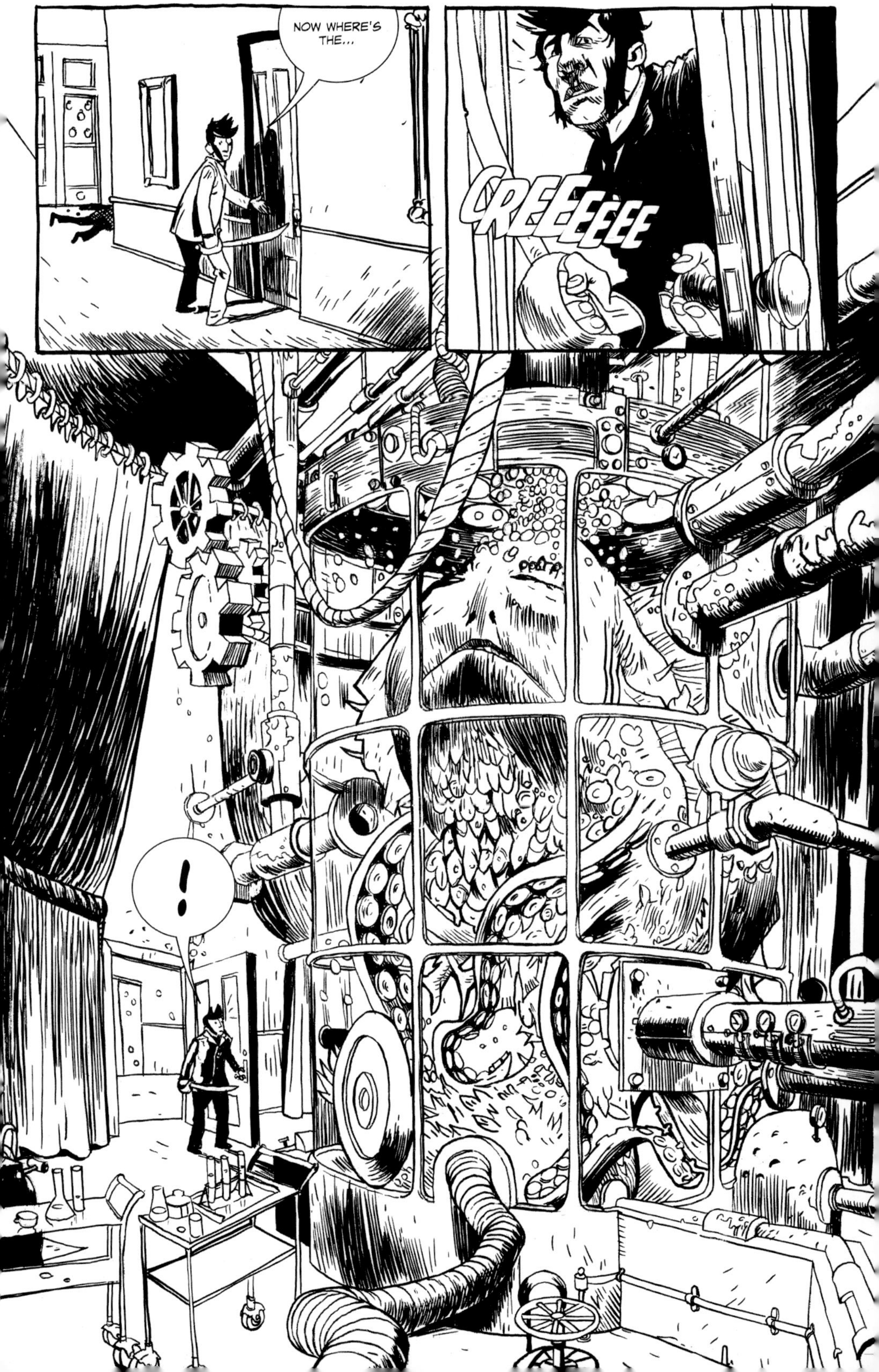
NOW WHERE'S THE...
CREEEEEE
!

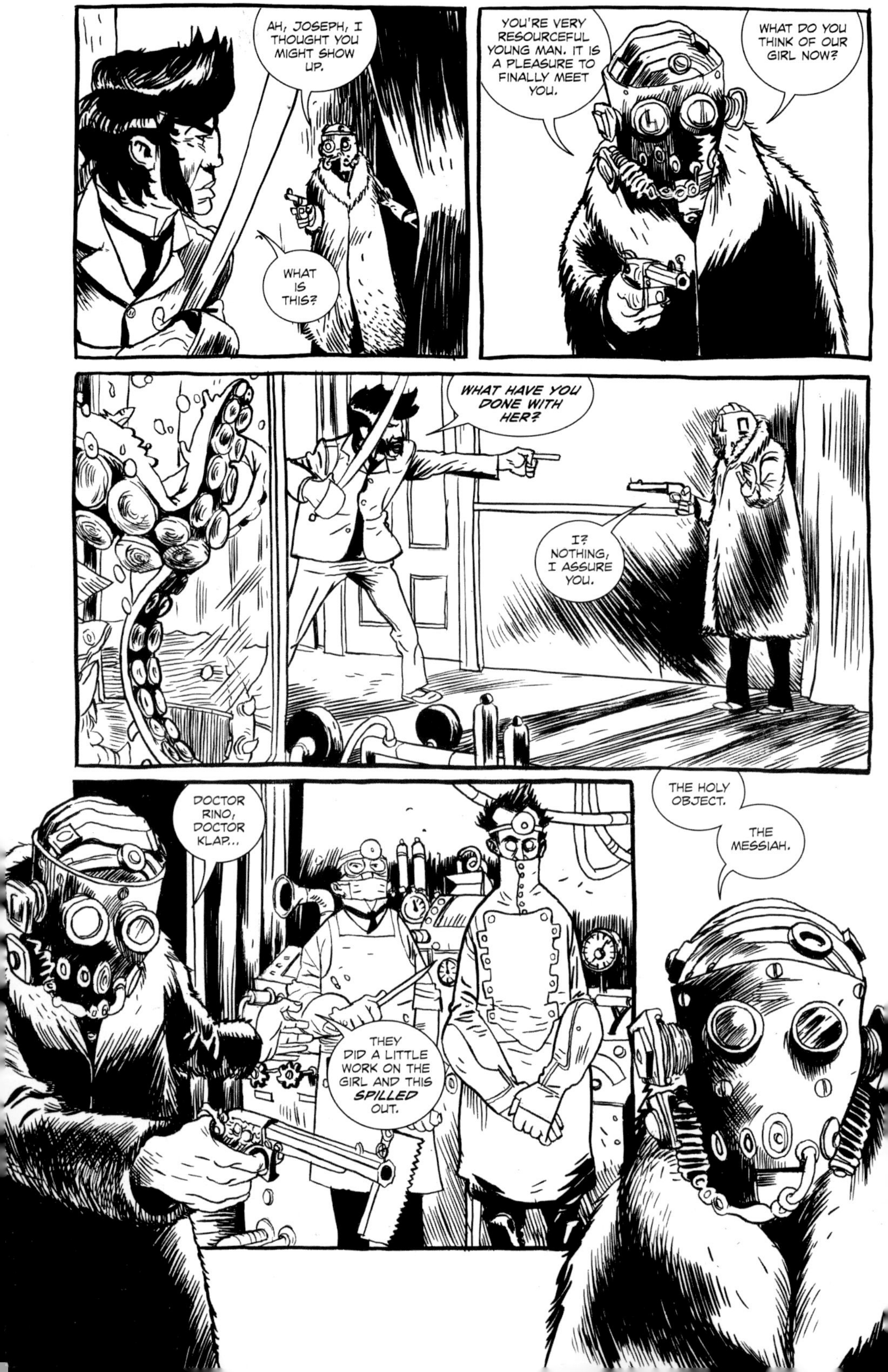
AH, JOSEPH, I THOUGHT YOU MIGHT SHOW UP.
WHAT IS THIS?
YOU'RE VERY RESOURCEFUL YOUNG MAN. IT IS A PLEASURE TO FINALLY MEET YOU.
WHAT DO YOU THINK OF OUR GIRL NOW?
WHAT HAVE YOU DONE WITH HER?
I? NOTHING, I ASSURE YOU.
DOCTOR RINO, DOCTOR KLAP...
THEY DID A LITTLE WORK ON THE GIRL AND THIS SPILLED OUT.
THE HOLY OBJECT.
THE MESSIAH.

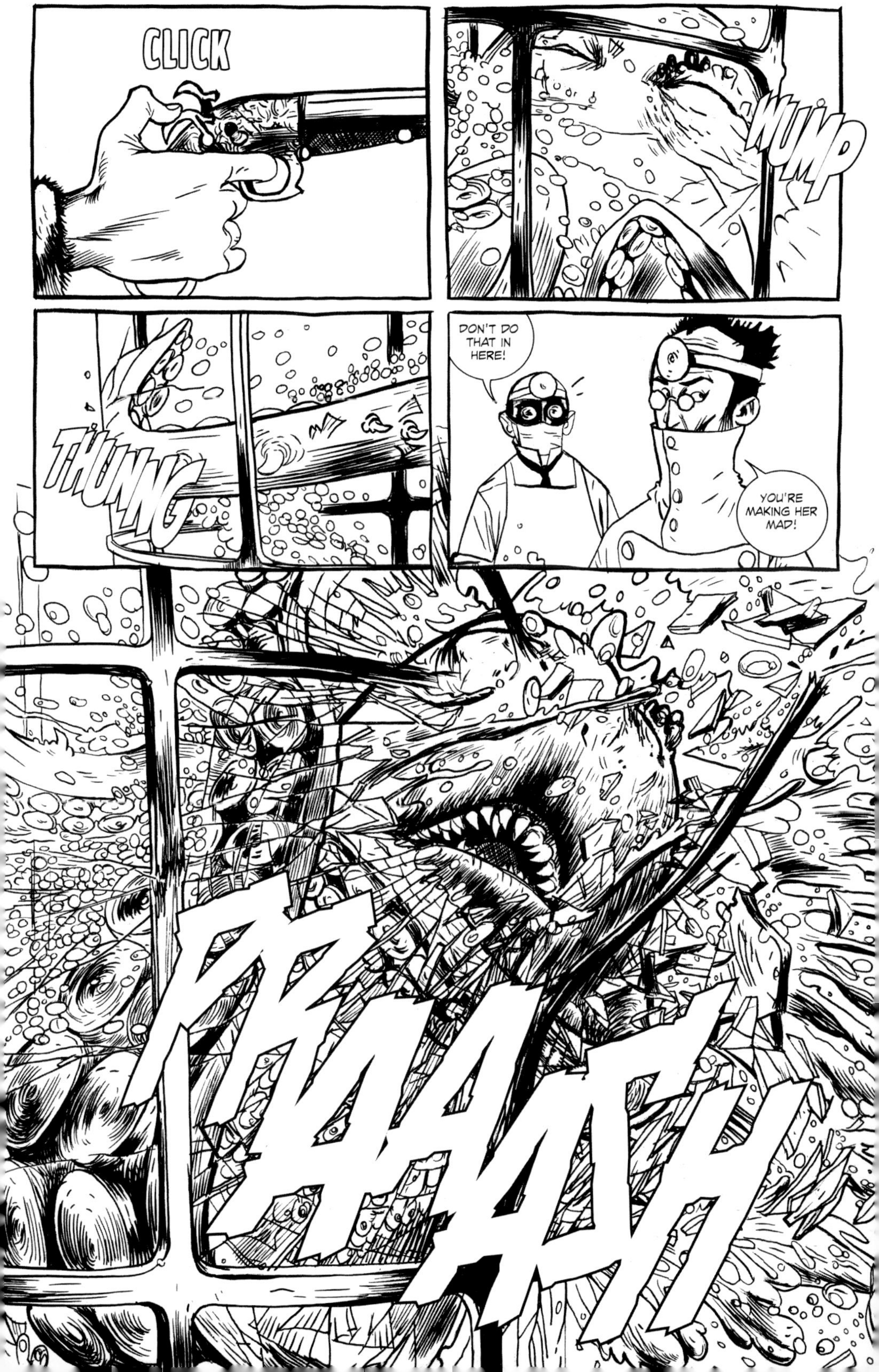
CLICK
WUMP
THUNNG
DON'T DO THAT IN HERE!
YOU'RE MAKING HER MAD!

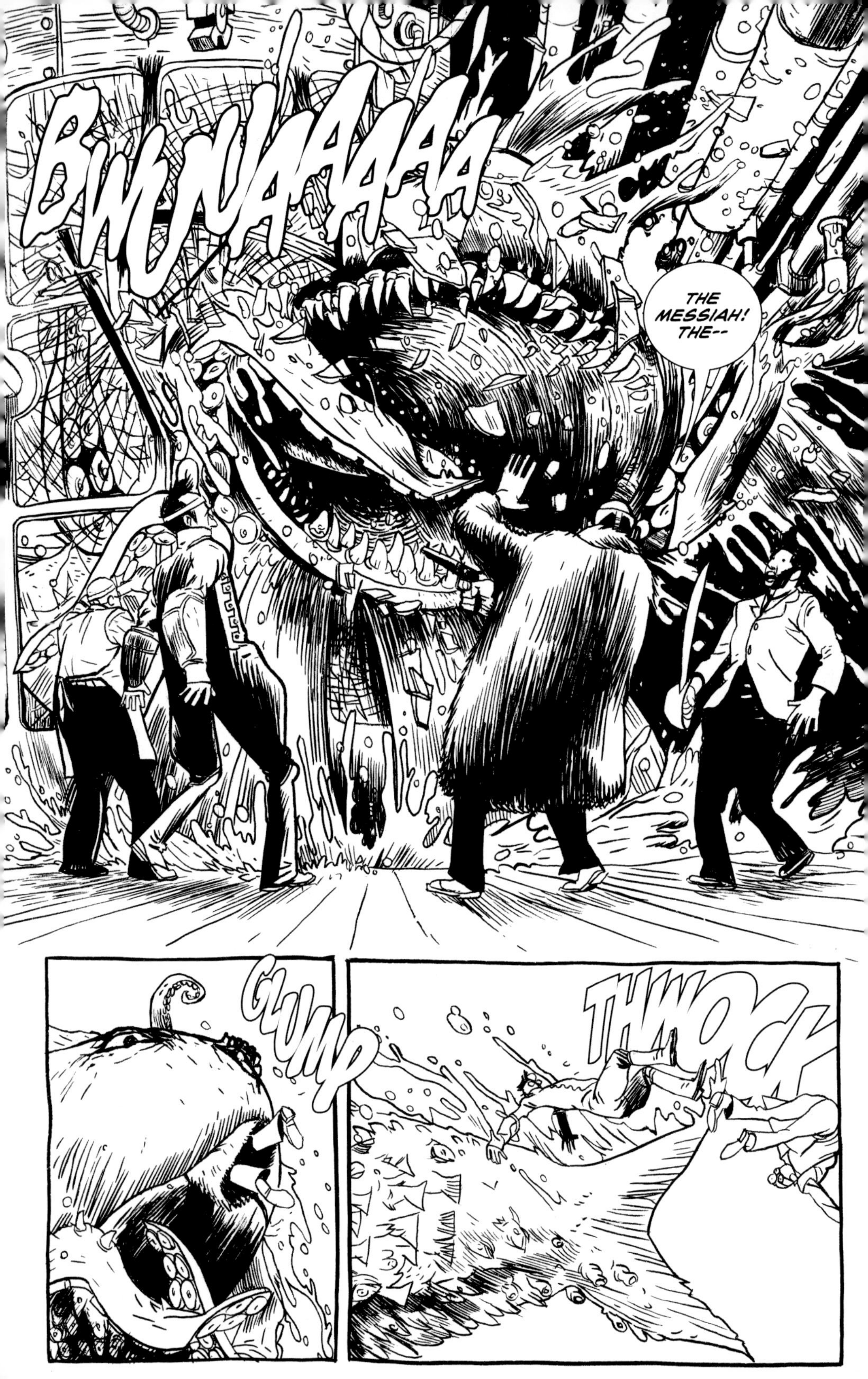
BWUAAAAAA
THE MESSIAH! THE--
GLUMP
THWOCK

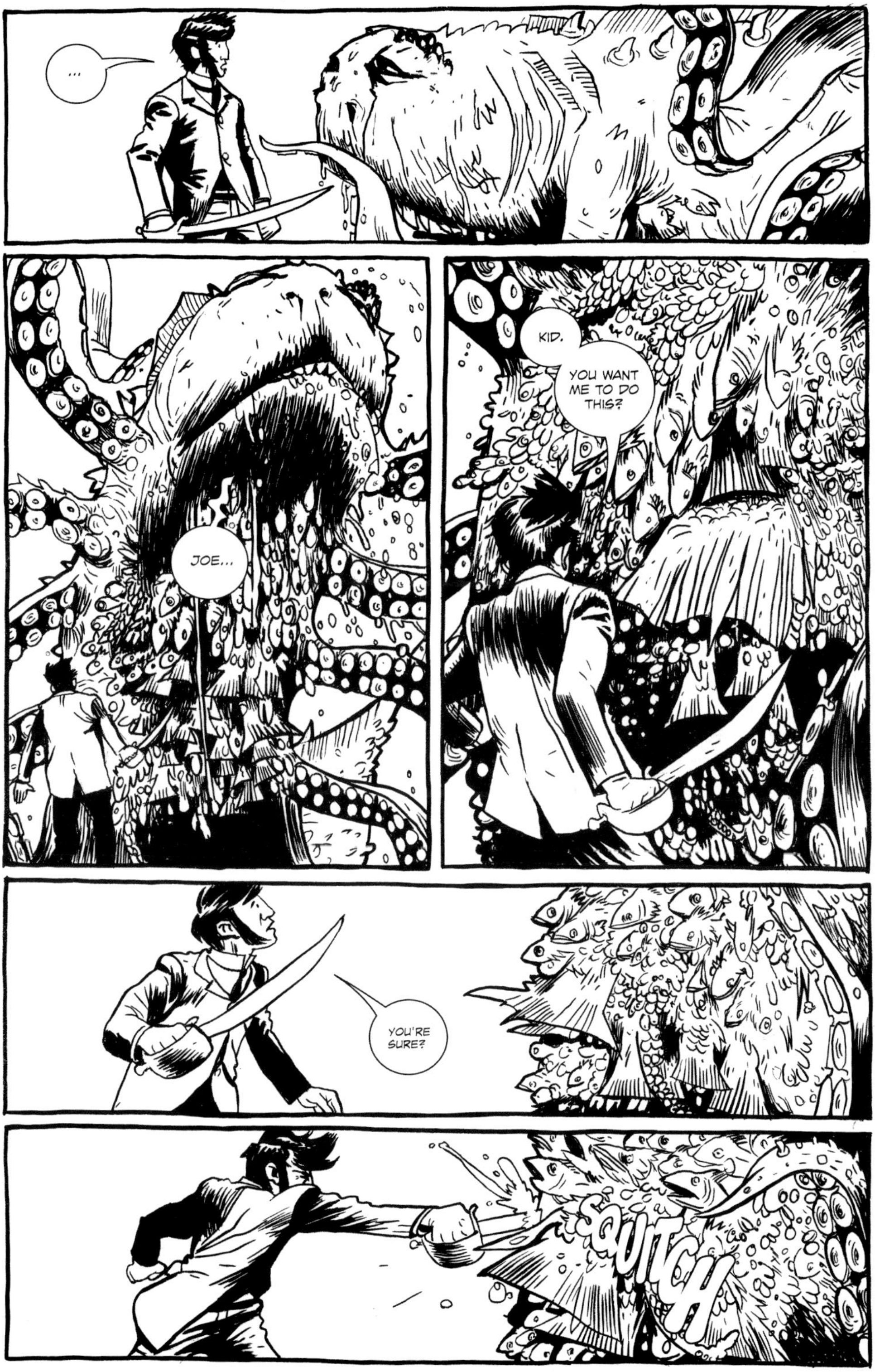
...
JOE...
KID.
YOU WANT ME TO DO THIS?
YOU'RE SURE?
SQUITCH

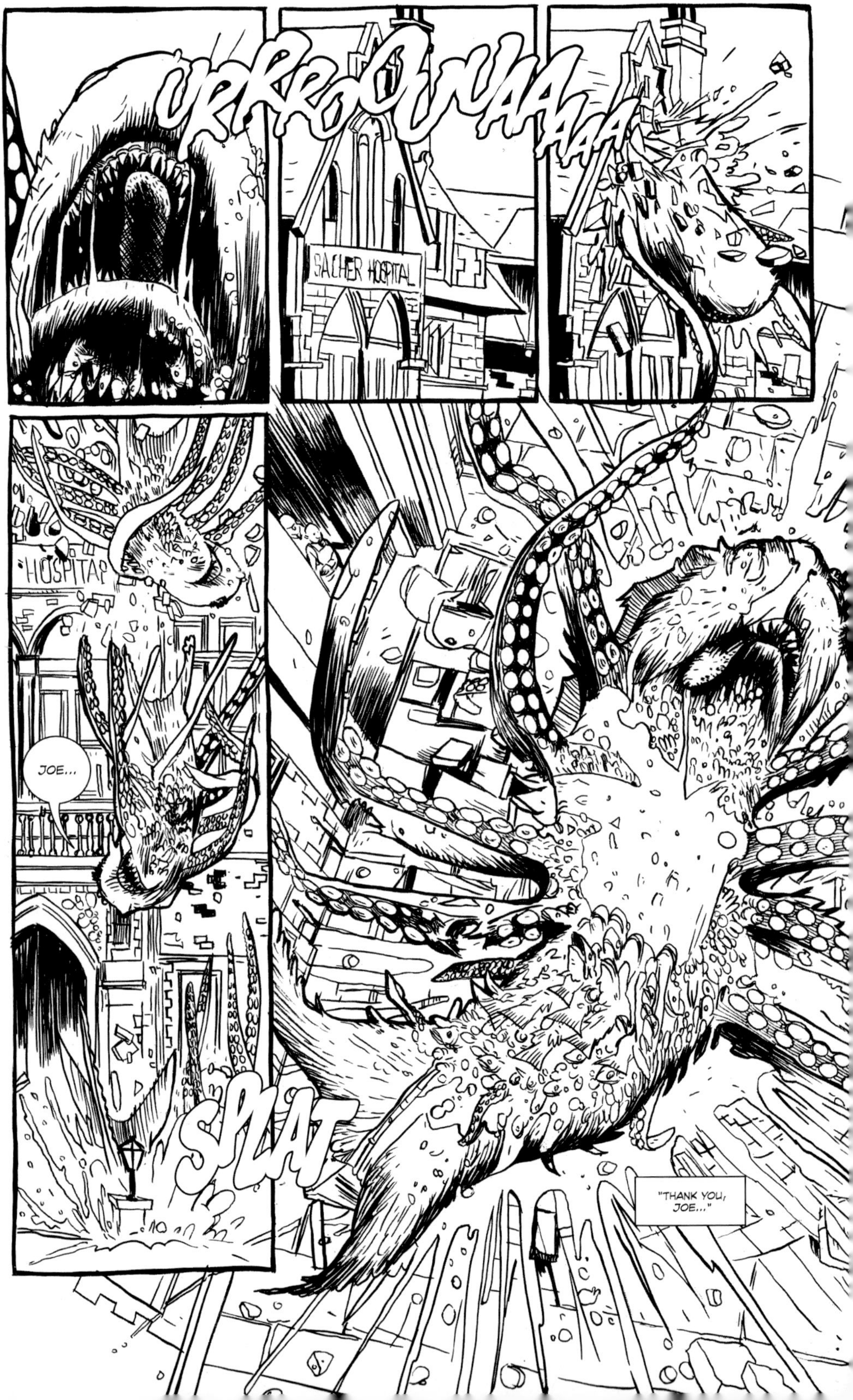

URRROOUUAAAAAA
SACHER HOSPITAL
HOSPITAL
JOE...
SPLAT
"THANK YOU, JOE..."

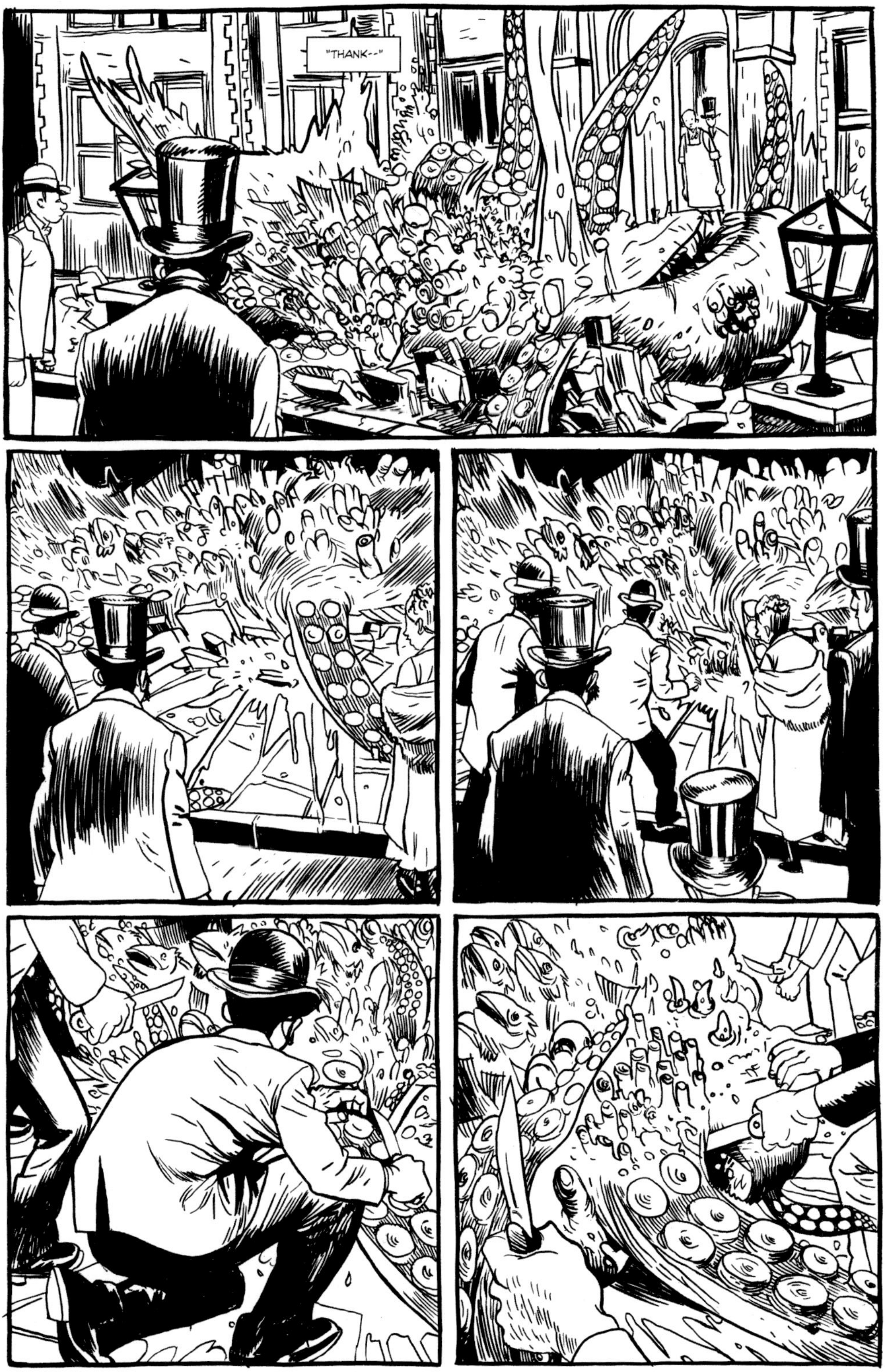
"THANK--"

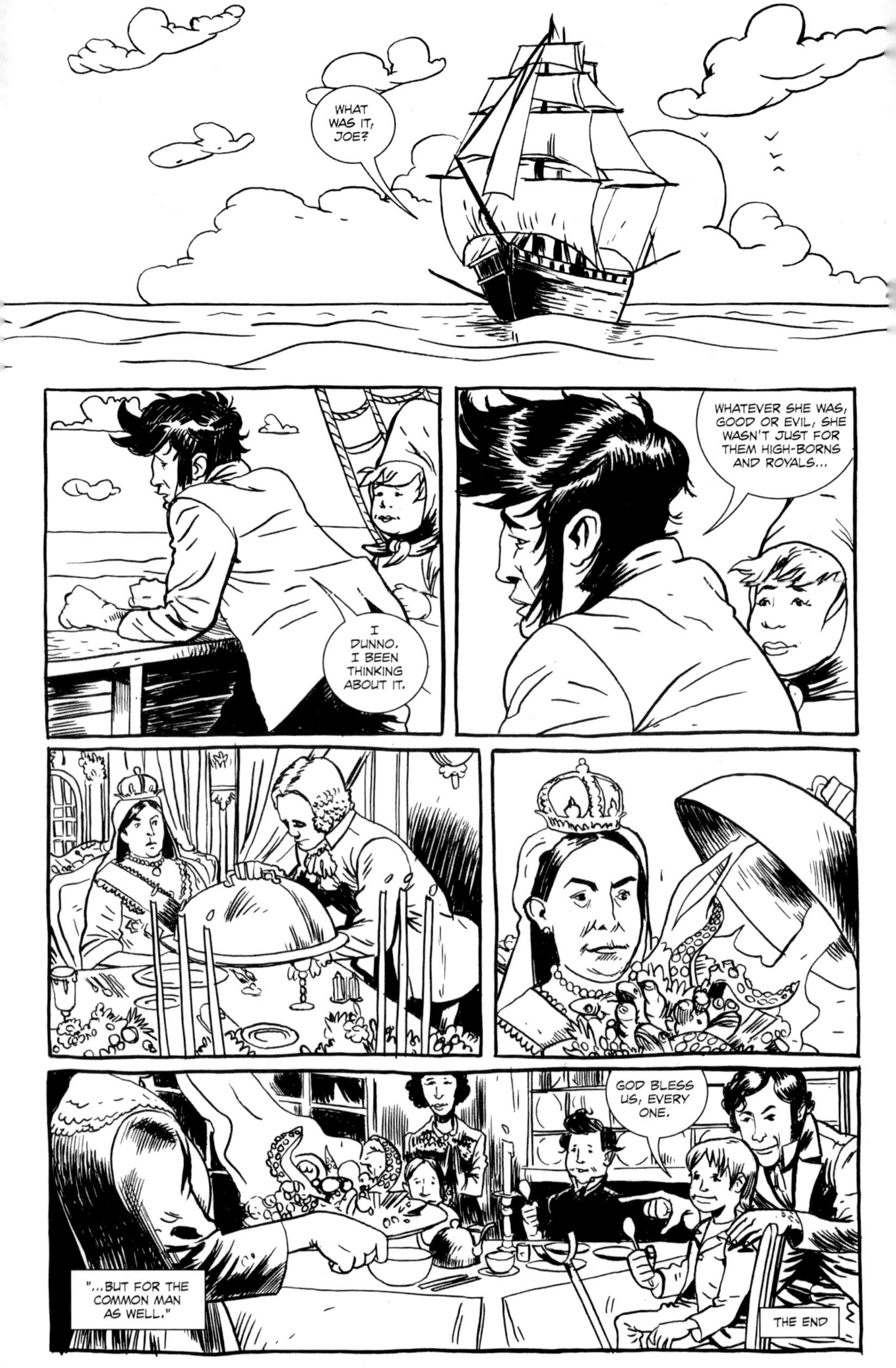
WHAT WAS IT, JOE?
I DUNNO. I BEEN THINKING ABOUT IT.
WHATEVER SHE WAS, GOOD OR EVIL, SHE WASN'T JUST FOR THEM HIGH-BORNS AND ROYALS...
GOD BLESS US, EVERY ONE.
"...BUT FOR THE COMMON MAN AS WELL."
THE END

SKETCHBOOK

ART BY TROY NIXEY

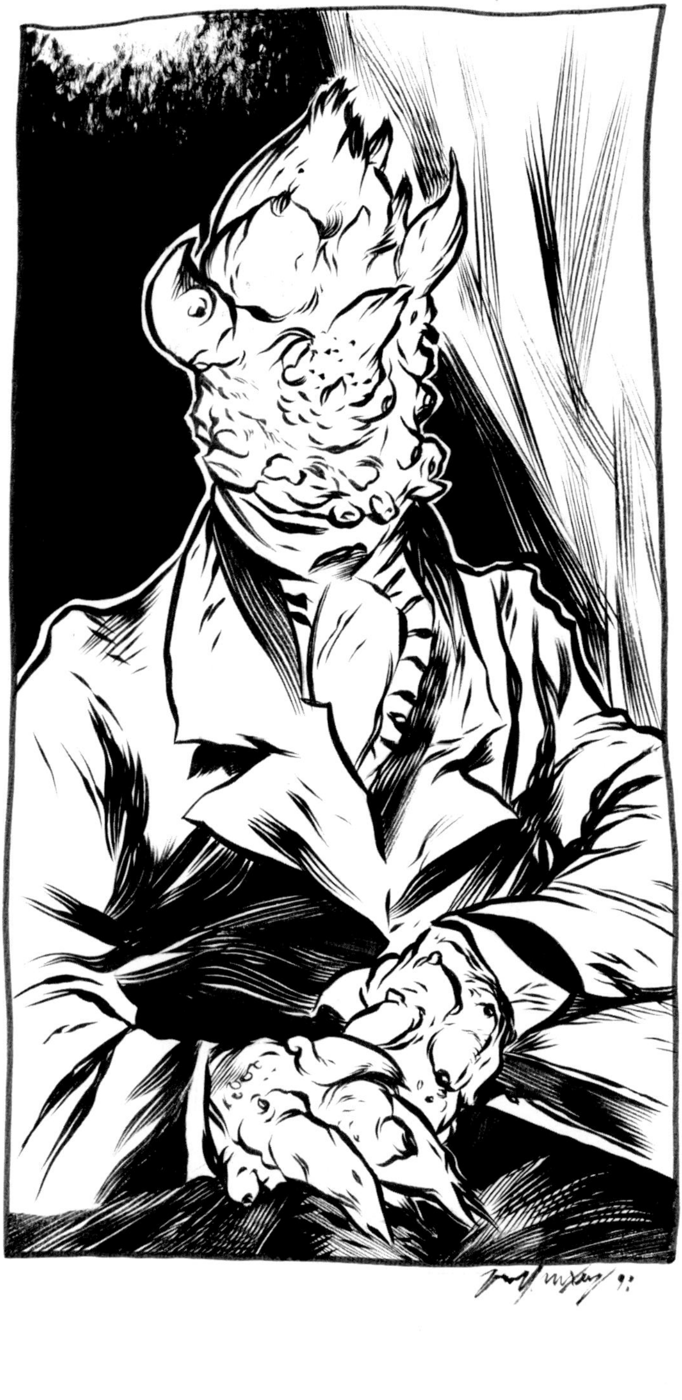

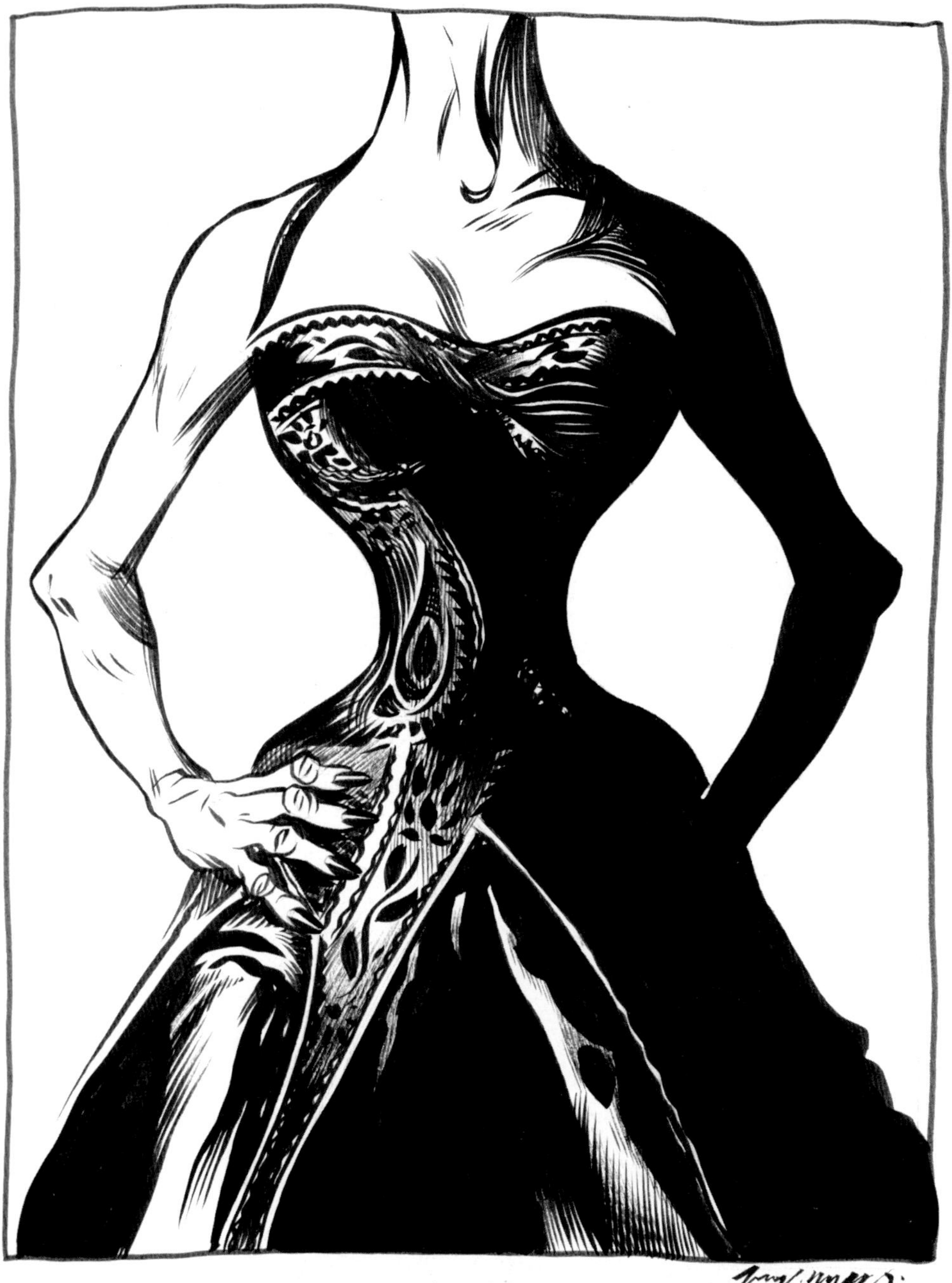
AFTER LIFE

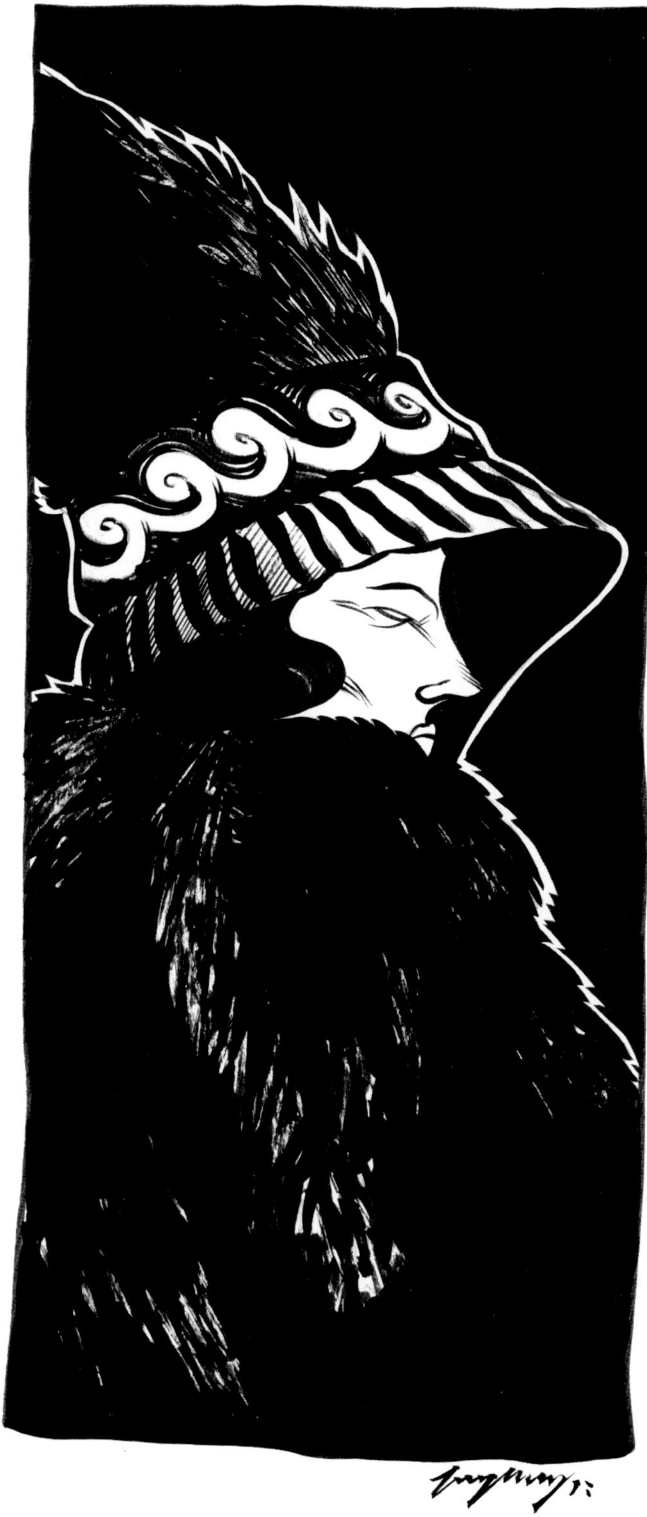

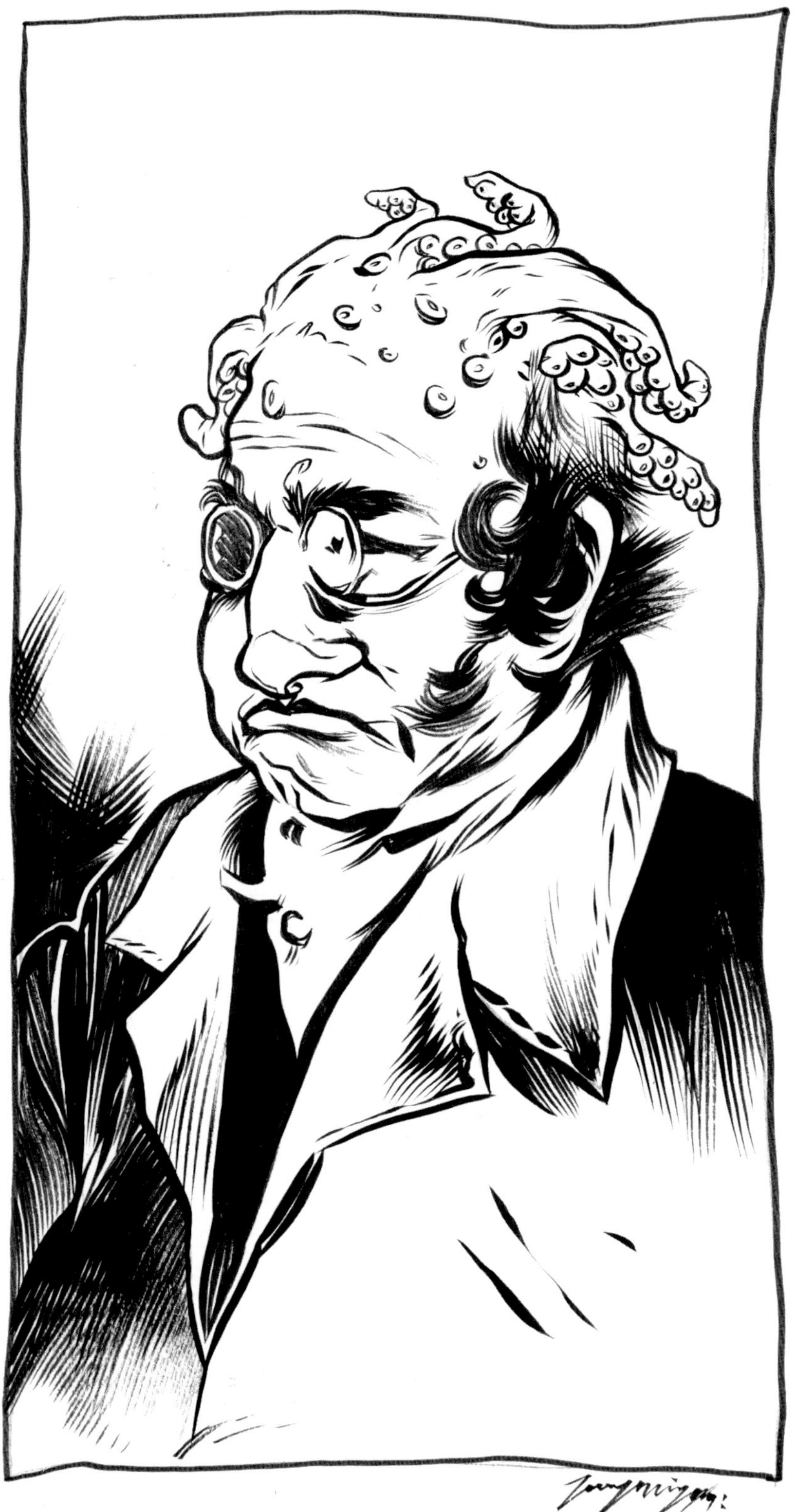

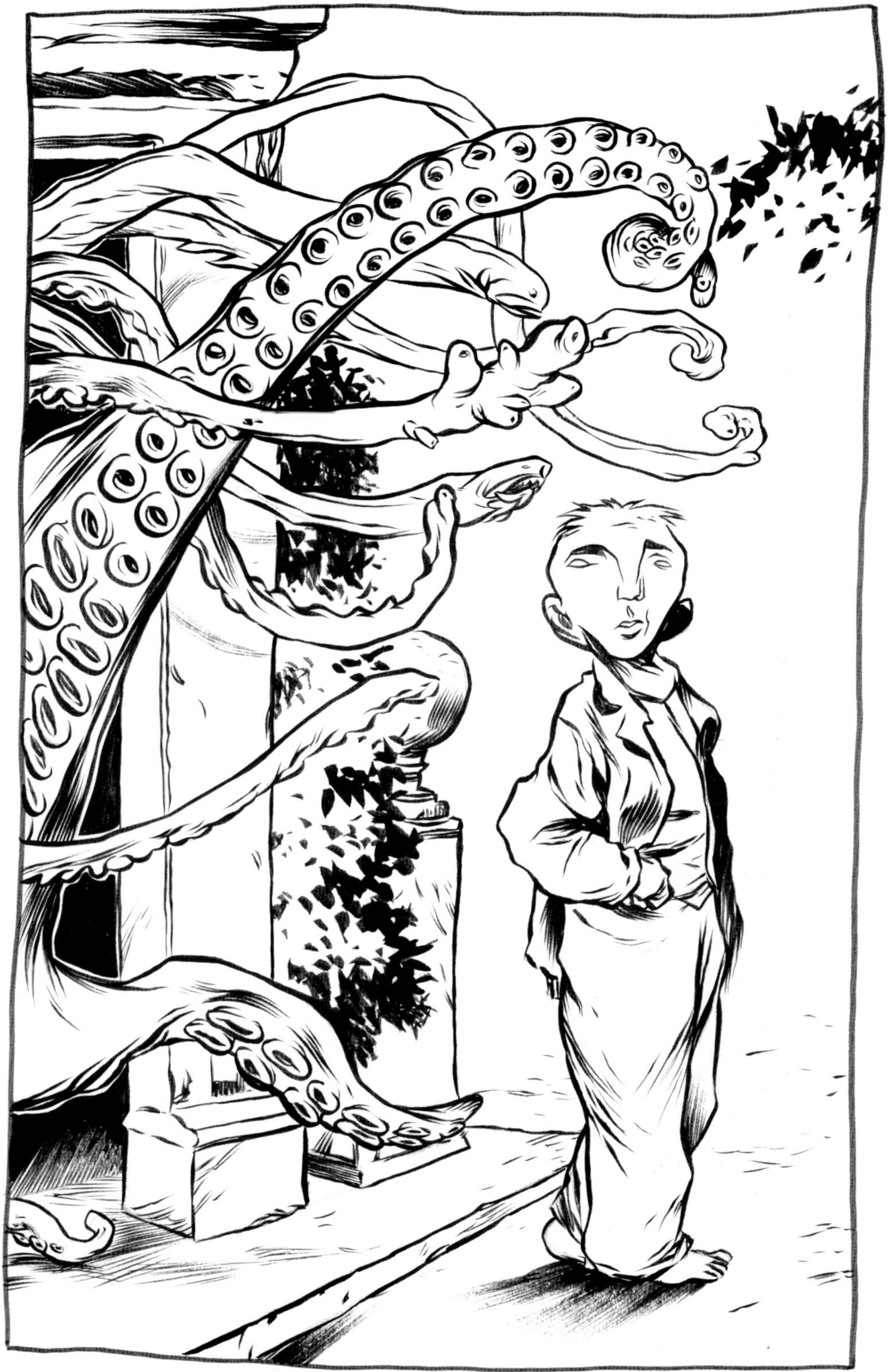

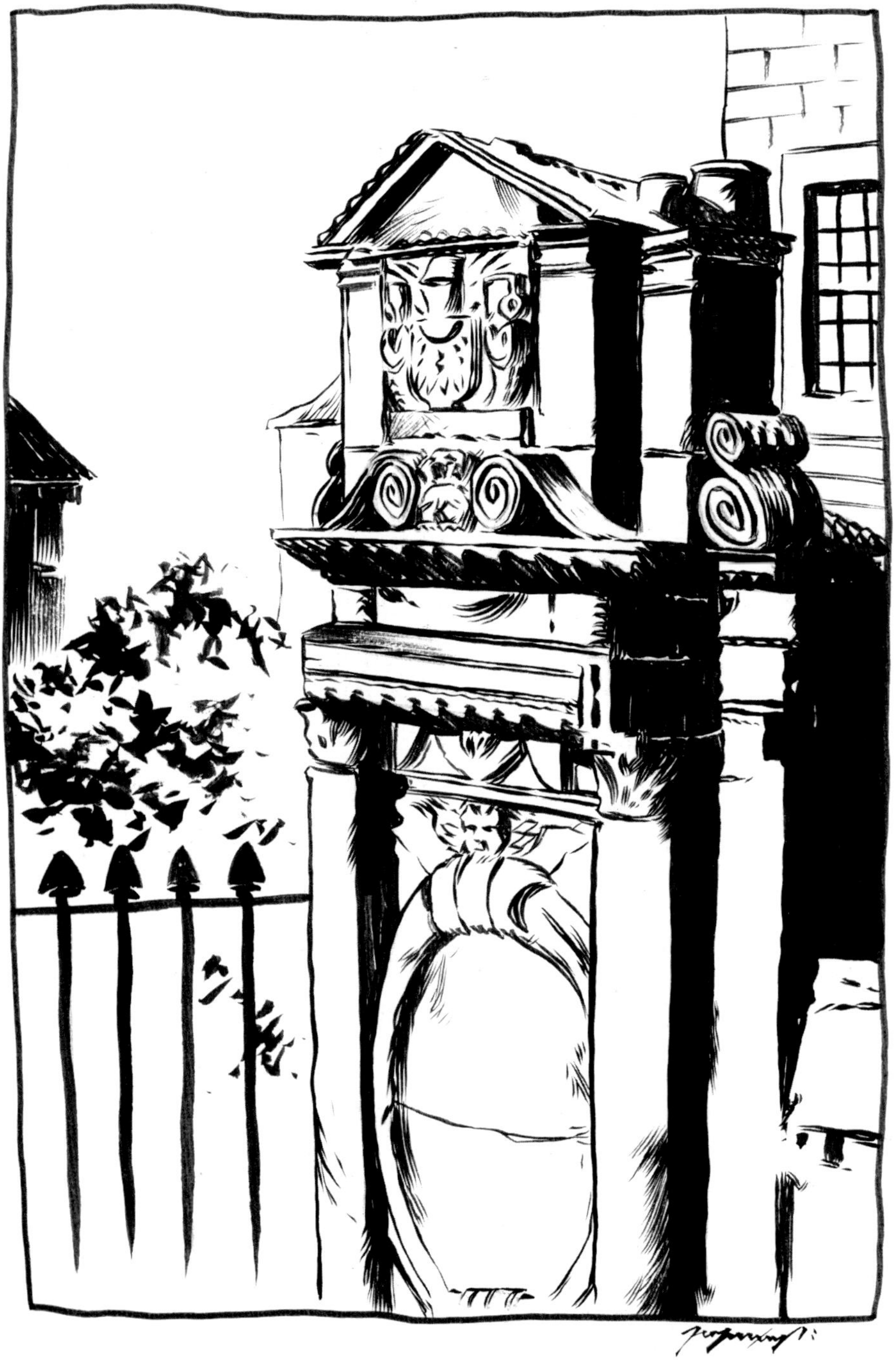

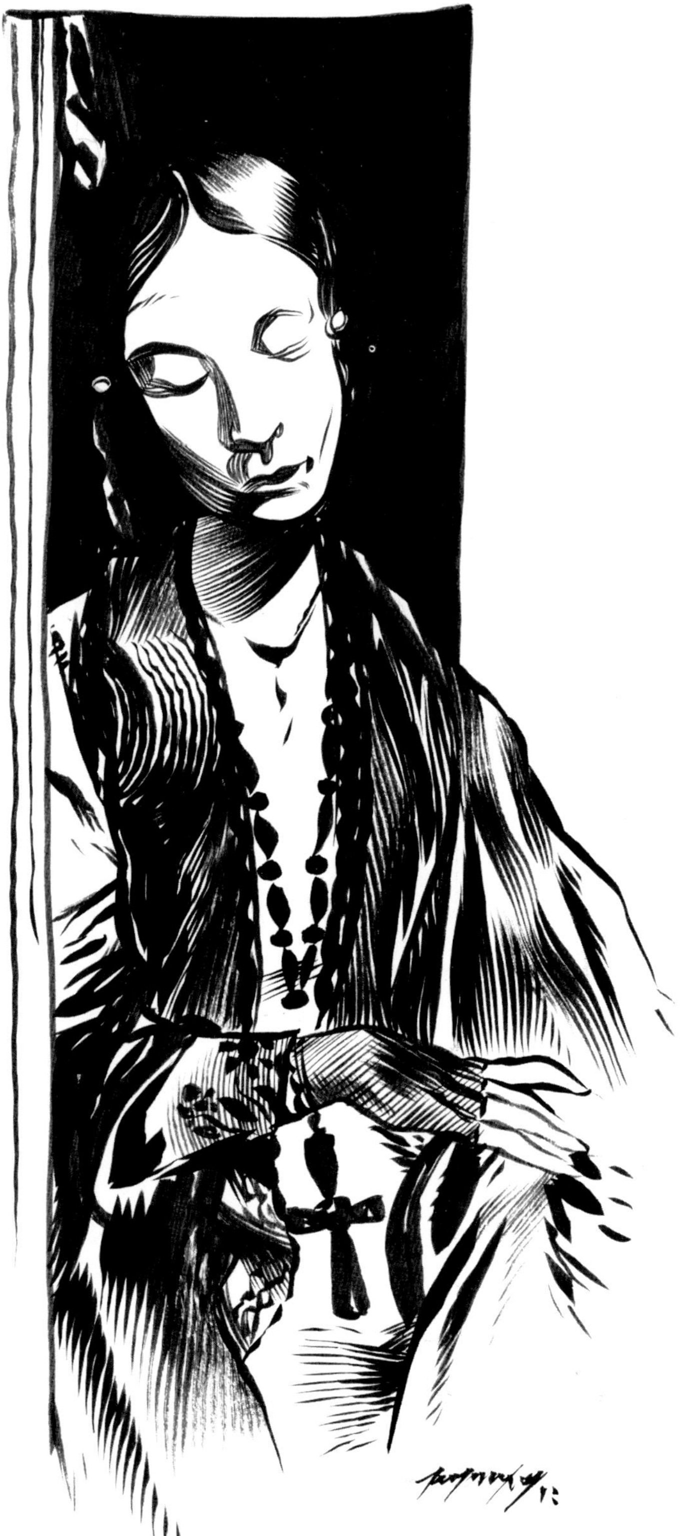

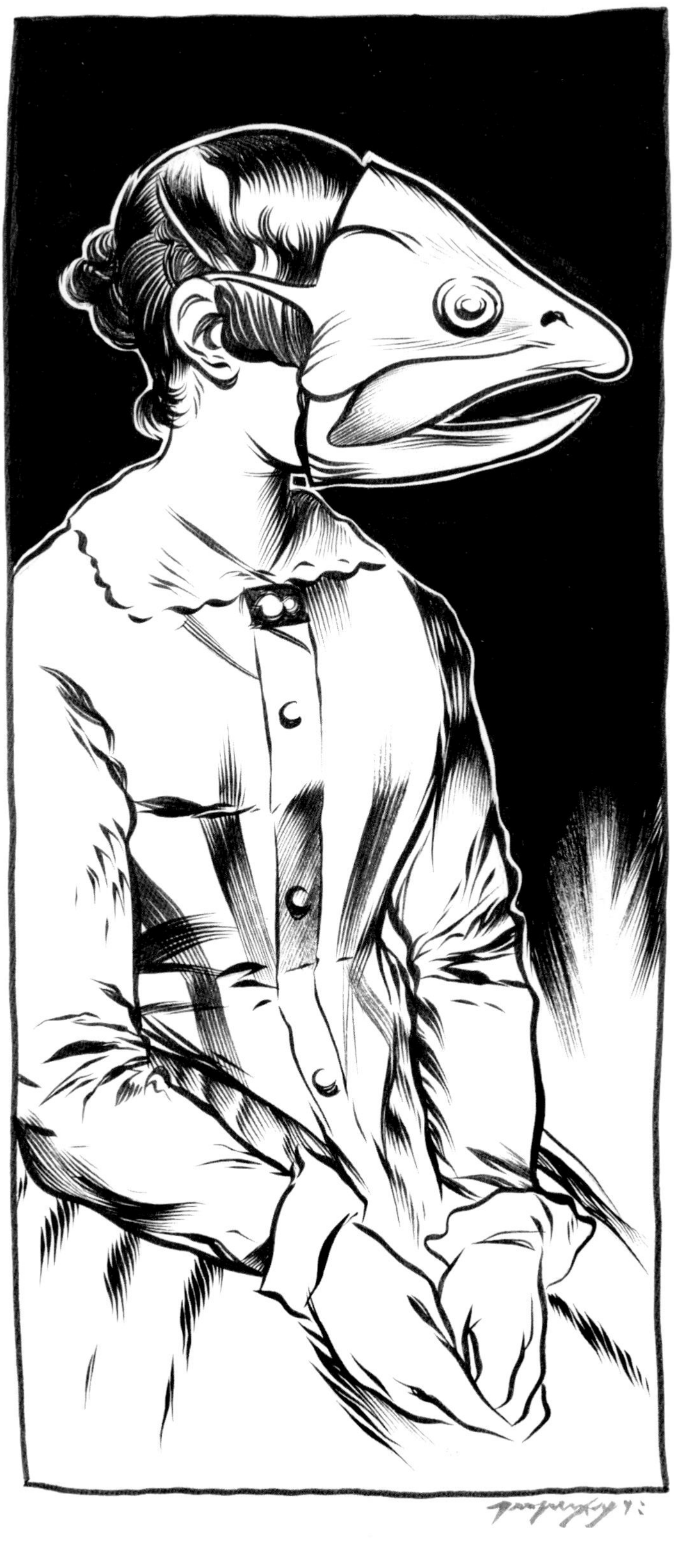

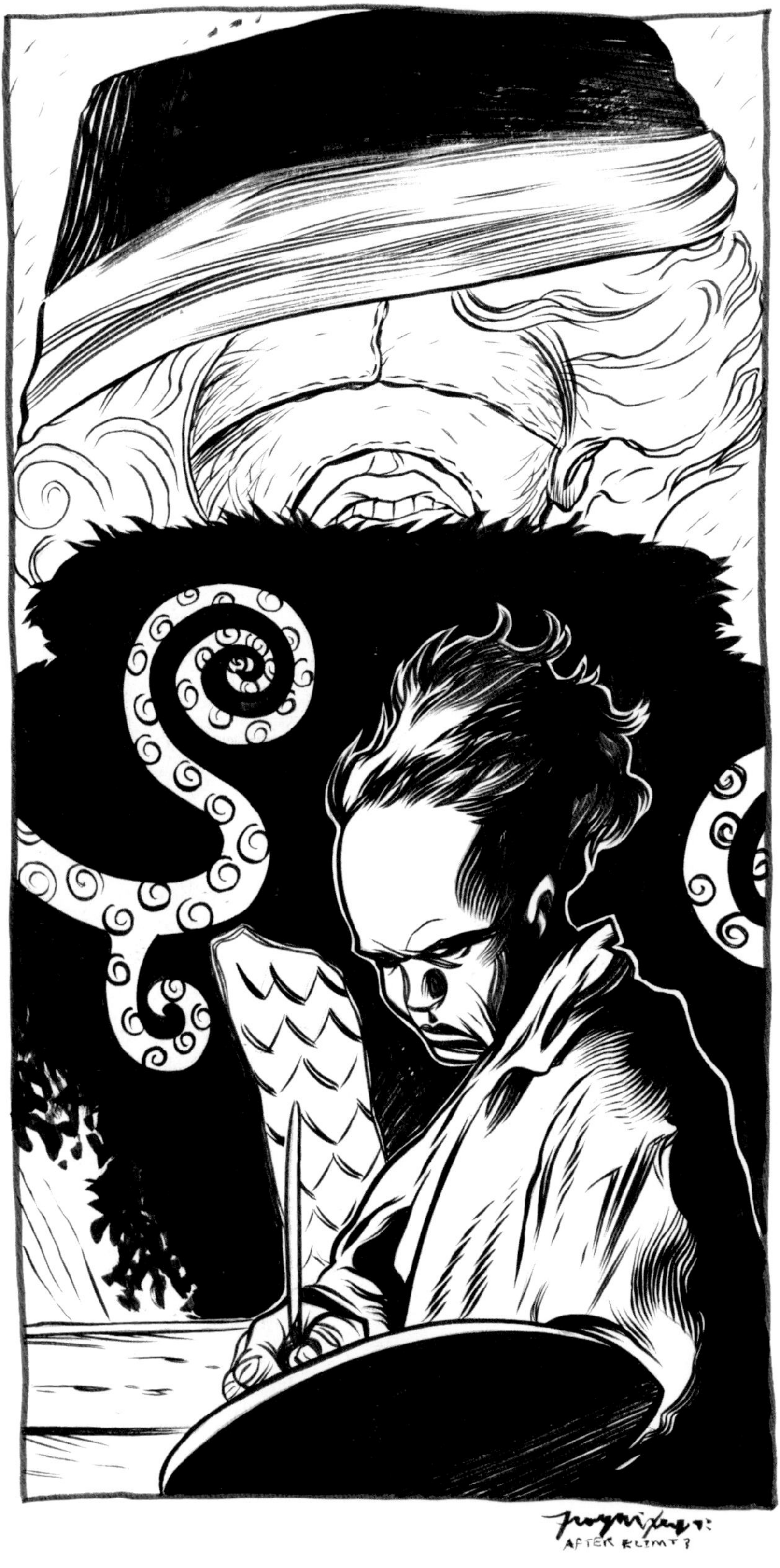
AFTER KLIMT?

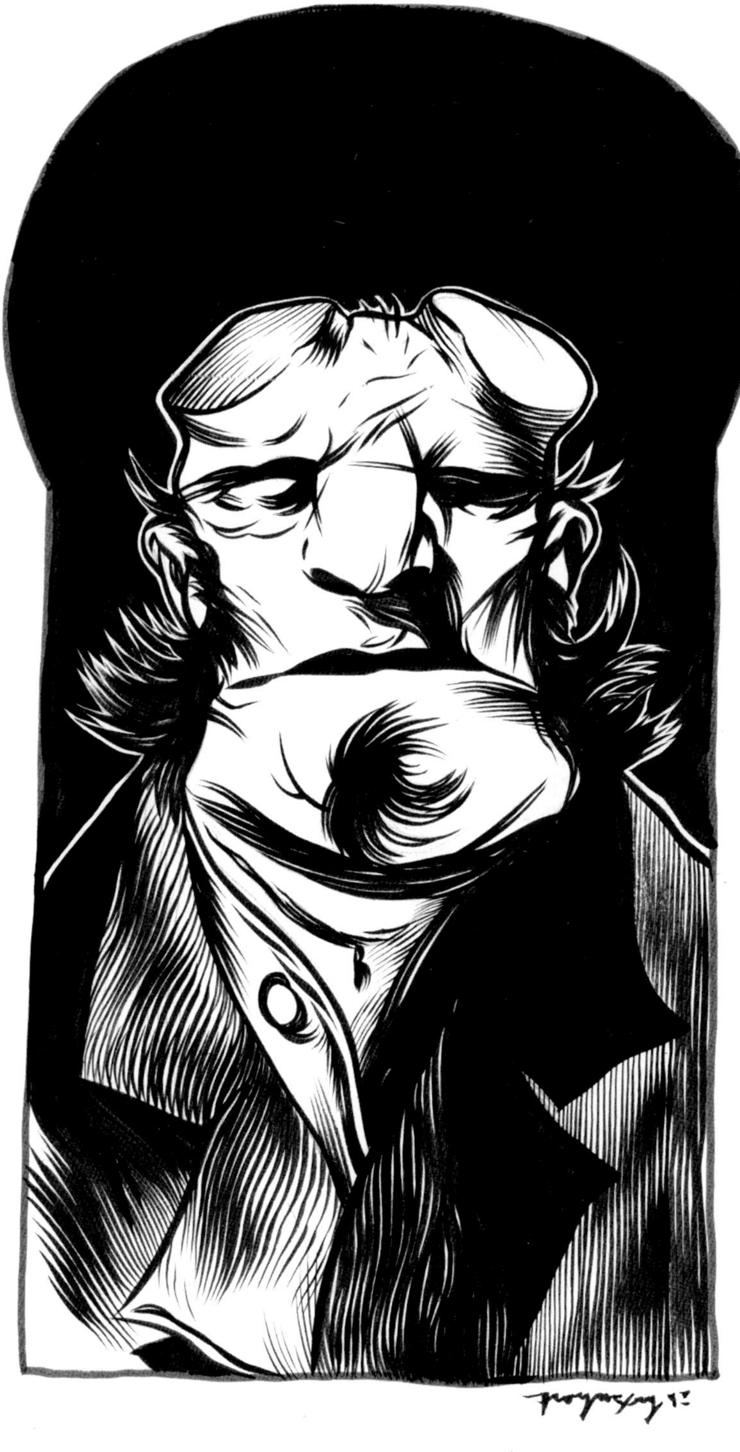

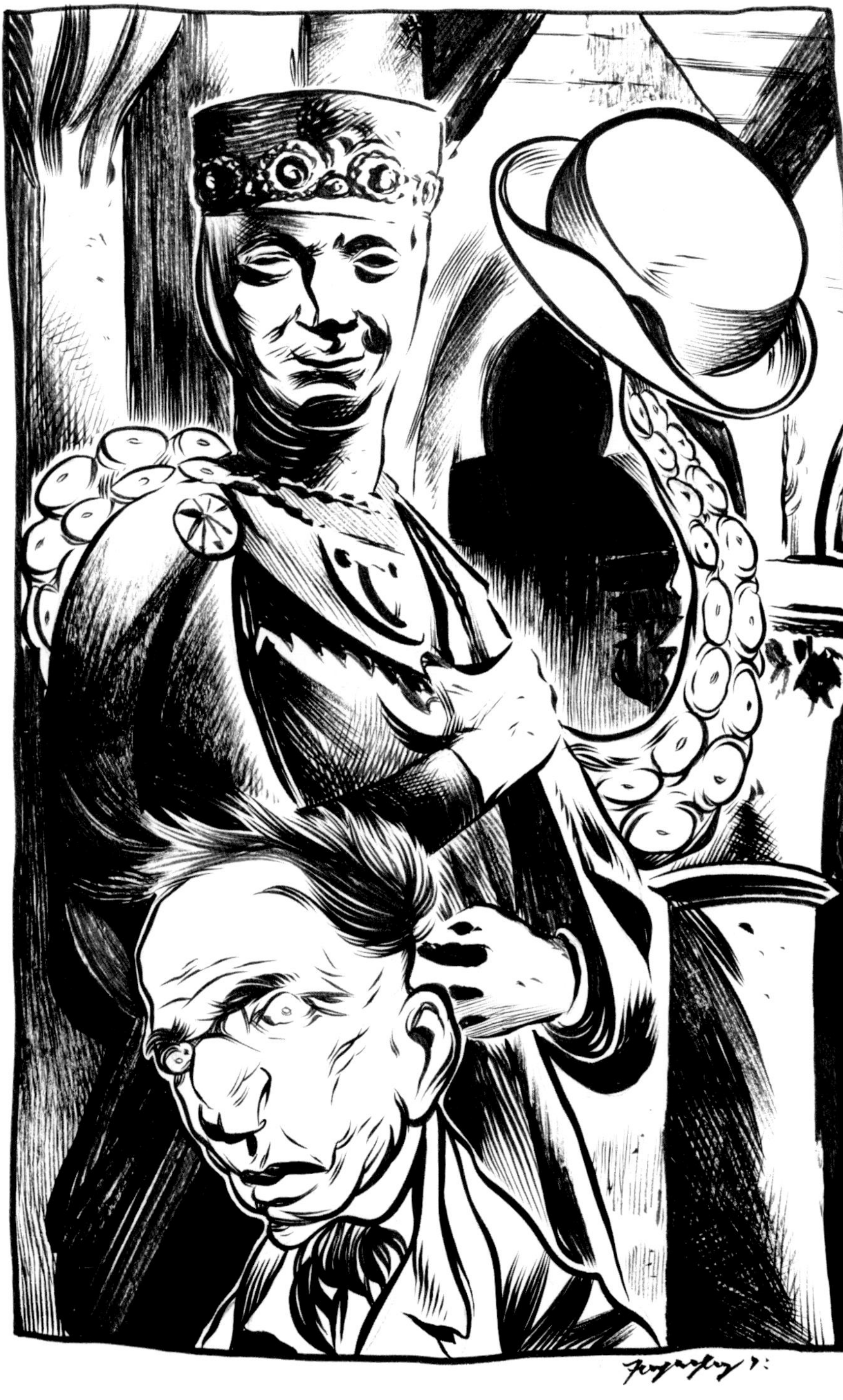

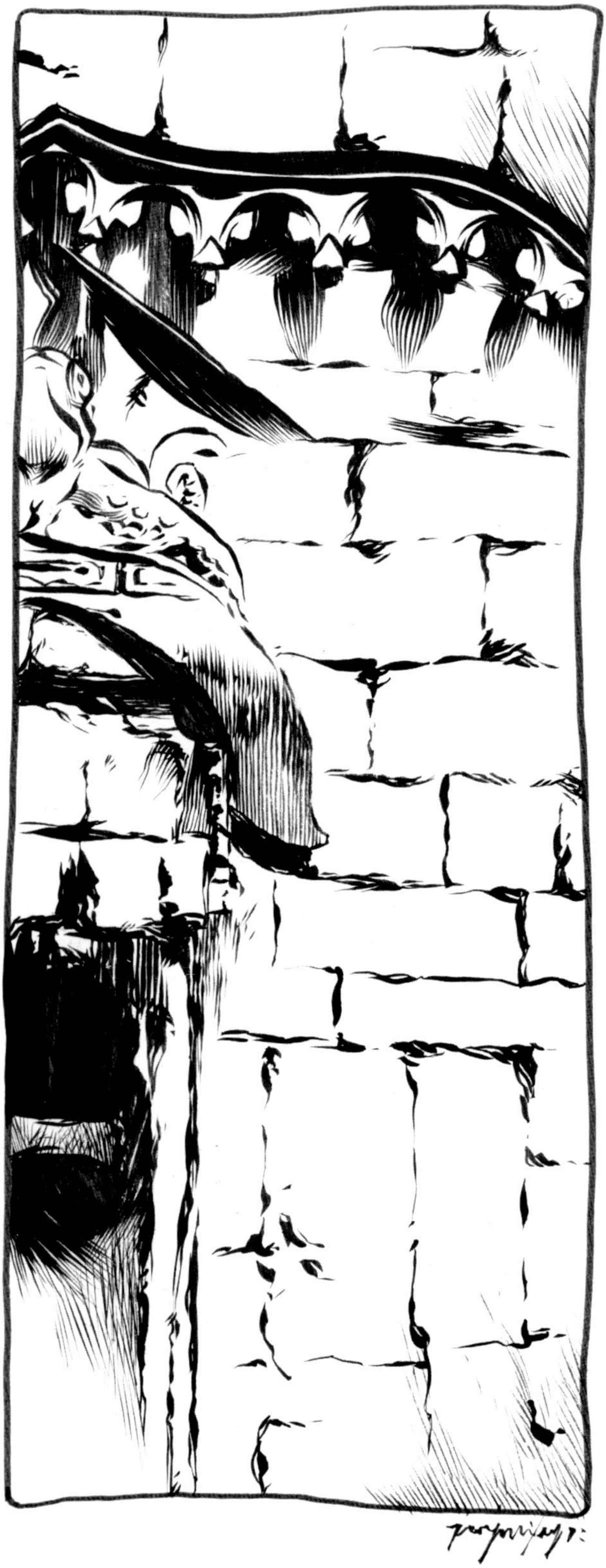

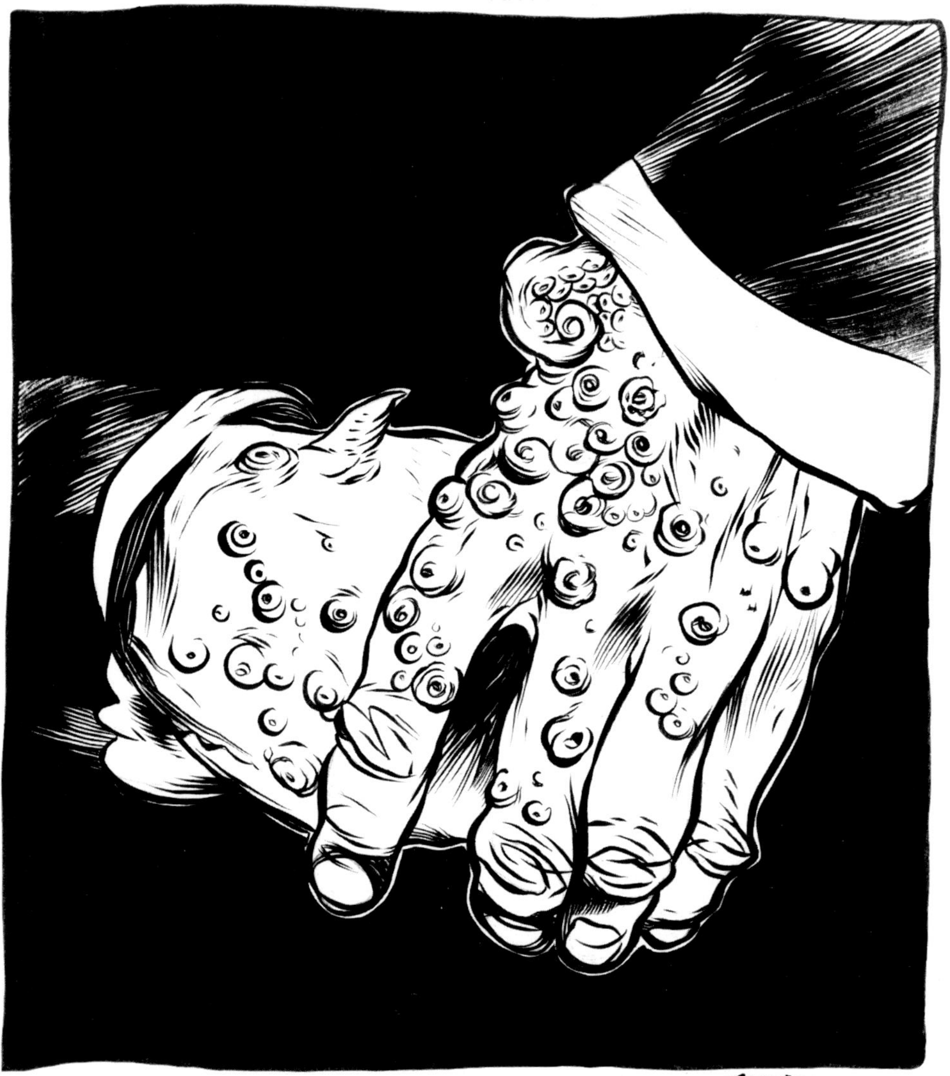

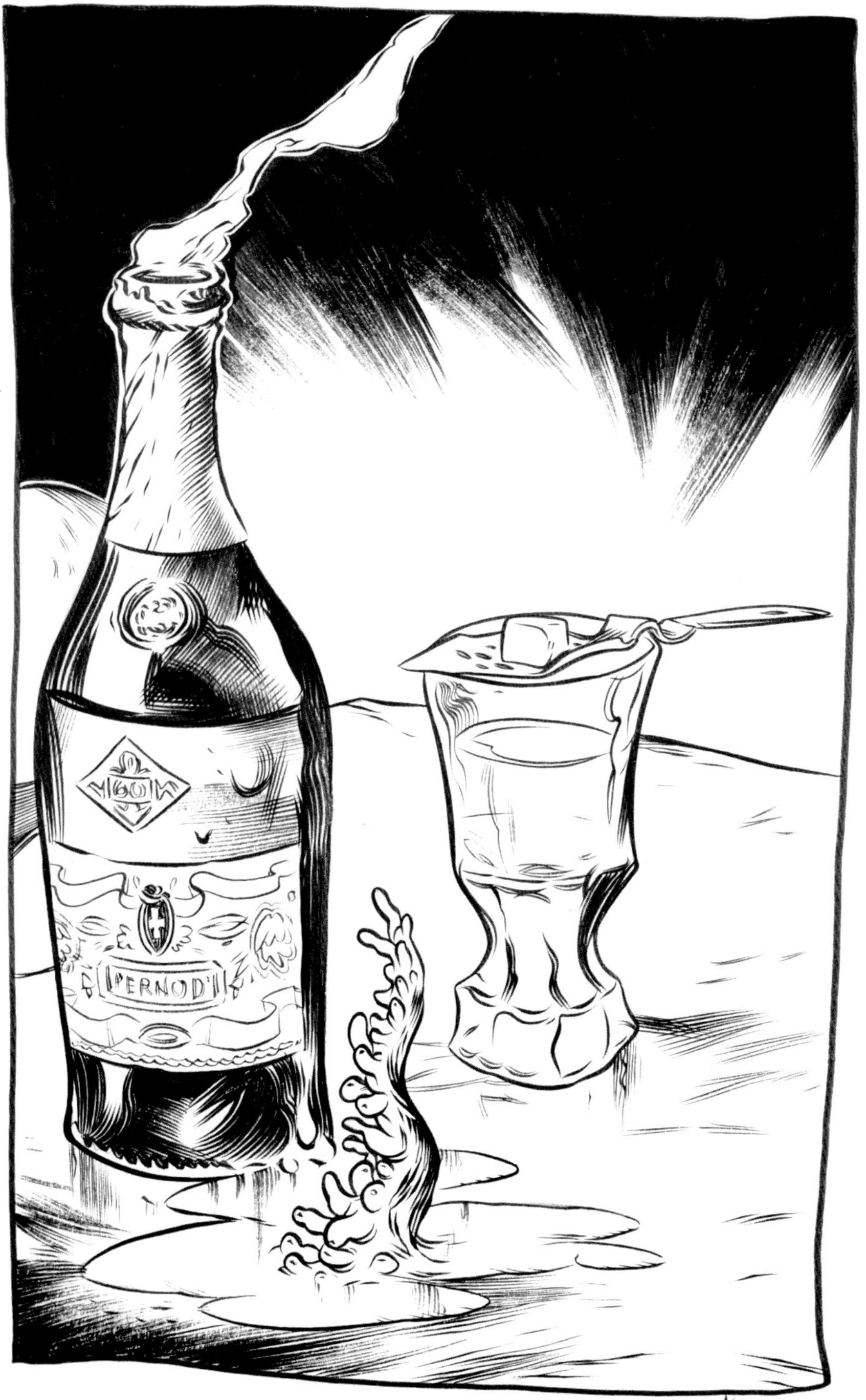
PERNOD

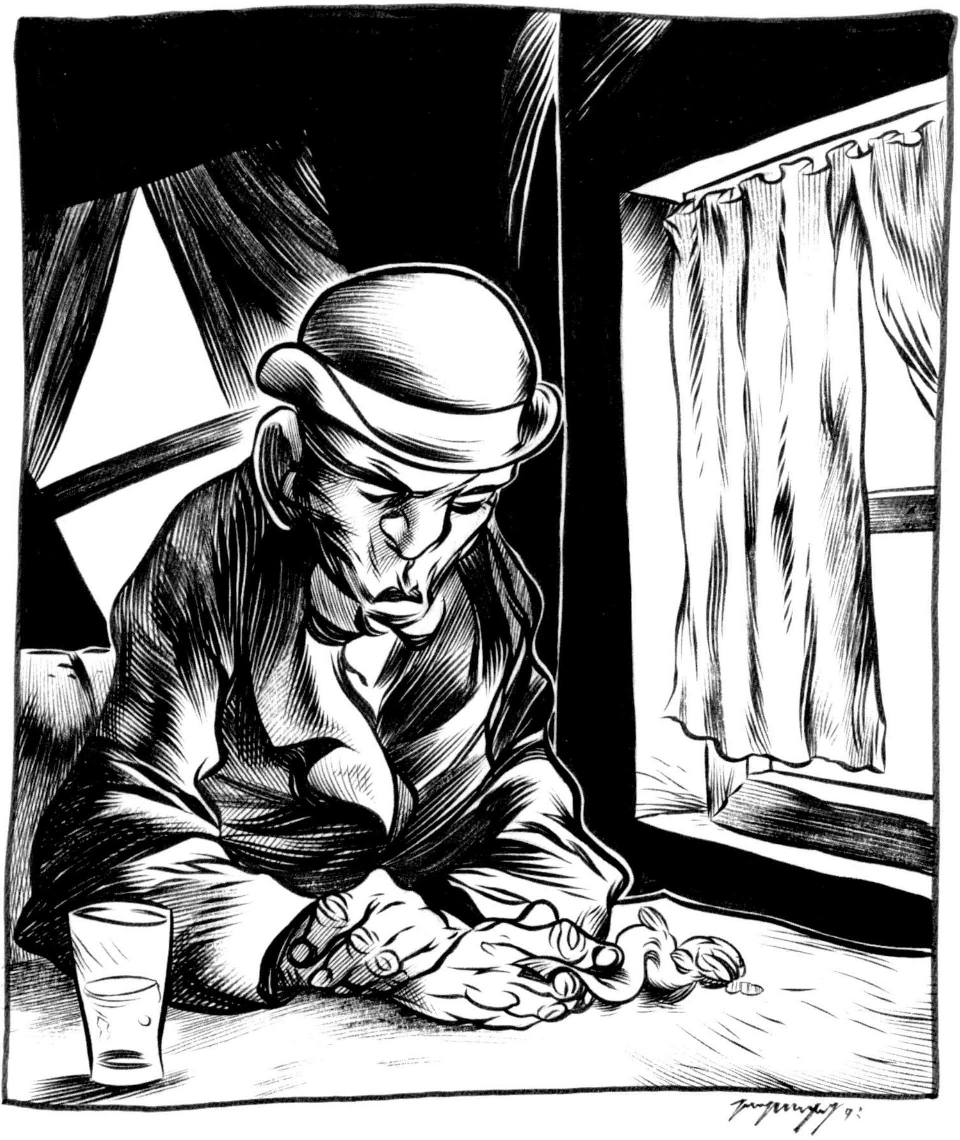

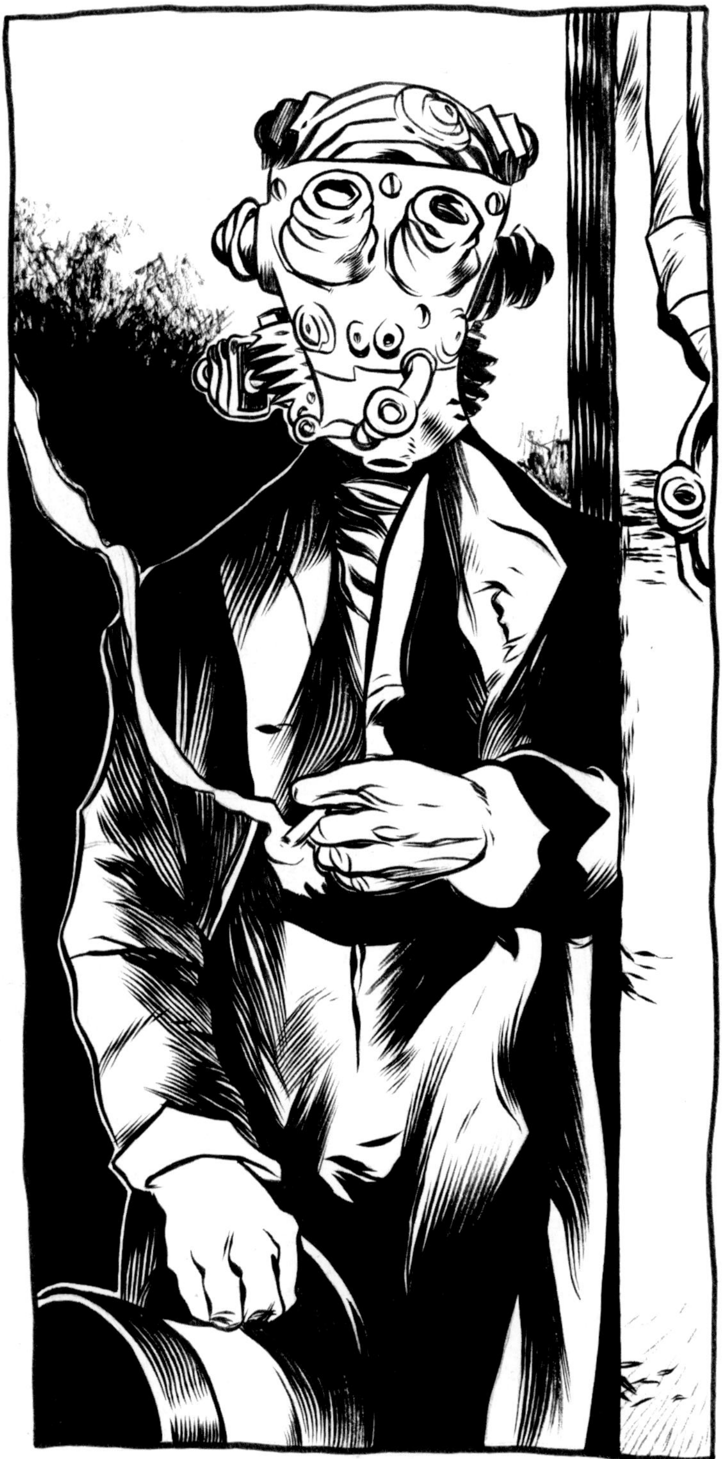

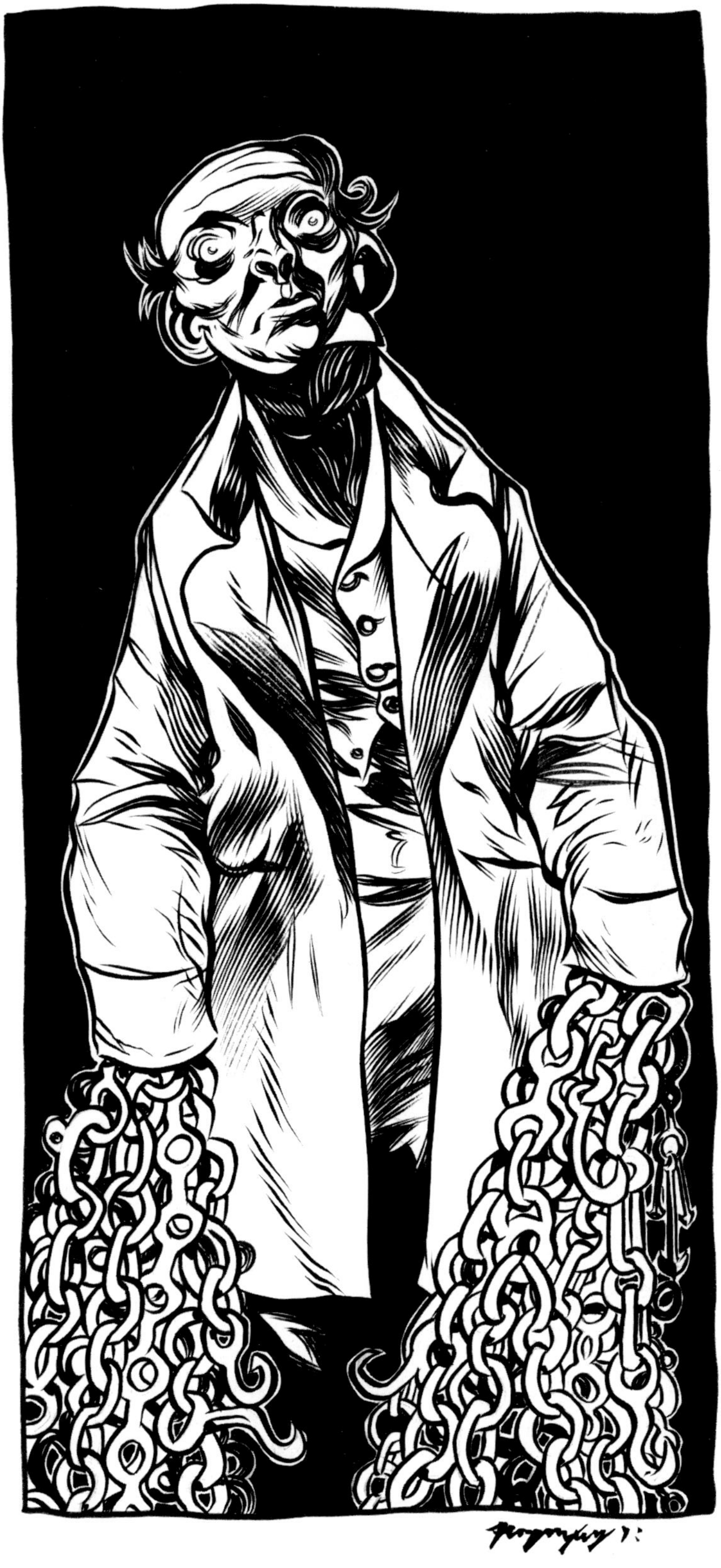

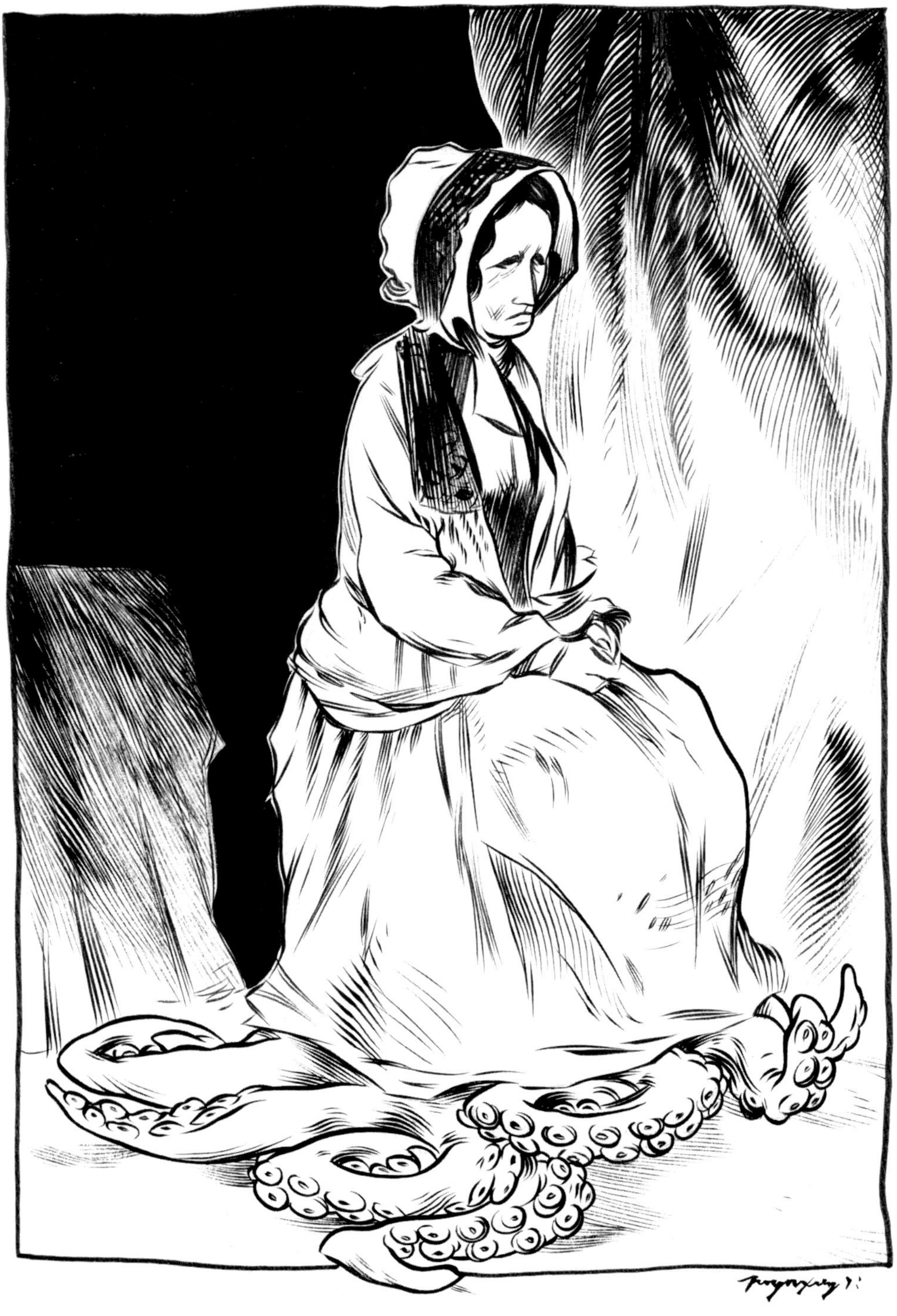

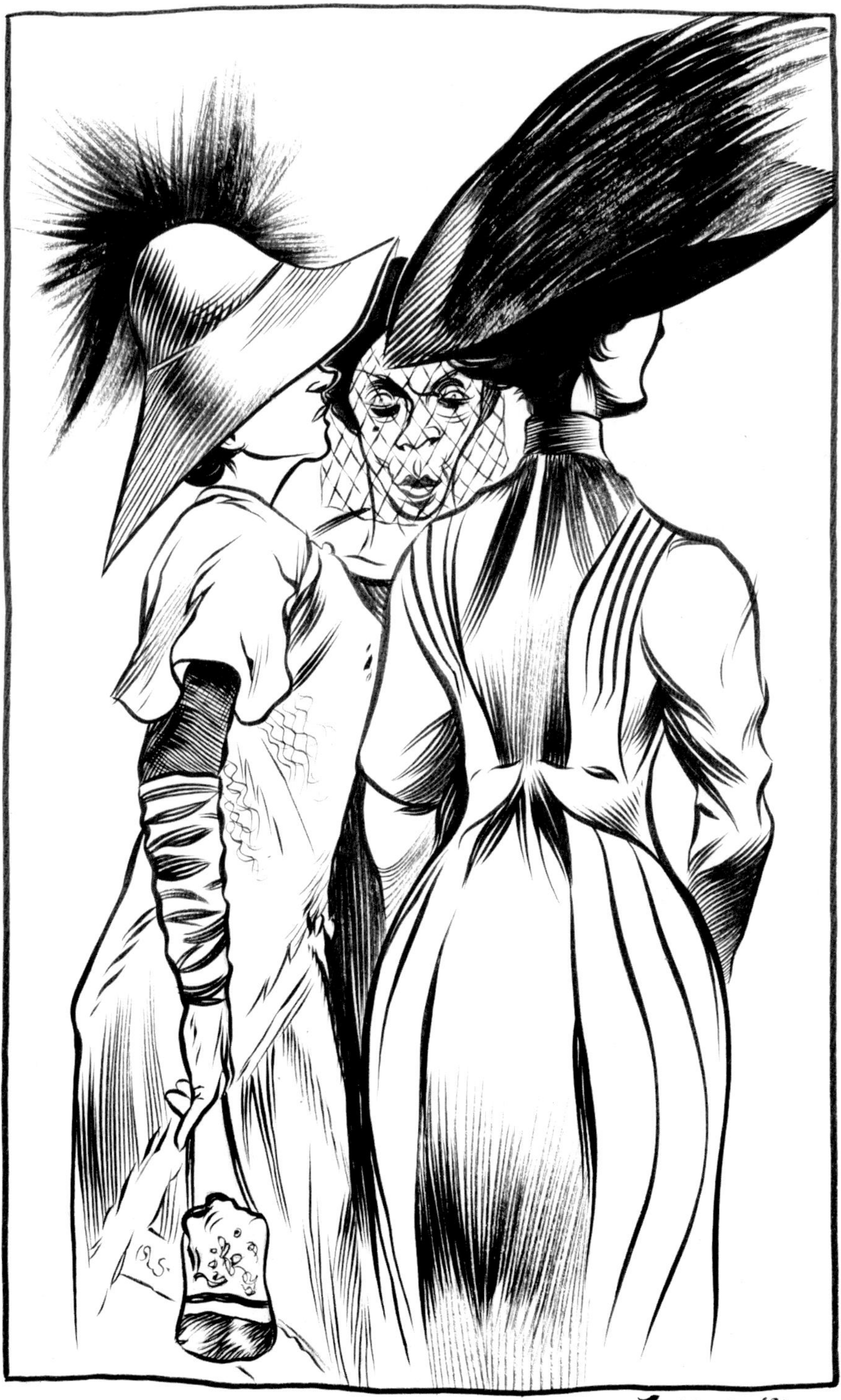